Tag

A Boy…
A Dog…
A Quest.

Dan Bomkamp

Lovstad Publishing
Poynette, Wisconsin
Lovstadpublishing@live.com

ISBN: 0692491007
ISBN-13: 978-0692491003
Previous ISBN: 0615752829

Printed in the United Stated of America

Cover design by Lovstad Publishing
Cover photo by Dan Bomkamp

DEDICATION

This book is dedicated to my Dad, Florian "Mike" Bomkamp.
Our time together was short, but he has been with me all my life.

ACKNOWLEDGMENTS

I want to thank Billy Silvers and Maggie Ziebarth
For portraying Tag and Bob for the cover photo.

I also want to thank my good friend and publisher
Joel Lovstad for all of the effort he puts into making my books
what they are.

Also a big thanks to Lorna Aigner for proofreading this
manuscript and for all the special order books she gets for me at
the library, one of my favorite places.

And, last but not least, I want to thank all of the great friends
who have made my life such fun. Without their friendship I'd
have nothing to write about.

Other books by Dan Bomkamp:

The Adventures of Thunderfoot
More Adventures of Thunderfoot
Thanks, Thunderfoot
The Gosey
Voyageur
Lost Flight
Big Edna

Tag

Chapter 1

The rain came down steadily, not hard and driving, but a rain that seemed like it would last forever, making a hissing sound as it hit the ground, trees and puddles. Occasionally a cold breeze would stir the trees making for a hard downpour from the sodden branches. An idling pickup truck with Chicago Cemetery stenciled on the rusting door sat a short way away on the narrow road, the exhaust from the motor spilling onto the damp ground like a stream of thin milk. The air was foggy with the humidity from the rain and the ground was slippery. Grass was mostly absent in this poor section of the County Cemetery and the bare ground was shiny with mud.

There were only five people at the grave. An elderly Priest wearing his cassock and surplus, with his purple stole was flanked by two altar boys, both wearing cassocks and surpluses, one carrying the Aspergillum holding the holy water. He held a large umbrella over himself and the Priest. The other altar boy held the Censer, swinging it slowly back and forth as the sweet scented incensed smoke billowed up and under the umbrella he held in his other hand. The three of them stood at the head of the casket. At the side of the grave stood a large heavyset lady wearing a black business suit and holding a large black umbrella over a small, thin boy. Water ran in little rivulets through the mud disappearing over the edge of the hole that had been dug into the ground. He stared at the casket, his eyes red, his nose running. Even with the umbrella over him, his blond hair was wet and spotted with drops of rain. He was dressed in a pair of dark gray pants that were a little short, making his black tennis shoes look out of place with the white shirt and a black clip-on tie. His hand-me-down sport coat was a couple of sizes too large for his thin frame.

"*Requiescat in Pace, in nominee Patre et Filii, et Spirite tu Sante.*" the Priest said, as he made the sign of the cross over the casket at the end of the prayers for the dead. He took the Aspergill and sprinkled holy water across the already water spotted casket. Then he took the Censor from the other altar boy and wafted incensed smoke over the grave. He nodded to the two altar boys and they turned and walked back to the waiting station wagon they had ridden to the cemetery in with the Priest. The one with the incense dumped the charcoal out onto the edge of the wet road before getting inside. The charcoal hissed as it was snuffed out by the water puddle. The Priest walked over to the boy and squatted down. Rain spotted his surplus. "Tag, is there anything I can do for you?" he said quietly.

The boy shook his head. The Priest stood and put his arms around the boy. "You call me if there is anything you need, Ok?"

The boy nodded. "Thank you Father," he whispered.

"He'll be fine Father," the lady said. "We've got a fine home for him to go to until we can find him a permanent place." She smiled down at the boy and put her arm around his shoulder. "Tag's gonna be just fine," she said smiling sadly.

The Priest squeezed the boy's shoulder, smiled down sadly at him, and turned toward the station wagon. He got in and started the vehicle and he and the altar boys drove slowly out of the cemetery.

Two workmen drove slowly up in the pickup truck and began to unload some tools. "The men have to finish up now Tag. We should go," the lady said to the boy.

He nodded. He stepped forward, his feet sinking into the mud, and put his hand on the wet lid of the casket. His eyes filled with tears and he rubbed his hand back and forth across the cold metal.

"Bye," he said quietly.

The lady put her arm around him, her eyes brimming with tears, and they slowly walked to her car which was parked a short way away on the cemetery road. She opened the door. He stomped the mud off his shoes and climbed in. She shut the door and walked around to the driver's side, got in and started the car. "Buckle up, sweetie," she said quietly. The windows were fogged so she turned on the defroster and waited silently as they cleared.

"What's gonna happen to me?" The boy asked quietly.

"We're going to go to your apartment and get all of your stuff, and then I'll take you out to stay in the suburbs with some people who are waiting for you to come and live with them for a while. We can't find any trace of your daddy, and so far we can't find any other relatives, so for now you'll be in a foster home."

"My daddy's been gone for forever," the boy said. "Mom never talked about him but I asked her once and she said he left before I was born, so I don't think you're gonna find him."

"Well, don't you fret your sweet little head now, we're going to take care of you," the lady said.

Tag nodded and looked out the window as the cemetery slid by, leaving his mother behind in the rain.

The lady, Janelle Hopkins was Tag's legal guardian now, since he had no other living relatives. She was his case worker for the Child Welfare Department of Cook County. She looked over at the boy sitting with his hands in his lap, his head bowed as if in prayer. He was about average height for a 13 year old, maybe a bit taller than most, but he was very thin. His light brown hair was almost blond on the ends and was cut in a longish style that hung down on his forehead in bangs and was long enough to hang to his collar. His eyes were a startling deep blue and were rimmed in red from crying. He had very long eyelashes and blinked away a tear that ran down his cheek. Her heart felt very heavy for the pain this small boy was enduring. He had a very sweet face, "Almost too pretty to be a boy she thought." He sat staring at his feet.

His mother had been killed while she worked her second job, as a cashier at a convenience store. She worked two jobs to make a decent home for her son, and her life had been taken over a couple of hundred dollars by some drug addled addict. The man had thought his need for drugs was more important than the life of a beautiful young woman. His mother was his only living relative as far as it could be determined. Now he had no one, and he was about to go into a foster care system that was overloaded, where he would probably spend his next five years, until he was eighteen, lost in the system. Then when he turned eighteen, he would be turned loose on the world, on his own. "Oh, how I wish I could just take you home with me," she thought. But she knew that was impossible. She had three children of her own, and the people who ran social services frowned on the idea of case workers getting too involved with clients.

After a drive of about twenty minutes they pulled up in front of an old, but well kept apartment building. "You ready to go get your stuff?" she asked.

Tag took a deep breath. "I guess so," he said.

Chapter 2

The apartment building was square and looked like a huge brown box. The builder had not worried about pleasing architecture, so no extra money was spent on anything but the necessities. It was four stories tall with four apartments on each floor, each a mirror image of the one across the hall, or the one above or below it. They walked across a cracked sidewalk that ran through a bare patch of earth. At the front entry there was a scraggly evergreen bush on one side and the stump of its former mate on the opposite side. The door opened to a hallway that showed four doors, two on each side. "We're up on three," the boy said.

They climbed the grimy stairs, listening to the sounds of different television shows on various sets, some rap music coming from 2C and some classical music coming from the apartment next to Tag's, 3A. "That's Mrs. Simonson," he said. "She listens to that kind of music all the time."

"I think it's nice," Mrs. Hopkins said.

"Me too, I kind of like it sometimes," he said.

They stopped in front of 3B and Mrs. Hopkins dug a key out of her purse and opened the door. The apartment, while small was immaculately kept. It was a stark contrast to the dingy hallway and the grimy stairs. The walls were painted a light mint green with off white trim. The floors were shined to a gleaming finish. The furniture, while old and mostly second hand was clean and everything was right where it should be. There was a large bookcase built of planks and decorative garden blocks that was filled with books along the far wall.

"Your mother was a good housekeeper," Mrs. Hopkins said. "Are those your books?"

"Some are Mom's but mostly they're mine. Mom bought

most of them at the used book store or at the Salvation Army. You can get them cheap there," Tag answered. He stood looking around the room, trying to come to grips with the fact that this was the last time he would ever be in this apartment. His life here was over. His new life was very uncertain.

"You go and pack your clothes and other stuff. I'll go talk to the Super about having the furniture and other stuff cleared out. We'll have someone come and pack everything up and then it will probably go to Good Will. So you make sure to get everything you want, ok sweetie?"

"What about my books?"

"You take the ones you want the most. I'll see if we can find a place to store the rest for you."

He nodded and walked across the living room/kitchen to his small bedroom. Mrs. Hopkins closed the door and walked down the stairs to the Superintendent's apartment to make arrangements.

Tag opened the door and stood looking at his room. His bed was made as usual. It was one of his chores to make it first thing in the morning. On top of his small dresser there was a picture of him and his mom taken a year earlier at a Cubs game by a family friend. Tag was wearing a Cubs cap and his mom was kissing him on the cheek, as he grinned widely. He stood looking at the picture and tears began forming in his eyes.

His mom had been the best mom in the world. She worked two jobs and devoted herself to making a good home for Tag. She was always there for him, whether it was helping him with homework or sitting and talking with him when he had something troubling him. They cooked together and sang silly songs while they stirred and chopped. They played Crazy 8's and Monopoly. Each night his mom came into his room and kissed him good night after he slid into his bed. Now she was gone and he'd never be able to tell her goodnight again. He slid the picture out of the frame and laid it on the bed next to his backpack. Then he began packing clothes and shoes into a trunk that had been delivered earlier for his stuff. Most of his clothes and shoes, he put into the trunk, but a few items, special things, he put in the backpack to make sure they didn't get lost. His favorite ball cap, his lucky tee shirt, and his favorite book all went into the backpack. Before he put the book in, he opened the cover looking at the inscription: TO TAG, WITH LOVE FROM MOM, MERRY CHRISTMAS. MAY YOUR LIFE BE FILLED WITH GREAT ADVENTURES. It was signed by the author. He put the picture of his mom and him between the pages of the book.

He remembered back when his mom had given him the book. She had sent a letter to the man who wrote it and he had signed it and mailed it to her. They had read the stories together over the next few weeks, one each night before bed and the book had become his favorite. He hugged it to his chest remembering how proud he had been to get it, with a special message in it just for him. He put it carefully in the backpack.

He slipped off his damp tennis shoes and socks and took off his pants, jacket and shirt and tie. Rolling the tie up, he put it into his sport coat pocket and then hung the pants and coat and shirt on a hanger and put them in the back of the closet. He didn't think he'd ever wear them again and didn't want to take them with him. He chose a pair of jeans, and a tee shirt and dressed. He put his damp socks in his backpack and put on a dry pair and then his tennis shoes.

In a half hour his stuff was packed and his room was empty except for the furniture. He had other thing that he wanted to get before Mrs. Hopkins returned and he went into his mom's room. He stopped in the doorway drinking in the smell of the room. He could smell her scent, the soap she used, the shampoo. He walked to the bed and pulled back the bedspread and picked up her pillow. He pressed it to his face, feeling her presence in the smell of the pillow. His eyes filled with tears and they soaked into the cotton pillowcase. After several minutes, he gently placed the pillow back on the bed, smoothed it out and then re-covered it with the bedspread. He opened his mother's closet door looking at all the clothes and shoes that would never be worn by her again. Standing there his heart felt like it would break and he backed away from the closet and closed the door. On top of the dresser there was a music box that held his mom's few pairs of earrings and a few inexpensive chains. As he opened it, the box played *Music Box Dancer.* He let the spring wind down until the box was silent and then he lifted up the shelf in the box. Under the inset shelf there was a compartment that Tag knew would hold some money, put away for a rainy day. He removed the shelf and pulled out a sheaf of bills held folded over with a rubber band. Removing the rubber band he counted the money. He was surprised to see that there was $187.

Just then he heard the front door opening, so he slipped the rubber band back around the money and stuck the wad into a pair of socks in his backpack. "Tag where are you sweetie?"

"In here," he answered.

Mrs. Hopkins came to the door. "What are you doing in here?" "I just wanted to see her room once more," he said quietly. "I can smell her in here."

Mrs. Hopkins choked back a sob and walked over to the boy and put her arms around him. Her eyes were moist with tears. "Oh you sweet boy, how I wish I could make this all right for you," she whispered. She took a deep breath. "Well, have you got all your stuff packed?"

He nodded yes. "I've got some stuff in my backpack and the rest is in that big trunk in my room."

"Ok, well I think we should go then. I've got everything set up for the rest of the stuff to be picked up and your trunk will be delivered to your foster home tomorrow. You ready to leave?"

"I guess," he said.

They walked to the front door and Mrs. Hopkins walked out into the hall. Tag stopped and turned back to the apartment for one last look, flipped the light switch off, stepped out into the hall and closed the door behind him. He put his backpack on his back and together he and Mrs. Hopkins walked down the creaking stairs and away from the only home he had ever known.

At the front door the sound of an apartment door opening caused him to stop and turn. Darius Clemmens his best buddy was looking out of his apartment doorway. "Hey Tag, you leavin'?"

Tag looked up at Mrs. Hopkins and she nodded. "I'll meet you in the car," she said.

She took his backpack and walked out. Tag walked down the hallway to Darius' doorway. "So you're goin'?" Darius asked.

Tag nodded, "I got to. I can't stay here alone."

"You gonna still be in school with me?"

"Don't know, I suppose I'll have to go wherever they send me."

Darius nodded slowly. He looked down at his feet, not knowing what to do or say.

The two friends stood a few feet apart looking at each other, feeling awkward. "Well, I hope you do ok, I'll miss ya man," Darius said offering his hand.

Tag nodded. "I'll miss you too Dari," he said.

He took Darius' hand in his and when he did they both pulled each other closer and their other hands went around each others back. They hugged and patted each other on the back, feeling awkward at the embrace. As quickly as he could, Darius, tears streaming down his face, let go of Tag and turned and stepped back into his apartment and closed the door. Tag stood for a minute, wiping the tears from his eyes. "Bye Dari," he said quietly and then walked down the hallway toward the front door for the last time.

Chapter 3

The rain had stopped but there were still a few drips falling from the street lights and the trees. The air was very humid, but the sky was beginning to brighten, looking like the sun would soon be shining. Tag opened the door of the car and strapped himself into the front seat. "Are you ready to go to your new home?" Mrs. Hopkins asked, trying to be as upbeat as possible.

Tag nodded yes. He looked out at his apartment building one last time as they pulled out onto the street. Darius was looking out his window and waved as the car pulled into the street.

Mrs. Hopkins talked about the foster family Tag was going to be with and tried to keep him occupied with conversation as they drove the streets of Chicago, moving east toward Lake Michigan. He listened, trying to be polite but his heart wasn't into it. He didn't want a new family or a new home. "I s'pose I'm not going to be at my old school, am I?" he asked.

"No Tag. You'll have to start at a new school but you will have four foster brothers and sisters there too, so it won't be so bad."

"I don't know them. How is that going to help?"

"Well, you'll know them soon. This evening you can all get to know each other and by the time you start school tomorrow you'll all be friends," she said smiling brightly.

Tag was silent for the rest of the trip and about twenty minutes later they pulled off the highway onto a side street and stopped in front of a two story brick house. All of the houses on the block for as far as he could see were exactly the same, except for the color of the trim and front door. Some had flower gardens in front, some shrubs. "They all look the same," he said.

"You're right, so be sure of the house number when you come

home. It wouldn't be a good idea to walk into the wrong house would it?" she said trying to make light of the situation.

They got out, Tag got his backpack from the back seat and they walked up to the front door. Mrs. Hopkins rang the bell and a half a minute later they heard footsteps coming. The door opened and a small lady wearing a print dress and an apron smiled. "I bet you're Tag," she said motioning them in. "Come in, please, I've been waiting for you."

The house was nice, not fancy but it seemed well kept and was inviting. They walked into the living room and the lady asked them to sit. "How about a glass of milk and some cookies?" she said to Tag.

"Thank you, that would be nice," he said.

"Coffee?" she asked Mrs. Hopkins who nodded yes.

The lady disappeared and Mrs. Hopkins said, "This is a very nice home isn't it Tag?"

He nodded yes.

"These folks have hosted foster kids for many years and are very highly recommended," she said.

Soon the lady came back with a tray of cookies, and two cups of coffee and a glass of milk. She set them on the coffee table. "So, you're Tag, I'm Alice Martin."

Tag shook hands with her. "Pleased to meet you Mrs. Martin."

"You call me Alice, and my husband is Roger. He's at work now and your foster brothers and sisters are at school but this will give us a chance to get to know each other."

"So, four other kids live here?" Tag asked.

"We have two girls, Heidi is 7 and LaShanda is 11. Then we have two boys, Angus is 13 like you and Clifford is 15."

"Isn't that nice Tag, you'll have lots of kids to play with and to help with homework," Mrs. Hopkins said smiling.

They sat and chatted for a while and then Mrs. Hopkins said it was time for her to go. "You have my phone number if there's anything you need. Don't be afraid to call me," she said to Tag.

She put her arms around him and hugged him. "Be brave, you're a good boy, things will work out for you, I'm sure."

After she left, Alice took Tag down the hall to his room. "You are going to room with Angus since you two are the same age. Clifford has this smaller room," she said pointing to a door as they passed. She opened a door to a nice sized bedroom with bunk beds and Tag walked in. "It looks like you get the top bunk,' she said. "There should be room for your stuff in this dresser. For sure there's enough room for what you have now, and when your trunk comes we'll see about getting more storage for you."

Tag nodded ok and stood looking over the room. It was much larger than his old room but he wasn't used to sharing. He hoped that Angus was going to be easy to get along with. Alice helped him put his things away and then he went with her to the kitchen. They talked for the next hour or so until they heard the front door open. "Someone is home...do you want to meet your new brothers and sisters?"

"I guess I have to sooner or later," Tag said.

A girl about Tag's height was coming down the front hallway. She was talking to a smaller girl behind her. "So I said, you just try it and I'll smack you upside your head." She stopped and the two of them giggled when they almost ran into Tag. "You must be our new brother," the taller girl said. "I'm LaShanda and this is Heidi."

LaShanda was a deep coffee brown with black hair and eyes. She wore her hair in braids and had a warm genuine smile. Her eyes were very beautiful and sparkled when she talked. Heidi was just her opposite. She was about a head shorter, blonde, and had blue eyes with light, almost snow white skin. She wore her hair in a pony tail tied up with a pink rubber band.

"I'm Tag," he said.

"That's a strange name," Heidi said smiling shyly.

"It's really Taggert Alan Gronert, but my initials *and* the short form of Taggert is Tag."

14

"Tag for short," LaShonda giggled.

"I guess yeah, Tag for short."

Heidi was blushing as she shook Tag's hand. LaShanda was smiling broadly. "Anyone ever tell you that you're a hot looking guy Tag?"

Now it was Tag's turn to blush. "No, I don't think so," he muttered.

"Well you are, man. Those big blue eyes of yours are really sexy, and those long eye lashes, I bet the chicks at your old school dug you."

"I uh," Tag's face was getting very hot and he could feel sweat forming on his forehead.

"LaShanda, you little hussy," Alice said laughing. "Quit embarrassing Tag." LaShonda and Heidi both giggled and hurried to their room. "Girls," Alice said shaking her head. "LaShanda is pretty outspoken, so don't be surprised when she says something outrageous. I think Heidi has a crush on you already too," she said winking at Tag.

Just then the door opened and in walked a boy who looked to be Tag's age. "Here is your roommate," Alice said. "Angus, meet Tag."

Angus smiled and held out his hand. "Hey man, cool to meet you."

"Same here," Tag said liking him instantly.

Angus was about Tag's height but had bright red hair, freckles and green eyes. He had a genuine nice smile and seemed very happy to meet Tag. While he wasn't fat, he was much huskier than Tag. "Where's Clifford?" Alice asked.

"He was fooling around with a bunch of guys at the grocery on the corner," Angus answered.

"Why don't you and Tag go to your room and get to know each other," she said stepping out onto the front stoop and looking down the street.

The two boys walked to their room and Angus said, "Boy I'm glad you're here. Now I've got somebody to hang out with.

Clifford is a big ass."

"Why's he an ass?" Tag asked.

"He's a bully, just likes to pick on everyone, I hate him. I hope Alice makes him stay in his room when he gets home. He's probably smoking with his buddies, and if she smells it he'll be in deep shit."

Tag laughed. "I can hardly wait to meet him," he said.

Angus changed out of his school clothes into a pair of shorts and a tee shirt and the two boys began talking about their lives. It turned out that Angus had been abandoned at birth and had spent his first 6 years in an orphanage. He had been in three foster homes before this one. "This place is the best I've had. Alice and Roger are really good parents."

Angus asked Tag about his past and Tag told him about losing his mother. "My dad has never been around, and all my grandparents are dead, so I'm alone," he said.

"What kind of name is Tag?"

Tag smiled. "I'm Taggert Alan Gronert, Tag for short."

"Taggert, never heard that name before," Angus said.

"I'm not sure where my mom got it, but it's what I'm stuck with."

Just then there was some shouting in the front hall and the boys looked out the door to see Clifford arguing with Alice. "You go to your room and stay there until I tell you to come out," Alice said angrily. Clifford stomped down the hall and stopped in front of the next door. He was a big kid for 15, nearly 6 feet tall and he looked like he weighed over 250 pounds. He had messy black hair and brown piggy-like eyes. He was scowling at them and growled when he saw them. "Oh boy, look at the two little baby faces," he smirked.

"Clifford! In-your-room!" Alice said from the end of the hallway.

He opened the door and walked through then slammed it shut. Alice shook her head and walked toward the kitchen.

"And stay in there until I call you for dinner," Alice said

angrily. Then she looked at Tag and Angus. "He smells like a brush fire, he's been smoking again." She walked toward the kitchen shaking her head.

Tag and Angus went into their room and closed the door. "See what I mean?" Angus whispered.

"No kidding, is he always like that?"

"Shhh, he's probably listening through the wall. He's a pig. Just stay away from him the best you can. With two of us, maybe he won't be so brave. He doesn't like fair fights, just like most bullies. He likes to have the odds in his favor."

The two boys busied themselves with Angus' Playstation. It was an older model but worked well. He had bought it at the Salvation Army store for very little, most likely discarded by some kid who had a newer model. They passed the time until dinnertime playing with the machine. There was a knock on their door about an hour later. "It's time for dinner gentlemen."

Angus opened the door and there stood Alice's husband, Roger. "Tag this is Roger. Roger this is Tag," Angus said.

"Glad to meet you Tag, that's an unusual name."

Angus laughed. "Tag for short, I'll explain later, let's eat."

Chapter 4

The girls were already sitting at the dining room table when Tag and Angus walked in. "Sit here," Heidi said pointing to the chair next to hers. LaShonda grinned as Tag sat down.

Angus sat on the other side of the table next to Alice while Roger sat at the end. Everyone looked toward the hallway, waiting. "You did tell him dinner was ready didn't you?" Alice asked Roger.

"Yes dear, I knocked and he said ok."

Three minutes later Alice got up and walked briskly to the hall. "Clifford, if you want to eat, get in here, otherwise your next meal will be breakfast." Alice came back to the table, muttering under her breath. The two girls giggled as they whispered to each other.

Shortly after she sat down as Clifford hulked into the room, glaring at everyone. He sat next to Angus and elbowed him. "Move over queer!"

"Clifford! If I hear any more talk like that you'll be going to bed without dinner. Are we clear?" Alice asked looking him right in the eye.

"Crystal!"

Roger began passing bowls and platters of food and soon everyone was eating. Angus began to tell Roger about Tag's name and Clifford butted in. "Tag, like 'you're it'? That's a stupid name!"

"Not tag you're it, you idiot!" Angus replied. "Tag, short for Taggert, also his initials, Taggert Alan Gronert. I think it's pretty unique."

"You would, sissy boy. Are you two boyfriends now?"

"Clifford, what did I tell you?" Alice asked.

"I didn't say queer, I said sissy, that's different."

"Don't say anything like it, ok?" Roger said. "We don't allow that kind of bullying in this house. So, how was your day at school girls?"

The conversation shifted to things that Clifford wasn't interested in and he shoveled food into his piggy-like mouth. Soon he had his plate cleaned off and he burped loudly. "May I be excused?" he asked smirking.

"By all means," Alice said.

Clifford elbowed Angus again as he got up and then he lumbered off to his room. Alice just shook her head. LaShonda mouthed the word PIG, to Tag who burst out laughing.

When dinner was finished, the kids, except for Clifford helped clean up the dishes and kitchen. Heidi made sure to be right next to Tag most of the time, asking him questions and talking about her dolls and other girl things. When they were finished, he and Angus went back to their room and the girls to theirs to study.

"I think Heidi has a crush on you," Angus said.

Tag blushed. "She's a little too young don't you think?"

"Yeah, I guess so, but it's kind of cute. Do you have a girlfriend?"

"Jeez no, I'm only thirteen," Tag said. "Do you have one?"

Angus grinned. "There's this girl who's a ninth grader who likes to study with me in the library. She lets me kiss her when nobody's looking."

Tag was surprised and he grinned. "You dog! You look so innocent."

Angus shrugged. "Don't underestimate the red haired kid."

Since Tag didn't have any homework, he got out his favorite book and began re-reading it. Angus was working on his math and looked up. "What's that book about?"

"It's about a kid and this guy and the fun things they do, like fishing and stuff, the man who wrote it put my name in it and wrote me a personal message too," he said handing the book to Angus.

"Wow that's cool," Angus said reading the words. "Did you meet him?"

"No my mom got that for me. She wrote to him. She didn't say so but I got the idea that she knew him for some reason. It's really a good book I've read it about ten times."

"It looks like it," Angus said looking at the worn pages.

As he paged through the book the picture of Tag and his mother dropped out onto the floor. Angus bent and picked it up. He looked at Tag. "Ok if I look at this?"

Tag nodded. Angus opened the picture and looked. "That's your mom?" Tag nodded. "She's very pretty," he said. Tag nodded again. Angus smiled sadly at Tag. "At least you had a mom who cared for you. Mine just dumped me off like garbage."

Just then Alice came to the door. "It's about bed time boys."

Angus put away his homework and got into his pajamas. He walked to the bathroom, brushed his teeth and then came back to the room. "The bathroom is open, you better get in there or you'll have to wait all night if LaShonda gets in first."

Tag went to the bathroom and was brushing his teeth when the door burst open. "Hurry up pretty boy," Clifford said pushing his way in.

"I'm almost done," Tag said.

"Wrong, you ARE done!" Clifford said grabbing Tag by the back of his tee shirt and pushing him toward the door.

"You big boar pig! Quit acting like such an ass!" LaShonda was standing in the hall glaring at Clifford.

"Don't tell me what to do ghetto girl!"

LaShonda's eyes bugged. "What did you call me you overgrown ox? You take that back or I'll come into your room and cut your balls off when you're sleeping!"

Clifford looked agitated. "You can't. I lock my room."

"A lock doesn't stop a ghetto girl, we can pick any lock we want to, now get out of the way so Tag can finish, and then when me and Heidi are done you can come in. Animals are last in line… after humans." She put her hands on her hips and nosed right up to the much larger boy, glaring at him.

Clifford stood there staring at her, but picked up his towel and walked down the hall to his room.

LaShonda grinned at Tag. "He thinks he big stuff, but he's not so sure about me."

"I'm glad you and I are friends," he said smiling at LaShonda. She grinned, "Hurry up, I gotta get my beauty rest."

"Yes Ma-am!" Tag finished and put his arm around LaShonda's shoulder as he walked past her. "Thanks."

"Anytime gorgeous," she said giggling. As Tag walked past, LaShonda pinched his butt. His face turned bright red and he hurried to his room.

Angus was grinning from ear to ear as Tag told him about LaShonda and Clifford. "She's only 11 but she acts like a big person," he said. "I bet Clifford is about to blow up he's so mad." The two of them giggled about Clifford for a while and then Tag climbed into the top bunk in his underwear since he didn't have any pajamas.

Angus turned off the light and got into the bottom bunk. "Night Tag. I'm glad you're here."

"Thanks Angus, me too."

Tag laid in his bed listening to the sounds of the house as things got quieter and quieter. He heard Clifford's door open and the bathroom door open and close. He could hear Heidi giggling through the wall about something LaShonda was saying. Soon he heard Angus begin to snore.

He lay on his back looking at the ceiling and folded his hands over his heart. "Hello God. This is Tag. I'm not where I usually talk to you, I moved today cause they buried Mom, but I spose you know that. I sure miss her. I spose she's up there with you now. If you see her tell her hi from me, ok? I'm doing ok here I guess. Other than for Clifford this is a good place. So I guess that's about it for today. Don't forget to say hi to Mom from me."

And then he slept.

Chapter 5

Morning was little more than organized chaos. There were 5 kids trying to get showers and breakfast all at once. The two girls were in the bathroom first, one showering while the other brushed her teeth and such. Then Tag and Angus did the same. The two boys and the girls were eating breakfast while Clifford used the bathroom. They were just about to get up from the table when he lumbered into the dining room.

"Time to leave, the pig is here," LaShonda said as she walked past Clifford.

The other three giggled as they filed out of the room. Clifford sat and poured himself some cereal and scowled at them. "Yeah, laugh it up you dorks."

Alice drove the four kids to school. Clifford went to high school and rode the bus which stopped a couple of blocks away. At the school office Alice helped Tag get registered and when he was done she left for home, while Tag rushed off to his class room. The day went pretty well, and Angus and LaShonda saw to it that Tag found his way around the new building. There was only a week of school left in the spring semester, so Tag was really just going through the motions. After school the four of them walked home together.

When they got home, Clifford was already there, in his room playing his music loudly. "He listens to that Hip Hop crap," Angus said shaking his head.

"Likes it loud doesn't he?" Tag said grinning.

The two boys began their homework. After a while Tag was stretched out on the floor reading when he noticed a balled up piece of paper under the bed. He reached back and pulled it out and opened it up. His heart almost stopped when he saw what it was. "Oh no!" he said.

"What's wrong?" Angus asked.

Tag's eyes were filled with tears as he smoothed out the first page of his beloved book. It was the page with the message to him from the author. He held it up so Angus could see.

"Oh no...your book! Who would do that?" Angus asked.

Tag looked toward the wall between their room and Clifford's room. "That fat pig did it, I'll bet anything. Who else would?"

Angus walked over to Tag and took the page from him. "Maybe we can fix it, where's your book?"

Tag opened his dresser drawer and everything was all messed up. His book was missing. He frantically searched the drawer and then thought about his money that he had hidden in a pair of rolled up socks. The socks were unrolled and his money was gone! "That bastard! He took my book and my money."

"What money?"

"I had a bunch of money that was from my mom, I hid it in a pair or socks."

"How much?"

"A lot. Almost $200."

"Holy crap. What are you going to do?"

Tag looked resolutely at Angus. "I'm gonna get it back."

"Maybe we should tell Alice."

"He'll just deny it."

"We'll show them the book. You can tell them about the money."

"Just let it go. I'm going to get it back... one way or the other."

At dinner that night Clifford was even more obnoxious than usual and smirked at Tag, enjoying the fact that he had stolen the money and ruined his book. Tag ignored him and acted like he didn't notice anything amiss. After dinner he and Angus tapped on the girls' door. LaShohda opened it. "Can we talk?" Tag asked.

"What's wrong?"

23

"I need your help, maybe we should talk out here so".....he motioned toward Heidi.

"Heidi's cool, come on in."

Tag and Angus sat on Heidi's bed while she and LaShonda sat on the opposite one. "What's wrong?" Heidi asked.

Tag told them about Clifford robbing him. "Why don't you just tell Alice?" Heidi asked.

"Because, if he has the stuff, he's got it hidden, he'll deny it and I don't have any proof. He could just take the book and throw it away if he hasn't already. And the money, he could have hidden that any place."

"What do you want to do?" LaShonda asked.

"You said last night that you could pick Clifford's lock. Was that just talk or were you serious?"

LaShonda grinned. "I can pick it."

"Good, that's all I want you to do. Later when everyone's asleep, I want you to pick his lock for me and Angus. Then you get back here to your room, so if there's trouble it won't be on you."

"I'll help you too," Heidi said.

"All I need is to get into his room quietly. I don't want you guys to get into any trouble. Angus will help me, he already has said so. Angus nodded his head.

"Ok, tap on the door when you want me and I'll have you in his room in under a minute."

The boys went back to their room and got ready. Angus had picked up a jump rope from the girls' room and Tag snuck into the kitchen and swiped the biggest butcher knife that was in the knife rack. They cut off the handles of the jump rope and tied a slip knot loop on one end. Then they waited for Clifford's music to stop. After everyone had brushed their teeth, they settled down to wait for Clifford to fall asleep. Tag sat with his ear close to the wall listening. Soon he heard heavy snoring from the other side of the wall. "He's sleeping," he whispered.

Tag and Angus quietly opened their door. Angus walked

carefully down the hall to the girls' room and tapped quietly. LaShonda opened the door, slipped out and grinned. Angus nodded his head and they snuck down the hall. At Clifford's door, LaSnonda knelt down and put a bent paper clip into the key hole. She listened and twisted and in less than a minute, there was a click as the lock opened. She looked up grinning. Tag nodded and motioned for her to get back to her room.

She stood up and put her mouth close to Tag's ear. "Be careful gorgeous."

When LaSnonda was back in her room, Tag carefully opened the door. It was very dark in the room and he and Angus snuck in and closed the door. They waited in the dark until their eyes adjusted. Clifford was lying on his back snoring up a storm. There were clothes and shoes and other junk lying all over the place. "What a pig!" Angus whispered.

They snuck over to the bed and Angus quietly moved dirty clothes and other junk from under the bed and then crawled under it. Tag very slowly lifted Clifford's left arm off his chest and moved it toward the edge of the bed. Clifford began to move and mumble. Tag stopped and waited for him to stop moving. Then he moved the arm to the edge of the bed. Angus reached up and slipped the slip loop over Clifford's left wrist and tightened it down. Then he crawled back to the front side of the bed.

Tag began moving Clifford's right arm toward the front edge of the bed while Angus held the rope ready. The plan was to pull the rope over his right wrist and pull hard enough to get both arms over the sides of the bed, tying the right one quickly, so Clifford was tied to his bed. Tag moved the right arm over the edge and Angus wrapped the rope around his wrist. Tag picked up some dirty socks from the floor and wadded them up. He leaned toward Angus. "Pull it tight and tie it fast," he whispered. Angus nodded.

Angus pulled down on the wrist, jerked on the rope which tightened and then tied a half hitch before Clifford could comprehend what was going on. His piggy eyes opened and got wide as he saw Tag kneeling on the bed above him. He opened his mouth to shout and Tag shoved the dirty socks into it. "MMMffffff"

Clifford thrashed around and was trying to shout out, when Tag swung his leg across Clifford's body and sat down on his chest. He pulled the huge butcher knife from behind his back. He let Clifford get a good look at it as he put it to his throat. Clifford didn't know that as Tag got close enough to his throat for him not to see, he turned the knife so the dull edge was against his skin.

"Now, you fat boar pig. You listen carefully," Tag whispered quietly.

Clifford's eyes were wide and he was beginning to sweat profusely. He nodded.

"I'm going to cut your ugly head off and roll it down the street if you don't tell me where my book and my money are."

Clifford shook his head back and forth.

"Clifford, I'm going to ask you once more and then, if you don't tell me in three seconds, your ugly head is gone from your fat ugly body. Where is my money and book?" Tag pressed the dull edge of the knife hard into Clifford's throat.

Clifford was freaking out. His eyes were wide and he looked terrified. Suddenly, he glanced down toward the foot of the bed. Tag's eyes followed Clifford's and he looked over his shoulder and watched as the front of Clifford's pajamas get wet. Tag shook his head sadly. "What a worthless piece of manure you are Clifford, now you've got one second left to live.... where is it!" Clifford motioned with his head toward the desk.

"I'm going to take the socks out. If you yell, I'll cut you." Clifford nodded that he understood.

Tag removed the socks from Clifford's mouth.

"Behind the second drawer," he gasped. It's taped to the back of the drawer." Tag shoved the socks back into his mouth and nodded for Angus to check the drawer. Angus walked over and pulled the drawer out. The money was taped to the back in an envelope with the book taped under it. He pulled it out and walked back to the bed.

Tag looked at the money and counted it. It was all there. He opened the book to see the remains of the torn page. "I ought to cut you just for tearing this, you pig."

Clifford was sweating and breathing hard through his nose. "Smmoory?"

Tag motioned to Angus and they walked to the other side of the room. "Do you think he'll retaliate if we let him go?"

"What else can we do? You're not going to kill him are you?"

Tag laughed. "No, but I'm gonna have to leave now, you know that. I don't want you guys to get into trouble for helping me."

"Leave? What do you mean?"

"I held a knife to his throat, you know he'll tell. I'll have to go to prison or something."

Angus was shaking his head. "You can't leave. If I'd have known you were gonna leave I wouldn't have helped you." He said, his eyes tearing up.

"Angus, I decided today while I was thinking about doing this that I'm going to Wisconsin anyway. I have a friend there who will be glad to help me. I've thought about going to see him for a long time. This just moved up my plans. I'm sorry, I have to go."

"What friend? You didn't tell me about a friend."

"The kid in my book...he's a real person. I decided when Mom died that I was going to go Wisconsin and find him someday. This just moved up my plans."

"Dang, I finally found a friend I really liked and now you're going to leave."

Tag hugged Angus around the shoulder. "Come on, let's let him loose."

They walked to Clifford who was looking terrified yet. Tag sat down on his bed. "Clifford, I want you to listen carefully."

Clifford nodded his head. "I'm going to leave now. I won't be coming back, unless..." Clifford nodded. "If you retaliate on Angus, he'll call me and I'll come back. I'm not going to be far away from here and next time I won't even wake you up. You'll be dead before you know what happened. You got that?" He put the butcher knife up close to Clifford's face so he could see it very clearly.

Clifford nodded.

"Remember, I'll be in the area waiting. Angus has my number and if Angus calls me, you'll be dead in less than 24 hours." He turned to Angus. "Untie him."

Angus untied the rope from Clifford's right wrist and let it go. Clifford pulled his left arm up and slipped off the loop while massaging both of his wrists. He pulled the socks from his mouth. Tag still held the knife near his throat. "Are we good here Clifford?"

"We're good."

"And Angus?"

"No problem."

Tag nodded. He and Angus walked from the room, closing the door.

They walked back to their room and closed the door and locked it. Tag began loading his backpack with some clothes and other stuff while Angus took his book and taped the torn page back into the front. "It's not perfect, but it's pretty good," he said handing the book to Tag.

Tag took it and put it into his pack. "Thanks Angus," he said. He turned for the door, and then stopped. He put his arm around Angus and hugged him. "I think we'd have been pretty good brothers," he said quietly.

"Are you sure about this Tag? I mean what if this guy isn't real?"

"He's real... it says so in the book. I even know his name. I've got to do this Angus. If I don't go I'll always wonder about him. For some reason this seems like the right thing to do.

28

Don't ask me why, it just does."

They walked to the girl's room and tapped quietly. Heidi opened the door immediately. "Did it work?" she asked excitedly. Tag nodded.

"Why you got your backpack?" she asked.

"I'm leaving. I held a knife to Clifford's neck. I'll probably get arrested for attempted murder, so I gotta run away."

Heidi's eyes filled with tears. "No! You can't leave already, LaShonda tell him!"

LaShonda looked sad but said quietly. "He's right Heidi, Clifford will make a big stink and Tag is gonna get put in juvie or someplace. He's got to go to keep from that happening."

Heidi was crying quite loudly. "Shh, Alice and Roger will hear," Lashonda whispered.

"I'm sorry Heidi," Tag said, "I wish I could stay but I'll be back some day."

Heidi put her arms around Tag and cried against his chest. He patted her back and held her until she pulled away. She stood on her tiptoes and kissed him on the cheek and then ran sobbing into the bathroom. LaShonda put her arms around Tag and hugged him.

"You take care of yourself you gorggeous guy. You sure prettied things up around here." She kissed him on the cheek and he returned the kiss to her cheek. Then she grinned, bumped her fist against his and turned and walked to the bathroom to console Heidi.

They walked back to the door of Angus' room. With tears in his eyes Angus hugged Tag. "You take care of yourself, Taggert Alan Gronert, Tag for short."

"I will Angus.'

Tag smiled as he shut the door. He walked quietly through the house and unlocked the front door, stopped and looked back into the house, and then stepped out into the night, and began his quest.

Chapter 6

Tag didn't know which way to go for sure, but remembered a bus stop just down the street from the school he had attended for one day with the rest of the kids. He began hiking down the street with his backpack on his shoulders. It was about eleven o'clock and most of the houses on the street were dark and silent. He couldn't help but feel very alone on the darkened sidewalk. After a couple blocks he saw a car turn onto the street two blocks down, so he stepped into the bushes as it passed. He was hoping it wasn't a police car looking for him. Clifford probably had already made a big stink about being threatened with a knife and they had called the police when they found Tag missing.

He saw the bus stop just down the block. There was a plexi-glass and aluminum shelter with a couple of benches under it. It was lit by several lights in the ceiling. An old lady sat on one of the benches clutching her purse to her chest. She was wearing an old dark blue sweater despite the fact that it was a warm night. She looked at him warily as he sat down on the other bench.

"What is a child your age doing out here at this time of night?" she asked.

"What? I'm sorry, did you say something?"

"Come over here child."

Tag got up and sat down on the same bench as the lady.

"What are you doing out here so late, and all by yourself, I asked."

Tag thought quickly. He looked at the wall of the shelter and saw a poster for the musical Oliver, so he said, "Oh, um, well you see I was at play practice at my school and we kind of got lost in time, what with dancing and singing and all that. My mom called the school and told me to take the bus cause my dad had to go out on an emergency call and she has to stay with my two little sisters, so I'm taking the bus home." He looked at her and smiled. In his mind he was quite proud of himself for the 'off the cuff' story.

"You're in a play? What play is it?"

Oh boy, she believes me, Tag thought. "It's um Oliver, have you ever heard of that one?"

"Oh my yes, I love that play, who are you playing?"

"I'm playing Oliver of course,' he said. Of course he didn't know any names of any other characters, so he had to be Oliver.

"Oh dear, how wonderful. I just love your solo song."

"Thanks, me too," he answered. He had no idea what song she was talking about so he was hoping that she wouldn't ask him to sing.

"*Where is love?* What a beautiful song, it makes me cry every time I see that play and that poor little Oliver sings that."

He smiled and nodded his head. "Please don't ask me to sing, please don't ask me to sing." He kept saying in his head.

"You must have a lovely voice to be able to sing that song, what's your name, so I don't have to keep calling you dear?"

"My name? Oh..." Tag was thinking furiously. He didn't want to tell her his real name in case the cops questioned her, so he tried to think of another name. "It's Jack, Jack London."

"Jack London like the famous author?"

"Crap," Tag thought. "I couldn't come up with a better name than that?"

"Same name, but he's no relation."

"He's been dead for many years."

31

"Well, I guess he was a favorite of my Granny London's, she wanted me to be named after him."

"It's a name you should be proud of, he wrote some very wonderful books, I suppose you've read them?"

"Yes ma-am, I've read both *The Call of the Wild* and *White Fang,*" he said. He had actually read both of the books, so he wasn't lying about that. He did hate lying to this nice old lady but if he told her his real name, she might remember it when the police put his poster up in the Post Office as one of the Ten Most Wanted. He didn't want any trace of himself to be left behind when he made his get away.

Just then, thankfully, the bus pulled up and they joined three other late night passengers. Tag had no idea how much the bus cost, so he watched as the lady put a dollar into the money box, and he pulled the same out and dropped it in.

"Can't make change kid," the driver said.

"What? I thought it was a dollar?"

"Dollar for adults, half a dollar for kids, but I can't make change."

"That's ok, my mom will give it back to me, so you keep the extra," Tag said as he walked toward the back.

The old lady motioned to him to sit by her, so he walked over and sat down. "So Jack, where do you live?"

"I live with my parents."

"I can guess that, but where? If you go to school in this area, what area do you live in?"

"I live where this bus is going of course," he said.

"Oh, by the lake, how nice," she said.

"Yeah, it's real nice, I just live a couple of blocks away, and I go down by the lake and fish a lot you know, that's when I'm not singing in a play or something." He was on a roll now and was getting pretty good at lying on the fly.

The bus rolled on and two of the passengers got off. A few blocks later the old lady got up. "Well Jack, I enjoyed our little visit. I hope you do well in the play. When is it being performed, maybe I'll go and watch you sing?"

"Oh, it's not for a while," he said. "Lots of the kids aren't very good yet, so we're gonna practice until everybody gets good and then we'll put up posters." Apparently she hadn't noticed the poster in the bus stop.

She smiled and patted him on the head. "I'll watch for them. You get home safely sweetie." And she stepped off the bus into the darkness.

Tag now was the only person on the bus. He walked up to the front and sat down behind the driver. "Mister? Where does this bus stop?"

"I go six more blocks east, and then turn north three blocks and head back to where I came from," he said, "Where are you trying to get to?"

"I'll get off where you turn to start back if that's ok sir."

The driver nodded. They drove on and soon he pulled over to the bus stop where two men were waiting. "This is where I start back kid. Are you sure you're ok?"

"Yeah, I'm fine, I just forgot, thanks for the ride," Tag said and walked to the back door to get off. He stepped off onto the sidewalk and the bus roared away, leaving a fog of diesel fumes. Tag looked around and could see in the distance, the tall masts of sailboats that were moored in the harbor. He began walking toward the lake, hoping to find someplace to spend the night where he would be safe.

The closer he got to the lake, the more he could smell fish and the unmistakable smell of the water. There was a small park next to the lake and several stores and restaurants across the street from the docks. The first on his right was a bait shop and tackle store, the next a restaurant, then there was a fish market and there was a bakery just beyond that.

He walked down the sidewalk and watched for any place that might be a suitable spot to sleep for the night. He was in front of the restaurant when he saw the lights from a car coming down the street toward him, so he stepped around the building and back into the alley between it and the fish market. He watched from the shadows as a police car drove slowly down the street past him.

"Oh no, they're after me already!" he thought to himself. "I better find a place to hide tonight and then tomorrow see about getting out of town."

He kept in the shadows as he walked to the back end of the alley. There were a couple of dumpsters and an old lean-to that was piled with empty cardboard boxes and bags of aluminum cans. "Must be their recycling stuff," he thought. "Maybe I can make a hidey hole in those boxes."

He snuck over to the shed and took his pack off his back. Then he pulled some of the boxes out and made a space behind them. He flattened out a few for a bed and then crawled in and pulled the outside boxes back. He looked around in the dim light from the streetlight down the alley a short way. "This is pretty nice," he said, feeling quite proud of himself. He put his backpack down for a pillow, took off his shoes and stretched out, pulling the boxes in tight, so his hidey hole was completely dark.

Tag lay on his back and folded his hands across his heart. "Hi God," he said quietly, "it's Tag again, and I'm in a different place again. I did something kind of bad tonight and had to leave the place I was staying. I don't know if you know about Clifford, but he's probably not a guy who talks to you too much. He's a real shit...oops, sorry I didn't mean to say that, but he's not a very nice guy. He stole my money and my favorite book and I got real mad and threatened to cut his ugly head off. Of course, I really wouldn't do that, you know me better than that. So anyway, I had to leave 'cause Clifford probably went to the cops and I'm probably on an APB right now. So, I'm kinda gonna lay low for a while, so if you see Mom, tell her I'm ok and I've got a cool place to sleep tonight. I'll let you know tomorrow night, how stuff turns out. Bye for now, your friend Tag."

Tag turned onto his side and closed his eyes. In just a few

minutes he was sleeping and he began to dream. He was standing along a road in the country. To the left there was a big hill that ran down along side the road ahead of him. On the right there was nothing but open land. The road ran ahead of him and where the hill met the road there was a rise that made it look like to road went off into infinity. He stood there looking around, wondering where he was and then he noticed a man standing on the edge of the road way down near the rise. He couldn't see his face or much about him but he knew it was someone he needed to meet. He started walking down the edge of the road.

Chapter 7

Tag walked along in his dream for a long time when he heard his mother's voice. He turned and she was walking along side him. She laughed when he turned, looking so surprised, and he was filled with joy at the sound of her voice. She put her arm around his shoulder and they walked along together smiling and talking. He told her about Clifford and she laughed at his story. Suddenly he could hear another sound, a scratc hing sound that was very out of place along the road. He turned to see if his mom heard it and she was gone. Consciousness was approaching as the sound got louder and closer.

Tag's eyes were still closed but he was awake, listening to the sounds of toenails scratching on the cardboard of his hideout. He could hear the sound of an animal of some kind working it's way through the cardboard maze. It was getting closer.

"Maybe it's a rat or a raccoon," he thought to himself as he opened his eyes. It was still completely black in the little space he had made for himself, so he couldn't see a thing. The sound came closer and he felt the boxes near his feet move. He could hear the animal sniffing as it smelled it's way toward Tag. Suddenly he could feel something touching his right foot. He pulled it back quickly and tucked both feet up under his body. The animal moved forward and he felt it again as it touched his foot.

This time it felt like the animal was licking his sock. He tried to move away from it but he didn't have any more room to move. Then he felt teeth scratching on his sock as the animal nibbled on his toes. "Oh no! I'm being attacked by rats!" he said to himself, panicking at the thought.

Just then the animal's teeth sunk into his sock and it began

36

pulling it off his foot. That was enough for Tag. He jumped and tried to stand up, shouting at the critter. "Get away! Let me alone!"

There was a scurrying sound as the animal backed away and stopped. Tag couldn't see anything and was almost afraid to slide the boxes open so the street light would shine into his nest. He could hear a whining sound coming from a short way away. Finally he moved the top box a little and a beam of light shined in. He looked near the end of his hideout and could see something crouched there. It didn't look like a rat, it was too large. "Maybe it's a raccoon," he thought. He moved the box a little more and then he could see plainly, it was a dog. Tag's sock was lying on the ground by the dog's feet. It whined and wagged it's tail.

Tag was relieved. "Hey fella, come here," he said extending his hand. The dog whined again but moved forward. "Come on, I won't hurt you," he said. The dog moved forward again, and he reached out and touched its head. The tail began wagging wildly and the dog moved up and climbed right into Tag's lap. "Hey see, I'm not going to hurt you," he said, as the dog began licking his neck and face. "I'm sorry if I scared you, but you scared me pretty bad too."

Tag petted the dog's head and back and in no time they seemed to be great friends. He took the dog in his hands and held it up in front of him. It was a small beagle, mostly black but with white and tan markings on it. "What's your name?" he said. "That was a stupid question, you can't talk."

The dog wagged and it's tongue was lapping at Tag joyously trying to lick him anywhere that got close enough to be licked. "You look like a friend of mine from my last school. He had big sad brown eyes like you and his hair hung down just like your ears. Maybe I'll call you Bob. That was his name, Bob Hartley. How do you like Bob for a name?" The dog wagged it's tail wildly. "Ok, Bob it is," Tag said putting the dog in his lap.

He peered out of the opening in the boxes and saw that the

sky was still very dark. "It's still night, maybe we should sleep for a while yet." He saw his sock lying on the boxes on the bottom of the nest and put it back on. Then he pulled the boxes back tight together and lay down. "Come on Bob, let's sleep a while yet."

Tag lay down on his side and Bob snuggled up next to his chest and lay with his back to Tag's chest. He put his arm around the warm little body. It felt good to have someone next to him. In just a short while, they both were sleeping soundly.

Tag woke several hours later when he heard the noise of someone out in the alley putting trash into one of the dumpsters. Bob woke up and yawned and then licked Tag on the face. "Hey Bob, good morning, did you sleep ok?" Bob wagged his tail.

Tag opened the boxes a little and saw that it was morning. He put his sneakers on and picked up his backpack. "I bet you're hungry....I know I am," he said to Bob. He pushed open the boxes and crawled out into the alley with Bob right behind him. Suddenly he could smell the most wonderful smell. The bakery that was just down the alley must have been baking bread or rolls already and the smell was making his stomach growl. "Let's go see if we can get something to eat," he said. He walked toward the street with Bob right on his heels.

They walked down the sidewalk and when they got to the bakery they saw a man coming out with a white paper bag full of baked goods. "It's open, you stay here and I'll go in and get us something to eat." Bob sat down and Tag walked into the bakery.

It smelled incredible in the shop and Tag walked up to the counter. There were glass cases filled with donuts, rolls, and all kinds of wonderful pastries. "Can I help you?" the lady behind the counter asked.

"Yes ma am, I'd like one of those, and those and those and two of those." The lady bagged up his choices.

"That's $2.90," she said. Tag pulled some money out of his

pocket and handed the lady $3. She made his change and handed it back to him. Then he noticed a machine that had milk and pop in it.

"Can I get change for the machine?" he asked.

She changed a dollar for him and handed him the coins. "Anything else?"

"I wonder if you might have an old container, like a margarine tub or something so I can get my dog something to drink," he said motioning to the street. He turned to make sure Bob was still sitting by the door and was surprised to see that he was gone. "Just a minute!" he said racing for the door. He stepped out and saw Bob walking down the middle of the street in front of the bait shop. "Bob! Hey Bob!"

The dog stopped and turned back, saw Tag and came on a run toward him. He squatted down and grabbed Bob as he jumped up to him. "Did you think I abandoned you? I'm sorry, you thought I left you didn't you? No way, you and I are buds. You wait here," he said patting the sidewalk. Bob sat and looked at him. "Stay there!"

He hurried back into the bakery and the lady had sat a small yellow bowl on the counter. "I think this will work don't you?" she asked smiling.

"That's perfect, thanks a lot," Tag said.

He hurried over to the milk machine and bought two cartons of milk. Then he picked up his bag of donuts and started for the door.

"Are you ok sweetie?" the lady asked.

"What do you mean?"

"Where are your parents? Are you lost or something?"

"Oh no, I'm fine, me and Bob were just hungry and my folks were still sleeping on the boat. Don't worry about us, we're good," he said smiling brightly.

"Ok, just wondering. You be careful now, you better get a leash on Bob or he'll get run over on the street."

"I will, thanks ma am."

Bob was very excited when he smelled the donuts. "I think we better go back to our hideout and eat," Tag said. "We don't want anybody to think we're lost or running away."

They went back to the alley and Tag crawled into his hideout with Bob right on his heels. He pulled the boxes partly closed so they were hidden and opened the bag of donuts. Bob's tail was wagging like crazy as Tag shared the donuts with him and then poured one of the cartons of milk into his bowl. "Looks like you were about starved," Tag said to the dog. Bob didn't even look up, but kept drinking milk until every drop was gone. "Umm, I feel better now, how about you?" Bob looked up, burped loudly and wagged happily and snuggled down in Tag's lap for a nap. "Not a bad idea," Tag said and soon the two of them were sleeping soundly again.

Chapter 8

An hour or so after they settled down, Bob began licking Tag awake. "Hey Bob, what's up?" Tag said sleepily. "You gotta go pee?" The dog began jumping up and down as if he understood what he had been asked. "I gotta go too, so let's see about that."

They opened up the nest and crawled out. It was mid morning already and there was the sound of cars and trucks on the street and the sounds of boats in the harbor. Tag went behind the dumpster and did his business while Bob just squatted in the alley. "Bob, what the heck?" Tag said looking at the dog squatting. He bent down and then looked surprised. "Jeez Bob, you're a girl."

Bob wagged her tail happily. "Well, maybe I should re-name you, what do you think?" Bob wagged as usual. "Well, I don't know, I kind of like the name Bob, so we'll just keep it. Let's go see what's going on."

They walked out to the front of the store and stopped on the sidewalk. There was a lot of traffic on the street and many people walking up and down the sidewalk. Bob trotted ahead of Tag and started across the street. "Bob, get back here!" Tag called. Bob stopped and came trotting back to Tag. "I think I better get you a collar and leash, or you'll get squashed by a car or truck." He patted his leg and the dog followed him down the street to the bait shop. "Wait here," he said patting the ground. Bob sat down.

Tag walked in and looked over the store. It was more than just a bait shack, with fishing tackle, nets, some rain gear, oars and a counter of snacks. He walked up to the counter. The owner walked over to him. "Hi young man, what can I do for you?"

"Hi mister, say would you happen to have a dog collar or a leash? My dog lost his collar and I'm scared he'll get run over."

"I do, right over here," the man said leading Tag to a shelf next to the fishing nets. "We have these leather collars or these chain slip collars, and several leashes from simple ropes to leather ones."

Tag looked at the collars and chose a slip collar which was only $1.99. He checked out the leashes and put the leather ones down right away since they were all over $10. He found a light red nylon one with a clip on one end for $2.29. "These will be good," he said handing them to the owner. They went back to the cash register and the man rang them up. "That's $4.28 plus tax for a total of $4.49." Tag dug in his pocket and got out a five dollar bill. He handed it to the man and got his change. "Thank you young man, take good care of that dog of yours."

"Thanks mister, I sure will." Tag walked out to where Bob was waiting patiently. Bob was very excited about what Tag had in the bag but seemed disappointed when it turned out to be something other than food. Tag slipped the loop collar over Bob's head and snapped the clip on the collar. "There, now you won't get smooched all over the road," he said leading the dog down the street.

They walked down along the lake and looked over the fishing boats and the big charter boats. "I wish we could find someone going north to Wisconsin to give us a ride on one of these boats," he said to Bob. They walked for a while and ended up walking out onto the breakwater pier. The breakwater was a long pile of big boulders with a cement sidewalk on top that stretched out into the lake for several hundred yards. The cement walkway on top was about as wide as a single lane road. It protected the harbor from the waves when the lake was rough on a windy day. About half way out on the break wall he stopped by an old man who was fishing. The man was sitting on a folding chair and had two fishing poles lying on the sidewalk. One was propped up on a small cooler and the other was propped up on his bait bucket. He was wearing plaid shorts and red tennis shoes. His legs were very skinny but quite tan making Tag think that he spent a lot of time in the sun fishing.   A very colorful Hawaiian shirt completed his attire topped off with a big straw hat. Each of his fishing poles had a large red and white bobber on the line that was out in the water. The old man was sitting reading a paperback book, looking up occasionally at his bobbers.

"Catchin any?" Tag asked.

The man looked up. "Nothing yet, but it's early, and I got no place to go anyway."

"What do you usually catch here?"

"I'm fishing for northern...but you can catch perch and sometimes small mouth bass too. Once in a while a brown trout or a salmon comes up in here too, but not very often."

Tag nodded his head knowingly. Just then one of the bobbers began bobbing up and down and then began to move away. "Holy cow, you got a bite!" he said pointing at the moving bobber.

The man looked up. "Yup, one's workin."

Tag was excited. He'd only been fishing a couple of times and that was for bluegills, so it was exciting to think of a big northern on the line. "Aren't you gonna pull?" he asked.

"Not time yet."

The bobber moved about ten feet and stopped. "Looks like he's gone, you waited too long," Tag said.

The old man chuckled. "He's there, he's scaling the minnow. Northerns will pick up the minnow, then swim a ways with it, and then stop and scale it and then turn it and swallow it head first," he said. "When he starts to move again, he'll be ready for a pull."

Tag sat down on a boulder nearby and Bob lay down and rested her head on her paws. Soon the bobber began moving again, slowly and steadily down along the rocky break wall. The old man leaned down and picked up the fishing pole and held it over to Tag. "Here, give her a hard pull."

"I don't know how to fish," Tag said.

"Ain't no *know-how* to it, just pull hard and then turn that handle and reel him in, I'll help you."

Tag took the rod and swallowed hard. "Reel up the slack and then give her a hard pull," the man said. Tag reeled up the line until it was almost tight between him and the bobber. "Smack him a good one now!"

Tag pulled hard on the rod and the fish began running so fast that he almost lost the rod from his hands. He held on for dear life as the line began to spin off the reel. "Holy smokes, it's a whale!" he yelled.

The old man chuckled. "Just keep the line tight, reel when you get some slack, and take your time, he's not going anywhere."

The fish ran toward the end of the break wall and then turned and raced back toward them. Tag reeled furiously as the line came his way. Then as fast as it had come, the fish passed them and kept going toward the shore. The line pulled off the reel again and soon Tag was reeling up the slack a second time. Bob was on her feet now, barking as the excitement grew.

"You're doing good, just keep the line tight, he's getting tired."

"So am I!" Tag said and the old man laughed uproariously.

Finally the fish began to slow down and the old man picked up a battered old landing net and walked carefully down across the rocks to the edge of the water. "Just lead him over here and I'll net him," he said.

Tag pulled and reeled and soon the fish could be seen just below the surface. "Holy smokes, it's huge!" Tag said excitedly.

"It's a good one, bring him a little closer...closer." The man slid the net under the tired fish and in a second it was thrashing, flinging water all over the place. The old man crawled up over the rocks with the fish in the net. He held it out to Tag. "There, what do you think of that?" he chuckled.

"Jeez mister, that's the biggest fish I ever pulled in," Tag said not believing how huge the fish was. "The only other fish I ever caught was a bluegill about the size of a potato chip."

"This one is a little bigger than that," the man said with a wide grin on his face.

"What you gonna do with it?" Tag asked.

"I'm gonna take it home and cook it for supper tonight, and if you and your friend here haven't got any dinner plans, I'd like to invite you to share it with me."

"Really? That'd be great. Me and Bob don't have any plans at all mister."

"Well, then I guess we should introduce ourselves since we'll be dining together," the man said as he took the hook from the fish and put it on a stringer. "I'm Fred Orchard, and you are?" He took the fish and put it in the lake and tied the stringer to a steel post that was driven in between some rocks, probably by a fisherman who used it for just the same purpose.

Tag thought for a minute furiously trying to come up with a name since we was still on the Most Wanted list in the area. All he could think of was the big fish so he said, "Me? I'm Ernest, Ernest Hemingway."

The man raised his eyebrows. "Ernest Hemingway, are you any relation to the author?"

"No, my grandma liked his books and when I was born, she talked my mom into naming me that," Tag lied. Again, he hated to lie to the nice man, but he didn't want anyone to know his real name or the cops would find him real fast. "And this is my dog Bob."

Fred looked over Bob and then at Tag. "You know Bob is a girl don't you?"

"Yeah, I had her named Bob before I knew that but when I found out I didn't want to change her name and give her some kind of complex or something, so I just left it at Bob."

The man shook his head and grinned. "So where do you live Ernest?"

45

"Oh, just up the road a piece. My parents are out on a sightseeing charter but Bob gets seasick, so we stayed on shore. They're going to be out all night, so we're gonna get a motel room later."

"I see, so you're free for the day so to speak."

"Yeah, free as a couple of birds."

Fred re-baited the hook on the pole that had caught the northern with a large minnow and tossed it back out into the lake. They sat down again and Bob began to snooze. "So, why is it that you're not in school today Ernest?"

Tag searched his mind for a reason and quickly came up with, "Oh, they're removing asbestos at our school so we have a week off, bad stuff that asbestos."

"Yes, it surely is."

They fished in silence for a while and then Tag asked, "Are you married Fred?"

"I was, my wife died six years ago."

"Sorry to hear that. Got any kids?"

"Yes I do, three boys and two girls, all grown up and living all over the country. I was a Professor of Physics at Northwestern University for thirty one years. Then six years ago my wife got cancer and died, so I decided to retire and fish the rest of my life. I lived in a big house near the University and didn't need it anymore, so I sold it and now I have a little apartment above the restaurant over there," he said pointing to the establishment. "I just work there part time, to keep myself busy, but mostly I fish and enjoy the quiet life."

Tag nodded knowingly. A seagull landed a short way away and screeched and Bob jumped up and took off chasing it, howling. Tag and Fred laughed as Bob raced down the break wall after the bird. "So how long have you had Bob?" Fred asked.

"I just got him...her, for my birthday."

"Oh? What are you twelve?"

"Thirteen, I'm skinny for my age."

Fred laughed. "Well, let's see what we can do about that. Are you two hungry?

"Now that you mention it, I'm starving and I know Bob is hungry, dogs are always hungry."

"Dogs and teenage boys are always hungry," Fred said as he opened the small cooler. He took out a loaf of bread and a package of bologna and some cheese. Then he took out a couple of cans of soda and handed one to Tag. "Help yourself to a sandwich and make one for Bob too," he said.

They ate and talked for a half hour or so and then got back to some serious fishing. Fred picked up his book again and Tag laid down on his side with his head on his back pack and watched the bobbers. Bob lay down next to Tag and went to sleep. Ten minutes later Tag was sleeping right along with Bob.

"Ernest, you want to pull in another fish? Ernest?"

Tag heard the man talking but it didn't dawn on him that he was talking to him. Then he realized that he was Ernest. He sat up quickly. "Yeah, what? We got another bite?"

"He's been working it for about ten minutes, I expect that he's on by now, you want to pull him in?"

Tag nodded and Fred handed him the rod. He wound up the slack and then hauled back on the rod and the fight was on. This fish headed out toward the end of the breakwater and began bulldogging across the lake toward the other side. The rod was singing as line was pulled out. "He's taking all the line... go with him!" Fred said excitedly.

Tag jumped to his feet and began walking quickly toward the end of the break wall, following the fish. Fred came along behind with the net and Bob was behind him, checking out all the new smells on the rocks. They came to the end of the rocks and the fish was still going. "He's gonna take all the line," Tag said looking at Fred for advice.

"Here, let me tighten up the drag a little to see if we can stop him," he said turning the knob on the front of the reel. The line slowed down but the pull from the fish was harder than before.

Tag held on as tight as he could and tried to plant his feet to keep from getting pulled over the edge and into the lake. "He's really strong," he said, his arms beginning to ache.

"Must be a big salmon, too strong for a northern," Fred said looking toward the lake at where the fish must be. Just then the line snapped with a bang like a pistol shot. Tag almost fell over backwards when the fish parted ways with him. "Dang! He busted the line!" he said. "Sorry Fred, I'll buy you a new line."

Fred just laughed. "Don't worry Earnest, that's not the first line I ever lost, and won't be the last. He must have been a dang whale, don't ya think?"

"Must have been Moby Dick," Tag laughed.

They walked back to Fred's chair and Fred said, "Well, one pole's out of commission and it's almost time for dinner, what do you think? I think we go and cook that fish up?"

"Sounds good to me Fred," Tag said smiling brightly. They gathered up the gear and Tag proudly carried the fish on the stringer up toward the crowds of people. He got a lot of smiles and compliments as they walked down the sidewalk toward Fred's place. Even though the fish was heavy and getting his jeans all slimy, he wouldn't have missed this for anything.

Chapter 9

Tag, Fred and Bob walked along the waterfront up the block and then Fred motioned Tag to turn into the alley next to the seafood restaurant. "My apartment is up over the restaurant," Fred said.

"I help in the kitchen, doing dishes four nights a week."

"Must be good pay to only have to work part time," Tag said.

"I have my retirement fund and get Social Security too, so this just helps me with some extra cash to buy fishing tackle and bait," Fred said pointing the way up a set of wooden stairs to a door with a little porch in front of it. "Besides, a guy can't just sit and do nothing all day. I enjoy a little work each day to keep me busy. They climbed the stairs but Bob was having trouble getting up one stair to the next, so Tag picked her up and Fred carried the fish. Fred unlocked the door and they walked into the small apartment.

"It's not much but it's all I need," Fred said. "This is the living room and kitchen, down that hall is a bathroom and a bedroom." Fred went to the sink and put the now dead fish in it and then put his fishing poles and tackle box in the corner of the room. He poured out the ice water from the cooler and threw away the empty cans and wrappers. "Make yourself to home," he said.

"Could I use your bathroom?" Tag asked.

"Sure, be my guest," Fred said.

Tag went to the bathroom and noticed several fishing magazines and a pile of books on a small table next to the toilet. He looked through the books and found several that he had read. "I see you have a nice library," he said to Fred as he walked back into the kitchen.

"Yes, that's the reading room I guess," Fred chuckled. "Are you much of a cook Ernest?"

"Yeah, I'm pretty good in the kitchen, I used to help mom a lot."

"Used to? What, you don't help any more?"

"Oh no, I meant that I help a lot, sure, I help whenever she wants."

Fred nodded slowly. "Well, how about you peel some potatoes while I clean this fish?"

"Just show me where they are," Tag said. Fred showed him the potatoes and he sat down at the table with a pan full of water and began peeling them with a knife that Fred had handed him. Meanwhile Fred laid some papers down on the counter top and began filleting the northern. It only took him a few minutes and he had four long thin fillets lying on the paper and the head and backbone and skin of the fish lying on another piece of paper. He rolled up the carcass and rinsed off the fillets in the sink. "That didn't take you long," Tag said admiring the fillets.

"I've done a bunch of them I guess, kinda gets to be pretty easy after a while. I see you've made short work of those potatoes too, how about you slice them into a pan and we'll get them going before we start on the fish."

Fred got a large frying pan out and poured in some cooking oil. Tag began slicing the potatoes into the oil and soon they began to sizzle. Bob was watching it all and began to whine. "Sounds like Bob is pretty hungry," Tag said.

"Won't be long now young lady," Fred said as he stooped and petted Bob on her head.

The potatoes had been cooking for ten minutes or so when Fred got out another deeper frying pan and filled it with oil. Then he cut up the fillets into smaller pieces and rolled pieces in flour and salt and pepper. He dipped his hand under the faucet and then let a drop of water drip into the pan. It jumped and skittered across the top of the oil. "It's hot," he said and began putting the chunks of fish carefully in the hot oil. The kitchen was filled with wonderful smells from the cooking food. "Those potatoes look about done," Fred said, "slice up that onion and put it in with them about now."

Tag did as he was told and soon the smell of the frying onion made the kitchen smell even better. Bob was whining up a storm and pacing back and forth during the next five minutes as the food finished cooking. Fred had set two places at the table and also had gotten an empty aluminum pie pan out for Bob. He filled a bowl with water and set it down next to the table for the dog. "About ready now Bob," he said.

They dished up the food onto two platters and sat down to the table. "Do you say grace?" Fred asked.

"Sure do," Tag said.

"Well, how about you do the honors then?"

Tag folded his hands and bowed his head. "Hi God, Tag here, just wanted to say thanks for this good meal that we're about to have. Thanks for letting me and Bob meet Fred too. Amen."

"Amen." Fred added, looking questioningly at Tag.

They filled their plates and Tag chopped up some fish and put a pile of potatoes onto Bob's pie pan and blew on them to cool them off. Bob was getting very impatient waiting and gobbled like she was starving when he set the plate down. "Boy I guess Bob likes fish," Tag said laughing.

They ate quietly for a while, savoring the great food. "Boy, Fred, you sure know how to make fish good," Tag said as he speared another piece of fish.

"Glad you like it Ernest, or is it Tag?"

Tag stopped eating. "Why would you call me Tag?"

"Hi God, Tag here?"

"Oh crap!" Tag looked over at Fred. "I'm sorry I lied to you Fred, I didn't know you'd turn out to ask us to supper and all. I feel pretty crappy about it."

Fred looked at the boy. "Are you in trouble son?"

Tag nodded and slid his plate away. "I'm wanted by the

police. I'm on the run and have to get out of town."

Fred looked mystified. "What are you wanted for?"

"Attempted murder."

Fred's eyes opened wide. "Attempted murder? Who did you attempt to murder?"

"A guy named Clifford. It's a long story Fred."

"I've got all the time in the world," Fred said leaning back in his chair.

Tag told his story and Fred listened intently. When he was finished Fred said, "So you really think this Clifford will press charges? It sounds like he's nothing more than a bully. I doubt he'd have the guts to go to the cops."

"Well, I can't take the chance, I've gotta lay low," Tag said.

Fred nodded and turned his head as if looking at the door, suppressing a grin. "So where do you plan to go?"

"I've got this friend in Wisconsin. I'm gonna go and see him. I think he'll help me, maybe he and I can take off for out west or maybe Australia or someplace together."

"I see," Fred said. "Well, it'd be pretty risky to stay in a motel. They might require an ID or something. Why don't you and Bob sleep here on my couch tonight?"

"Are you sure? You know, you might be arrested as an accessory or something?"

Fred stifled a grin. "I'll take the chance," he said.

"Ok, that'd be great Fred. I don't want to be any trouble."

"No trouble Tag. That's a strange name, I've never heard it before."

"It's really Taggert Alan Gronert. My initials are TAG, so I go by Tag for short."

Fred grinned. "Ok Tag for short, I'll clean up these dishes. Why don't you and Bob go and get a bath and get ready for bed?"

"Ok, that sounds good."

Tag took his backpack to the bathroom and he filled the tub with warm water. He stripped off his clothes and climbed into the tub. He lay back enjoying the warm water and closed his eyes. Bob began whining and stood up with her front paws on the edge of the tub. "Want a bath too?" Tag asked. Bob began wagging wildly, so Tag reached over the side and lifted the dog into the tub with him. Bob loved the water and soon the two of them were having a great time soaping up. Bob was barking and Tag was laughing when there came a tap on the door. "Are you two ok in there?" Fred asked.

"Yeah Fred, Bob's having a bath too."

Fred chuckled.

A while later Bob came scampering out into the kitchen where Fred sat at the table sipping on a bottle of beer and watching a baseball game on TV. He reached down and petted the still damp dog. "You look quite bright and shiny young Bob," he said. Just then Tag walked in, his long hair still damp, wearing a pair of boxer shorts and a tee shirt. "I hope it's ok just to wear this," he said.

"We're very informal around here," Fred said. "Do you like baseball?"

"Yeah, it's ok, I like fishing better though," he said grinning.

Fred went to the refrigerator and got Tag a pop and opened another beer for himself. "I'd offer you a beer but I believe you're a little too young,' he said.

"Pop is fine Fred."

They watched the game and Bob fell asleep on the floor next to the TV lying on her back with all four feet sticking up. When it ended Fred got up. "Well, I think I'll have a bath and then go to bed. Maybe Bob needs to go out before we turn in."

Tag agreed and slipped on a pair of shorts and his sneakers and woke Bob up. She yawned and stretched and then he took her down the steps to the alley so she could go potty. When he got back upstairs Fred had laid out a sheet and a blanket and pillow on the couch. He could hear water running in the bathroom. He took off his shorts and shoes and made his bed on the couch. It was real nice and soft and plenty big for both him and Bob, who snuggled right next to him. He was just about to nod off when Fred poked his head around the corner. "Good night you two... sweet dreams."

"Night Fred, thanks a lot for everything."

Tag turned over on his back and folded his hands over his heart. "Hey God, Tag again. I had a pretty good day today. I met a nice man who let me go fishing with him and gave us a good supper. I'm going to sleep here on his couch tonight. I know, Mom probably is having a fit with me staying in a place with a stranger, but Fred's not creepy at all. Tell her he's been married and had lots of kids and stuff, so he's ok. I'm careful with stuff like that. Anyway, I'm safe tonight, so thanks for that and for everything else. I'll talk to you tomorrow again. Oh I caught a really big fish today too. Tell Mom. Good night from Tag."

The dream he had the night before came back again. He was walking along that long road that seemed to go forever. He noticed a person standing along the road just a short way up ahead but couldn't tell who it was. The person at the top of the knoll still was there, as if he was waiting for Tag. He had no idea who it was but he was sure he'd find out in time.

Chapter 10

Bob's warm body was pressed up against Tag's chest and he just barely woke as the dog moved away from him. He was still too deeply asleep to hear Bob jump down from the couch and go out the door with Fred for a morning potty break.

Tag didn't hear them come back but did begin to stir when the smell of frying bacon began to fill the room. At first he thought he was at home with his mom, but soon he was awake enough to remember that he was in Fred's apartment.

"Good morning young Tag," Fred said from the kitchen. "How did you sleep?"

"Morning Fred, wow, I slept good. I guess I didn't know how tired I was with all the running from the cops and stuff. Did Bob go out?"

"Yup, Bob and I have been out and her business is finished. How do you like your eggs?"

"Over easy if you don't mind," Tag said sitting up on the edge of the couch. He stretched and yawned and then got up and went to the bathroom, did his business and then splashed some water on his face and returned to the kitchen. Fred was just setting the plates of food on the table.

"Sit and eat, while it's still hot," he said.

There was a large plate with eggs, hash browns, bacon and toast sitting waiting for him, so Tag dug into the food and shared bites with Bob who was sitting next to him waiting for her share.

"I have to work this morning," Fred said. "I stopped into the restaurant when Bob and I were downstairs and they asked me to come in and work most of the day. The regular day guy is home sick, so I guess I'm elected."

"That's ok, Bob and I should be on our way to Wisconsin anyway," Tag said.

Fred ate silently for a couple of minutes. Then he said, "You know Tag, maybe you should find out about all that attempted murder stuff before you go off to Wisconsin. Maybe the police aren't after you. I'd be happy to put you and Bob up for a while, until you get things worked out."

"Thanks Fred, that's real nice of you, and I'm sure we'd have a fine time together, but this friend of mine in Wisconsin is really a good guy and I know he'll help me out. We've known each other for a long time and did a lot of stuff together. You've been as nice as anybody ever has been to me, but I really think I gotta get out of here or I might be in jail or some kind of youth home."

"This friend, how do you know him," Fred asked.

"Well, I don't actually know him personally, but he's the main character in this book of mine that I've read many times. My mom met the guy who wrote the book I guess. He signed the book for me and in the front it says that this character is a real person. I know where the guy who wrote it lives, so I'm going there to meet him."

"You're going to meet a character from a book?"

"Yeah, but he's a real person too."

"But you're sure he's real?"

"Yeah, I'm sure. Ever since I read the book the first time, I just knew that this guy and I were going to be friends someday. I can't explain it but it just seems like it's something I have to do."

Fred nodded but he was not convinced. "Ok, but just remember, if things don't work out, I'll be here, and you can come back anytime." Fred put his hand on Tag's shoulder and gave it a squeeze. He got up and walked to the counter. "Here," he said taking a slip of paper from the counter and writing his phone number on it, "if you get in trouble, call me anytime of the day or night."

"Thanks Fred, I'll do that," he said folding the paper in half and sticking it into his pocket.

56

They cleaned up the breakfast dishes and Fred got dressed for work. "Why don't you guys hang around for a while, maybe another day or so and get your plans worked out. Kind of lay low and watch for the cops. I'll be right downstairs, give me a holler if you need anything."

"Ok, we're gonna look around a little today and see what we can do about finding a way to get to Wisconsin."

Fred left and Tag brushed his teeth and got dressed. Then he put Bob's slip collar on and hooked it to her leash and they went down the stairs and walked to the street. They walked along the street checking out the businesses and stores. He was trying to figure out a way to get to Wisconsin that didn't cost very much and was safe. As they walked, they came past the bakery and the wonderful smell of fresh baked cookies wafted out through the front door. "Ummm, smell that Bob?" Bob's nose was working full throttle.

Tag tied Bob's leash to a bike rack. "You wait here, I'm gonna get us some cookies." Bob sat down and Tag went into the bakery. He walked up to the glass case and looked things over.

"Can I help you young man?"

"Yes ma-am, I'd like three of those chocolate chip cookies there."

The lady put the cookies in a white paper bag and rang them up on the cash register. Tag paid and went out and untied Bob's leash. "Lets' go over to the park and have a snack," he said to Bob who was sniffing the bag furiously.

They crossed the street and sat down in the grass alongside the waterfront park. The park was long and narrow and ran all along the docks where dozens of boats of every size and shape were docked. Tag slipped off Bob's slip collar and let her run and play. Bob didn't go far, wanting her share of the cookies.

Tag took a bite and then broke off a piece of cookie and tossed it to Bob who caught it and slurped it into her mouth. "Good catch Bob!" He broke off another piece and said, "Bob, back up a little," while he motioned her back. Bob backed up and he tossed her another piece of cookie. She caught it and devoured it. "Bob, you're a good catcher," he said laughing.

Now they had a new game, so Tag kept working Bob back farther and farther to catch her cookie bite. Soon she was about twenty feet away. Tag broke off a piece of cookie and tossed it to her. He had to lob it high into the air so it would reach Bob and about half way there, a sea gull swooped down and grabbed the cookie right out of the air. The bird took off flying down along the waterfront, with Bob in hot pursuit.

"Bob! Get back here!" Tag yelled as he jumped to his feet. Bob had a good head start and was half a block away following the sea gull and howling her head off. "Howoooo, howoooo,"

Tag started running after the dog but soon she was a block away and showed no signs of stopping. Suddenly he stopped short. A police car stopped at the curb and an officer got out and began coaxing Bob toward him. She stopped and looked curiously at the cop and he reached into the squad car and came out with a doggie biscuit which perked her interest. By now the sea gull had a half mile lead, and Bob was tired out, so she allowed herself to be picked up by the cop and put into the back seat of the car. The officer got back in and they took off down the street. Tag stood there horrified.

He saw that it was a local cop car as it went past. He turned his head so they wouldn't see his face and recognize him as a wanted person. "Holy crap! They got Bob," he said to himself. He was standing there trying to figure out what to do next as a couple of teenage boys came walking past, one talking on a cell phone. Tag walked up to them.

"Hey guys, can you help me?"

"What's up kid?"

"The cops just picked up my dog. She was running loose. Do you know where they take dogs?"

The two boys looked at each other. "No man, we don't, but you can use my phone to call the cops if you want."

"Do you know the number?"

"How about 911?"

Tag thought that this was surely an emergency, so he took the phone and punched in 9-1-1.

"Police department, what is your emergency?"

"I um, the police just picked up my dog when we were in the park, and I was wondering where I go to get her back?"

"Sir... this is an emergency number, it is NOT for lost dogs."

"She's not lost, you guys have her. I just want to know where to go to get her back."

There was a pause. "How old are you son?"

"Thirteen."

"What's your name?"

"John."

"John what?"

Tag thought furiously, "John Grisham."

Another long pause. "John Grisham, like the author?"

"Same spelling, but I'm not him. How about my dog?"

"The city pound is at the corner of Port and Euclid Mr. Grisham."

"Ok, thanks, sorry for using the emergency phone but I thought it was an emergency."

The operator chuckled, "That's ok, hope you find your dog."

Tag closed the phone and handed it back. "Thanks a lot, do you know where Port and Euclid is?"

The kid pointed across the street. "Two blocks that way is Port. Then about 18, 20 blocks east is Euclid. There's a bus stop on Port and the bus will take you right past Euclid."

Tag took off across the street. He turned back. "Thanks, I really appreciate your help."

"No problem John, hope you find your pooch."

Tag found the bus stop and waited for about ten minutes when the bus came along and stopped. He got on and asked the driver to let him know where to get off at Euclid. They drove for about ten minutes and the driver told him the next stop was Euclid. He thanked the man and got off the bus. Right across the street was the City Pound. He crossed the street and walked in the front door.

"How may I help you?" A large black lady standing behind the counter asked.

"Um, I'm looking for a dog to adopt, for my little sister."

"Well, you're a little young for adoption."

"Oh no, I mean I'm scouting, my parents will be doing the adopting."

"Oh, well, come this way," she said leading him through a door into a large room with rows and rows of pens holding dogs. 'What kind of dog are you looking for?"

"Well we like to hunt in our family, so maybe a hound of some kind."

"Your little sister hunts?"

"Oh no, I mean, she comes along but doesn't carry a gun, but she likes to go and watch. The dog will be hers but we'll all use it for hunting." Boy, he was getting good at this lying stuff.

"We have several hounds," she said leading him down the aisle.

They came to an area that held many large hound dogs. There were mostly coon hounds and one large black blood hound with a face that was all saggy, looking like it had melted. They all began howling and barking. "Loud aren't they?" Tag asked. "Anything smaller?"

"We have one that just came in," she said leading him farther down the aisle. "This one has to stay at least 7 days, before we can adopt her out."

There was Bob! Sitting in a cage all alone, looking very forlorn. She jumped to her feet and began wiggling when she saw Tag. "Well she seems to like you," the lady said.

"Yeah she sure does," he said. "So we have to wait 7 days for this one?"

"Yes, is that a problem?"

"Well Susie, my sister, has a birthday coming up in a couple of days, but no, I don't think it will be a problem, I'll have to talk it over with the family."

They started back down the aisle and Tag noticed a little dog all alone in a cage near the end. It was sitting in the back corner of the cage with his head hanging low. By the look of it one of his parents was a long haired dog, maybe a Yorkshire Terrier, and the other was probably a Chihuahua or Daschund. It wasn't the cutest dog in the world but it did tug at Tag's heart strings. "Why's that one all alone?" he asked.

The lady looked very sad. "See that red card on the cage? It's his last day," she said quietly as if she didn't want the dog to hear.

"What do you mean?"

She motioned Tag away from the little dog. "He's been here three months. Today is his last day. Tomorrow he gets put to sleep."

Tag's mouth dropped open. "Why? What did he do?"

"It's not what he did, it's what he didn't do. He didn't get adopted. We have hundreds of dogs and cats that come in here. We can only hold them three months and then they have to go."

Tag was shocked. "Why didn't somebody adopt him? He looks cute to me."

"He's pretty old. I think he's ten or eleven. Most people don't want an old dog that will be expensive to take care of with Vet bills and stuff. He's a sweet little thing but he just didn't find a home."

Tag walked back to the cage and stooped down. The little dog came up to the wire and he stuck his finger in. The dog licked it and wagged its tail. "Don't worry," he whispered to the dog, "I'll be back to save you." Tag was working on a plan.

Chapter 11

Tag walked, deep in thought down the sidewalk and had just arrived back at the bus stop when the bus drove up. "Are you going back the other way?" He asked as the driver opened the door.

"I go six more blocks this way and then up three blocks west and back around. Where do you want to go?"

"I'll get off back where I was the last time." The driver nodded and Tag climbed aboard. On the ride back he was formulating his plan for rescuing Bob and the dog on death row. By the time he got back to his original stop he had worked out a pretty good plan. He got off and trotted back to Fred's apartment. He thought about going downstairs and talking to Fred but decided to leave him a note, so he wouldn't try to talk Tag out of his plan. He gathered up his clothes and his backpack and sat down and wrote a note to Fred.

Dear Fred,

Thanks for being so nice to Bob and me. Sorry to leave without saying goodbye but something came up. I'll send you a post card from Wisconsin.

Your friend Tag.

He searched through the kitchen and took a large garbage bag from a drawer and put all of his clothes and stuff in it, put his empty back pack on his back and walked down the steps and onto the sidewalk. A few blocks down the street he had noticed a Dollar store so he walked to it and went inside. "May I leave this stuff here?" he asked as he put his sack and back pack next to the door.

"Sure, I'll keep an eye on it," the lady behind the counter said.

Tag went to the party supplies isle and saw exactly what he was looking for. Then he searched until he found the dog supplies and bought another slip collar and leash and a chew bone. He went to the counter and paid for his purchases and then walked across the street to the park to get ready for his mission to rescue the dogs.

He waited for the bus to come back around and then got back on and rode back to the Dog Pound. "Going back the other way again later?" the bus driver asked.

"No, I think this will be my last trip. Thanks for the ride," Tag said waving as he walked toward the Pound.

"You're back already?" the lady at the Dog Pound asked as Tag walked in.

"I just wanted to bring the beagle a little treat," he said producing the chew bone.

The lady smiled. "She's a lucky girl if she goes to your home. You can go back if you want to."

Tag gave her his most dazzling smile and sat his garbage sack next to the door. "I'll just leave my soccer stuff here if it's ok," he said. He left his back pack on his back and walked through the door into the kennel area. Looking around to see if there was anyone else in the room, he walked down the aisle to where Bob was waiting in her kennel, wagging her tail furiously. "Bob, you gotta be real good now," Tag said. "I'm gonna smuggle you out of here in my back pack." Bob whined and howled.

Tag took his back pack off his back and opened the snaps on the top. Inside were four party balloons about the size of a small soccer ball that had made the back pack look like it was full of books or clothes. He checked the door which was at the far end of the room and could see it was still closed. He dumped the balloons out onto the floor and opened the door to Bob's cage. She was very glad to see him, smothering him with wet kisses. "Bob, be good, you gotta calm down or we'll get caught." He sat Bob down and petted her and talked calmly to her. She settled down.

He lifted her into the top opening of the back pack and said, "Now you lie down and be still!" Bob sat very quietly. He gently pushed down on her head and she lay in the bottom of the backpack. He carried her down to the end of the row to the cage with the small dog who was on his way to death row. "Hey fella, I told you I'd be back."

The dog looked frightened. Tag opened the cage and checked over his shoulder to see if anyone had come into the room. They were still alone. He stepped into the cage and picked up the little dog. It was shivering. "It's ok, I'm not going to hurt you," he said quietly. He held the dog over to Bob so she could sniff it. Both of the dogs sniffed each other and it seemed that they liked each other. Tag slipped the little dog into the back pack with Bob. "You guys sit real quiet," he said as he snapped the top cover over them. He lifted the back pack onto his back. It was pretty heavy but not much heavier than it was when he carried his school books in it. He walked back to the pen where Bob had been and then stooped and picked up two of the balloons. He kicked the other two into Bob's pen and shut the door. Then he went to a pen with a litter of what looked like Doberman puppies in it. He opened the door a crack and tossed the two balloons into the pen with the puppies. Then he hurried out to the reception room.

"Well, did she like her chew bone?" the lady asked as he walked through the door.

"She sure did, she's chewing on it like mad," Tag said.

Just then there was a loud bang from the kennel room. "My Lord! What in the world was that?" the lady said, startled.

"Sounded like a gun shot," Tag offered.

"Was there anyone back there besides you?"

"No I didn't see anyone," he said. There was another loud bang.

The lady opened the door carefully and peeked through. Seeing nothing out of the ordinary she walked tentatively through the door. Tag grabbed his garbage bag and hustled out the front door of the Dog Pound.

The lady was walking slowly and carefully down the aisle of the kennel not knowing for sure what she was looking for when she spotted a piece of pink material on the floor outside the Doberman kennel. There was obviously no one else in the kennel, so she walked to the pen where the rubber was and picked it up. It was rubber from a balloon. She looked at it curiously and then saw bits of rubber in the bottom of the kennel with the Doberman puppies. "What the...?" She stood there looking at the bits of rubber. Suddenly she turned and walked quickly to the pen where Bob had been. There in the cage were two party balloons. "That little..."

She started back to the reception room and then had a thought. She walked down to the end kennel and found it empty. She smiled to herself. "That little kid. He snuck out that beagle and that little dog that was to be put to sleep."

She walked back to the front room and opened the front door, knowing that she wouldn't see anyone, especially that kid. She stood there looking across the park and smiled. "You take good care of those puppies," she said quietly.

Meanwhile, Tag, Bob and their new friend were walking quickly along the edge of the breakwater wall several blocks from the Dog Pound. The little dog from death row had his slip collar on and was walking along with Bob like they were old friends. Tag had his clothes and stuff back in his back pack and they were going north... toward Wisconsin.

Chapter 12

Tag and his two dogs walked for many blocks. They kept close to the lake and stopped now and then so the dogs could get a drink and rest in the shade. It was long past noon and Tag was getting hungry. Up ahead he saw a Burger King. He tied the dog's leashes to a fence around the outside playground of the Burger King and went inside for some food. The dogs waited expectantly smelling the food smells coming from the restaurant and accepting pets and pats from people going to and coming from the place.

A few minutes later Tag came out carrying a large bag and a cardboard tray with two paper cups on it. He sat the bag down and untied the dog's leashes and they headed for a small park next to a public boat landing. Tag slipped off the dog's collars and they all sat down and he began breaking up burgers and feeding pieces to Bob and the new dog. He'd break a burger into three pieces, give Bob one, the new dog one and eat the other. It didn't take long to make five burgers disappear. Then Tag took a drink from his Coke and poured some water from the other cup into Bob's water pan. Both of the dogs took a drink and then laid down next to Tag for a nap.

He smiled as he stroked their soft heads. "You don't have to worry any more little guy," he said to the new dog. "Bob and I will take care of you."

The dog looked up and licked Tag's hand. "I guess we gotta give you a name," he said. "What do you think Bob? Any suggestions?" Bob rolled over on her side and groaned.

Tag picked up the new dog and looked it over. "Hmm, what to call you," he said, more to himself than to the dog. Suddenly he smiled. "Harley, yeah, I think you look like a Harley." The little dog sneezed, and Tag laid him down in the grass. "Have a nap Harley."

They rested in the shade for nearly an hour and then Tag began to think about where they'd sleep tonight. They were miles from Fred's place and he really wanted to keep going north, so going back there didn't seem like a good thing to do. "Well, let's walk north a while and see what we can find," he said to the two dogs. He put their collars back on, slid his backpack onto his back and they began walking along the lake shore toward the north, and Wisconsin.

They weren't walking fast but kept at it steadily and soon Tag began to notice it was starting to get dark. "We better get something to eat for supper and then find a place to sleep," he said to the dogs. Up ahead there was another small park and boat landing. The park had the usual playground toys including a large yellow covered slide. Tag walked over by the slide and looked inside. It was a large tube, about thirty inches wide. It wound around up and down from the ladder and platform at the top to a long flat section, then a turn to the right and out onto the grass. Tag tied the dogs to a swing set and crawled inside the slide. After he got in about ten feet there was a nice area about ten feet long and level that would make a great place for them to sleep out of the wind and rain if it happened to rain. It would also be hidden, so it should be pretty safe. He crawled back out and got the dogs. They walked down the street to a gas station and he tied them outside while he went in and bought a package of ham, some string cheese and a loaf of bread. He picked up a box of brownies and a bottle of Coke as he went to the counter. He had saved one of the soda cups from Burger King, so he asked the man at the counter if he could fill it with water for him. He did, and Tag paid for the groceries and off he, Bob and Harley went to their little house. On the way they went past a dumpster full of boxes and Tag reached over the side and took a couple of them out. Everyone went potty and then Tag crawled into the tube. He had a little trouble coaxing Bob and Harley inside but they cooperated when Tag offered them a slice of ham. Once they were all inside, he put his back pack behind him between them and the outside opening. Then he tore open the boxes he had taken from the dumpster and filled in the space around his back pack, with cardboard, sealing up the opening. "There, now we won't have to worry about some skunk or stray cat coming in here," he said to the dogs who were sniffing the groceries, oblivious of his home making efforts. Since the tube was yellow, there was enough light coming through it from the street lights in the park so Tag could see what he was doing. He made sandwiches for the three of them and shared a couple of string cheeses. Then they had a brownie and a drink and he took off his shoes and socks, and settled down on the floor of the tube. Bob lay next to Tag's chest and Harley stood back. "Come on Harley," Tag said patting his hand next to Bob. Harley lay down and snuggled up next to Bob and closed his eyes.

Tag listened as the breathing of the two dogs slowed. Bob began to snore quietly and Tag grinned. "Well God, it's Tag here again. I know it's pretty hard to keep track of me but I'm doing ok. I kinda did a bad thing today. I broke Bob out of jail, but I also kinda stole another dog from the Pound. His name is Harley and he was going to be killed tomorrow, so I couldn't let that happen, so I took him. I don't know if it's technically stealing since he was going to be dead tomorrow anyway. I guess I'll let you decide that one. We're heading north toward Wisconsin and we're doing ok. Please tell Mom. Bye for now...Tag." He closed his eyes and sleep came quickly.

Tag was dreaming the now familiar dream where he was walking down the long road in Wisconsin when he heard a low growling noise. He thought it was part of his dream until he felt Harley jump to his feet and run toward the barricade that he had made with his back pack and the cardboard boxes. He was much too tired to open his eyes, so he tried to ignore Harley and get some more sleep. The he felt Bob jump up and she began to bark too. Tag sat up quickly and hit his head on the top of the tube. Just then a piece of cardboard on top of the barricade was pushed off into the house he had made and Bob and Harley began making a heck of a racket. "Hey, what's wrong? What are you guys barking about?"

Tag jumped when he saw a hand come through the opening and begin to feel around inside his little house. Harley jumped forward and clamped his teeth onto the wrist of the intruder and suddenly the air was full of yelling and cussing. The barricade collapsed and Bob jumped up and grabbed onto the arm of a boy who was now falling forward, being dragged by two snarling dogs. "Wait! Wait! I'm not going to hurt you! Call your dogs off!" the kid screamed as the two dogs sunk their teeth into his arm and wrist. "Get them off, please!" he screamed again.

"Bob! Harley! Come back here!" Tag shouted. Bob let go and looked over her shoulder. "Come on Bob, let him go!" Bob jumped back toward Tag and began barking while Harley held on tight. The intruder took hold of Harley with his free hand and began to talk to him. Harley was growling and holding on tight but he was so little that it wasn't too terrible for the kid. "Here, here, come on, I'm not a bad guy," he said stroking Harley's fur. "Harley, let go. Harley, come here," Tag said. Harley opened his mouth and looked back at Tag. The intruder picked him up and held him. "Hey little man, you're brave like a lion, but small like a mouse." Harley's tail began to wag so the boy put him down on the floor. "Sorry man, I didn't know anybody was in here. I sleep here now and then and I was surprised by your barricade when I crawled in."

Tag looked at the kid. He was a couple years older than himself, maybe 15 or 16. They were about the same height but this kid had pretty good muscles. His blond hair was kind of spiked up and he wore a gold ring in one ear and a couple of gold chains around his neck. He was wearing a sleeveless red tee shirt and white shorts with white sneakers. His teeth were very white and he had a handsome face.

"You sleep here?" Tag asked.

"Yeah man, now and then, I crash lots of places, I was in the neighborhood tonight and this is usually a good place to sleep. I didn't know it would be filled with snarling dogs."

Tag laughed. "I hope they didn't hurt you, they were just protecting me."

"The little one just got my wrist all full of slobber but that beagle pinched my arm pretty good," he said massaging his upper arm. "I think I'll live though."

The kid stuck out his hand. "I'm Corey," he said.

Tag shook hands with him. He was going to give one of his usual aliases but thought he could probably trust this kid, who seemed to be a runaway like him. Besides he was beginning to run out of authors. "I'm Tag."

"Tag, huh, that's a new one, never heard that name before."

"Taggert, Tag for short," he said not bothering with the whole initial thing.

"Well Tag, sorry about waking you up, I'll go find someplace else to crash."

"Why don't you stay, we've got plenty of room, I'm sure the dogs will leave you alone now."

"You sure you don't mind?"

"No, it's really your place in the first place. Come on in, I'll slide up a little and there's lots of room." There was thunder off in the distance and rain was probably coming soon. "It sounds like it's gonna rain, you don't want to be out in that. Besides, it's nice to have someone to talk to besides the dogs."

Corey crawled in and turned around and pulled in a back pack similar to Tag's. He stacked one on top of the other and then packed the cardboard around them and sealed the entrance. "There, just like down town," he said. He slipped off his shoes and socks and lay down on his side with his hand under his head. "So young Tag, have you run away?"

"Yeah, my mom died and I got put into a foster home and things went real bad." And Tag told Corey the tale of Clifford and the butcher knife. Corey was wide eyed when the story was over.   "Wow, maybe I don't want to sleep here after all," he said.   Tag looked surprised and then Corey began laughing. "Sorry, just kidding, I bet that Clifford sleeps with one eye open from now on just in case." They both had a good laugh.

"How about you Corey? Did you run away too?"

"Yeah, almost two years ago. I lived in Wisconsin, came down here to the big city where there was more action."

"Why'd you run away?"

"My old man caught me in my bedroom with someone. He went ballistic. I had to get out or he'd have killed me."

"Jeez, that's crazy. Was it your girlfriend?"

Corey looked at Tag for a long minute. "No Tag, it was my boyfriend."

Chapter 13

"It was who?" Tag asked, even though he knew what Corey had said.

"If you'd rather I'd leave, I'd understand," Corey said.

"Uh, no that's ok, I just didn't expect that, you look so normal." Tag said shrugging his shoulders.

"You're ok with it then?"

"Sure I guess so....you just surprised me I guess."

"I surprised the heck out of my dad too," Corey said. "But he didn't take it as well as you did."

"Well, I don't guess you'd do anything to me anyway....would you?"

Corey grinned. "Of course not, I'm gay, that doesn't mean I'm a molester. Of course, you're pretty cute."

"What?"

Corey began laughing. "Sorry, just messing with you. You're safe Tag, I wouldn't think of doing anything like that. I'm serious, if it bothers you, I'll go sleep someplace else."

"Uh uh, that's ok, I'm cool with it. Let's talk about it in the morning, I'm beat right now."

"Cool, night Tag."

"Night."

The sun had come up and warmed up the inside of the tube quite quickly. In no time the dogs began squirming around pestering to be taken out for a morning potty break. Tag woke to Bob licking his face. He looked over to see Corey still sleeping on his side. He moved carefully past Corey so he wouldn't wake him and moved the barricade. He put the dog's slip collars on them and they all crawled out of the tube. He led the dogs to a patch of bushes and then slipped back in behind them and did a little business of his own. When he and the dogs got back to the tube, Corey was sitting barefoot on the top of it straddling the yellow tube. "Beautiful morning,' he said.

"Yeah, gonna be a nice day again," Tag said.

"What you guys up to today?" Corey asked.

"Nothing real urgent," Tag said. "I'm working my way toward Wisconsin, but I'm not in a big hurry to get there, you wanna do something?"

"No plans man....I thought maybe we could hang out. It'd be nice to just take a day off and kick back."

"Yeah, we could do that," Tag said. "Do you have a job that you usually do every day?"

"Well," Corey said, "not what you'd call a steady job, but I do have clients that I see now and then. But that's mostly at night."

Tag nodded, but had no idea what Corey was talking about.

"There's a public swimming pool up about three blocks from here. Let's go have a quick swim and get a shower there. Then I'll spring for breakfast."

"Sounds like a good plan."

They gathered up their backpacks and put on their shoes. They left the cardboard in the tube as a surprise for the first kids that came sliding down the slide that day, and hiked up along the waterfront to the public pool. They tied Bob and Harley in the shade where they could see them from the pool and filled their water pan for them. Then Corey paid for two admissions and they went into the changing house, each put on a pair of shorts and jumped into the pool. They swam and laughed for about a half hour and then went into the shower and Corey produced a bottle of shampoo/body soap and shared it with Tag. After they were clean, they dried off and dressed in clean clothes. Bob and Harley were glad to see them.

"Come on, there's a little diner down the street. I eat there quite often." Corey said. "We'll get some breakfast to go so we can share with the dogs."

Tag stayed out in front of the diner with the dogs while Corey went in and ordered food. The waitress was a friend and she looked out the window at Tag. "Who's your friend out there?

Are you breaking in a new recruit?"

"No, just a kid I met, he's just passing through."

A few minutes later she sat three take-out boxes of food on the counter, and then put them into a large plastic bag. She added three cartons of milk and two orange juices. Corey paid for the food. "Thanks, Shirley," he said.

He started for the door. "Hey sweet boy, maybe you should do that too." Corey looked confused. "Just pass on through. Move on kiddo, you make old Shirley worry a lot."

"I know how to take care of myself Shirley," he said, giving her a big smile.

"You be careful sweetie."

Tag and Corey walked to the park and sat beneath a big tree at a picnic table. Bob jumped up on the seat next to Tag but Harley couldn't make the jump. Corey reached down and sat him on the bench beside him. "I should let you go hungry for attacking me," he said to the dog. Harley licked him.

They opened the plastic boxes and took two paper plates and some plastic silverware out of the bag. One box had scrambled eggs in it, the next fried potatoes and the last bacon and biscuits. "Oh man, what a feast!" Tag said as he filled his plate.

They ate like they hadn't been fed in a week and in a short time all of the food was gone. The dogs had gotten their share and were both stretched out on the grass beneath the table.

"Whew," Tag said patting his belly, "That was great. How much do I owe you for half?"

"My treat," Corey said.

"No way, that must have cost $20. I'll pay half, I've got some money."

"Keep your money Tag, I had a good night last night, I'm buying."

Tag looked confused. "What do you mean had a good night?"

Corey thought for a minute. "Tag, do you know what a hustler is?"

"I know there's a magazine named that, but otherwise I'm not for sure."

"Tag, I told you about my boyfriend. Well, I make my living by hustling. I do favors for guys. They pay me for stuff. Do you understand?"

Tag's eyes got wide. "You mean?"

Corey nodded. "I'm not proud of it, but it's a living."

"But aren't you afraid that someone will do something bad? I mean there's some weird people in the world."

"I'm real careful. And I have quite a few regular customers. They like me and they pay well for my services. But I'm real careful."

Tag didn't say anything but looked perplexed.

"Does that make you disgusted to think that I do that?" Corey asked.

"No I guess not. I guess I don't quite understand it. It sounds scary to me. Couldn't you get a normal job?"

"Don't understand hustling or understand being gay?"

"I guess either. How did you know?"

"When I was about your age, I guess I just knew I was different. It wasn't like one day I woke up and said, well today I'm gay. It just seemed like it was what I was. Does that make sense?"

"Yeah, I guess so. So maybe I'm gay too?"

Corey laughed. "Do you think you are?"

"No but I don't think I'm not either. I've never kissed anyone besides my mom, so I don't know for sure I guess. LaShonda is the only girl I ever got kissed by, so I got nothing to compare that to either."

"Well, I wouldn't worry about it. Whichever way you turn out to be, you'll do good."

"You think?"

"Yeah, with those big blue eyes and that pretty face, you could get any girl or boy you wanted."

Tag blushed. "Don't say that, boys aren't pretty."

Corey laughed. "Tag believe me you're pretty, and I'll just bet some girl will grab you one of these days and then you'll find out which team you are playing on."

Tag's face felt hot but he said nothing.

They sat silently for a while taking in the nice day. "How about let's walk down to the water and let the dogs go for a swim?" Corey suggested.

They cleaned up their food containers and Tag took Bob, while Corey led Harley and they walked down to the lake. They took off the collars and the dogs began wading and paddling around in the water while the boys took off their shoes and waded along in the shallows poking around. "Corey, do you think you'll hustle for your whole life?" Tag asked.

"No, I hope I can get some money ahead and go to some kind of school so I can get a normal job. When you're sixteen, with no diploma, it's impossible to get a job. I'd like to meet someone to settle down with, you know like everybody, I'd like to find love and happiness. Just because a person is gay doesn't mean he doesn't want love and someone to be with... to love."

Tag nodded. They called the dogs, and walked up into the park again and laid down under a shade tree, propped their heads on their backpacks and dropped off to sleep with the two dogs between them. Later at mid-day they ate hot dogs from a street cart and as evening came on, Corey got them a huge pepperoni pizza for supper. "Want to sleep in the tube again tonight?" he asked as he came from the pizzeria.

"Sure, that's a cool place."

They ate their pizza and shared it with the dogs. It was getting dark so they crawled in and barricaded the entrance. They took off their shoes. The dogs settled down. Tag lay on his back and folded his hands across his chest. "Hi God, Tag here again." He said silently in his mind. "I've got a new friend tonight. His name is Corey and he's, well, he might do stuff that might not be too good in your mind. He's a good guy though, so I want to put in a good word for him. Keep an eye out for him. Maybe you could help him find someone to love? Say hi to Mom.

Good night from Tag."

He rolled over on his side. Corey was looking at him. "Were you praying?"

Tag nodded.

Corey smiled. "I hope you put in a good word for me," he said.

Tag nodded. "I did. Good night Corey."

"Good night Tag."

Tag's dream came again that night just as it had the past several nights. This time though, there was another person standing along the road. As before Tag couldn't tell who it was but he could still see the person standing at the top of the knoll. It was impossible to see their faces, yet he felt he knew all of them.

Chapter 14

The sunshine had warmed up the tube and Tag was awake but felt like snuggling for a while longer. He could feel the warm body of one of the dogs next to him and he began rubbing the soft fir with his fingers. A couple of seconds later he felt a wet tongue on his face. He began smiling and opened his eyes to see Harley's little face right next to his, his little pink tongue flashing out onto his cheek. "Morning Harley," he said quietly.

He raised his head and saw that Corey was sitting cross legged just down the tube from him looking at him. "Hi Corey, you been up long?"

"About half an hour or so."

"What were you doing? Watching me sleep?"

Corey smiled. "Yeah, I guess I was. You looked so peaceful and nice. I guess I was thinking about what it would have been like to have a younger brother, like you."

"Don't you miss your family?"

Corey sighed. "I miss my mom a lot and my grandparents. I've got an older sister too and she and I got along really good. She knew about my sexual preference and was cool with it. But my dad, shit he's just not cool. He just freaked, he couldn't stand the idea that his precious boy, who he thought should become a football player or a baseball pitcher would turn out to want to kiss other boys. I don't miss him, but yeah, I miss the rest of the family."

"Maybe someday you can work it out," Tag said. "I don't have anybody to work it out with. My mom's parents were the reason we moved to Chicago. They were real strict with her and she left just before she graduated from high school. They died in a fire when I was a little kid, and other than them I don't have anybody else to call family."

"Your mom never talked about your dad?"

78

"Not really, when I asked her about him she just said that he was a great guy, but things had worked out that he couldn't live with us. I never understood it, and I think when I got a little older she planned on talking about it, but then she died and so I'm pretty much all that's left of my family."

Corey shook his head slowly. "I'd give anything to have a family, someone to love. If you weren't going to Wisconsin I bet we could be a family for each other."

"That'd be good Corey. I'd like you for a big brother. But you know, we can't live in a tube forever, and you sure don't need any more people to take care of. I've got to go to Wisconsin and find my friend. If that doesn't work out, maybe I'll come back here and we can figure something out."

Corey smiled. "I'd like that Tag."

They collared the dogs and went out into the sunshine. Just as the day before, they went to the public pool, swam and then showered and washed up. After they were dressed they repeated the breakfast of the previous day. As they were eating Corey said, "I don't know about you, but I'm getting short on clean clothes. These backpacks don't hold enough to carry a big wardrobe around. How about we go to a Laundromat and wash some clothes after breakfast?"

"That sounds good to me. I'm down to one last pair of underwear,"

They gathered up their breakfast waste and then walked along the sidewalk to a small coin laundry a few blocks away. Tag tied the dogs to a small tree with a metal cage around it on the edge of the curb and he and Corey went inside. They dumped their backpacks into a metal cart and Corey pushed it over to a front loading washer. "This one will take all of our stuff in one load."

Tag watched as Corey stuffed the clothes into the machine, and then went to a soap dispenser and bought a little box of soap, added it and then fed quarters into the machine. In no time it was filled with water and began to spin around sloshing the clothes back and forth.

"It's a good thing you know about this stuff," Tag said. "I didn't have a clue about how to wash clothes."

Corey laughed. "You learn a lot of stuff when you're on your own Tag." Corey noticed the book Tag had taken from his back pack and picked it up. "This looks like you've read it a few times," he said paging through the book.

"Yeah, it's a little beat up and that fat ass Clifford ripped the front page out."

"So what's it about?"

"It's about this kid, about my age and the man who wrote the book. They become friends and do all kinds of cool stuff together. There're stories that make you laugh like crazy and then some that will make you cry. I've read lots of books, but this one is my favorite of all times."

Corey began paging through the book, reading here and there. Suddenly he began laughing. "Wow, you're right this is a funny book. Are these true stories?"

"Yeah, these are real people, and the stories are real stuff that they did."

"I can see why you like it," Corey said. Just then the washer beeped and Corey pushed the metal cart over and pulled the wet clothes from the machine. Then he pushed the cart to a dryer and loaded the clothes in, shut the door and fed some quarters into the machine. The clothes began spinning around. He sat down next to Tag. "So Tag, I'm wondering, is this the friend you're going to see in Wisconsin?"

Tag nodded.

"Are you sure this is about a real person? You know books are made up most of the time. What will happen if you get there and this guy isn't real?"

"He's real, I know he's real."

Corey nodded. "Well ok, that's good. I hope he turns out to be as good of a guy in real life as he is in the book."

"It says right in the front that this is a real person, and the guy who wrote it is real, so I'm sure he's real."

They watched the clothes go round and round and about half an hour later the dryer stopped spinning. Corey pulled the clothes into one of the metal carts and they went to a big table and began sorting and folding their clothes up. When they were just about finished, Corey's pocket began making a beeping sound. He reached in and pulled out a pager. He looked at the number on the pager and a big smile spread across his face.

"Who's that?" Tag asked.

"It's Eric, he's one of my clients, but were really tight friends too. Just a sec, I gotta give him a call." He dug in his back pack and pulled a cell phone out. He pushed the power button and turned on the phone. "I don't keep this on much cause the battery runs down and I don't have a lot of places to charge it. Jeez look, I've got nine voice mails." He opened the phone and scrolled down to Eric's number and punched it. "Hey dude, you been trying to get hold of me?" he said with a wide smile on his face.

Tag watched as Corey's smile got even wider. "No kidding? Sure that sounds great. I'm at the Laundromat by the park on Lakefront Ave. Yeah, the one with the yellow slide." He nodded a couple of times and grinned. "You sure know how to talk to a guy," he said laughing. "You know, I don't have any nice clothes for a place like that. Really? Way cool man. Ok, I'll be out front, see you in ten."

Corey snapped the phone shut. "That's Eric...he's a broker at a big firm downtown. He and I get together a quite a bit. He's really cool, and we're real good buddies as well as... well you know. Anyway, he's going to New York for a week and he wants me to come along. You know, stay in big hotels....eat in fancy restaurants. He even said he'll buy me some nice clothes for the trip."

"That's great Corey. It sounds like a lot of fun," Tag said.

"I hate to take off on you though," Corey said.

"Hey, no problem, I should be heading north again anyway."

Corey smiled. "You know Tag, Eric could be the one. He really is nice and he treats me like no one else. I'm just wow, this is... maybe it's my chance for more than hustling."

Tag hugged Corey's shoulder. "I hope it's just what you are looking for Corey. You're a cool guy."

They walked outside and sat on a bench in front of the Laundromat. The dogs lay at their feet snoozing when a red Lexus pulled up and stopped. A guy who Tag thought looked to be about 25 got out with a big grin. "Hey gorgeous, you need to turn that phone on more often."

Corey ran up to the guy and put his arms around him and kissed him. "Come here, I want you to meet my friend Tag." He and Eric walked over to Tag. "Tag, this is Eric, Eric, Tag."

Eric was a very nice looking man, wearing an expensive looking dark gray suit with a pale blue shirt and a red tie. He was a little taller than Corey with stylish dark hair, brown eyes and a handsome smile. He held out his hand. "Tag, nice to meet you."

"Same here," Tag said.

Eric looked at Corey, "Is Tag..."

"No, he's on his way to Wisconsin to meet a friend. We met in the yellow tube. He was sleeping there the other night and we've been hanging the last couple of days. This is Bob and Harley, Tag's dogs."

Eric stooped down and scratched the dog's ears. "Well, I hate to rush you, but we've got to go buy you some nice duds for the trip and then get a good nights sleep so we can leave at six tomorrow morning."

"Ok, just a sec, I'll be with you." Corey said.

Eric walked back to his car. "Good luck Tag, nice meeting you."

"So Eric's...?"

"Gay? You can say it Tag, it's not a taboo word. Yeah, he is, does that surprise you?"

"I guess not. He just doesn't look different than any other

guy. He looks so....normal. So I didn't know for sure."

Corey laughed. "What are we suppose to do? Wear some kind of uniform, or a nametag that says, Hi I'm Corey and I'm gay!"

Tag laughed. "No that's not what I meant. You don't look gay either, I just didn't expect you to be so normal either."

Corey smiled. "We're all normal Tag. Some are just a little different kind of normal than others. Here," he said handing Tag a scrap of paper with his phone number on it, "if things don't work out with Wisconsin, call me." He stepped forward and put his arms around Tag and hugged him. "I'm real glad we got to know each other Tag. You're a good kid. I hope you find what you're looking for." He leaned forward and kissed Tag on the cheek. Then he laughed. "There, now you have a boy kiss and a girl kiss to compare."

He trotted over to the Lexus, tossed his backpack in the back seat and climbed in. The window went down. "Be safe cutie, and if Wisconsin doesn't work out, look me up."

The car pulled out into the street and Tag watched as it turned the corner and disappeared.

He felt kind of empty and lonely after the car pulled away. Although he had only known Corey for a couple of days, he knew he was going to miss him. "Well," he said to the dogs. I guess we better start looking for a way to get to Wisconsin."

Chapter 15

Tag was feeling kind of lonely as he walked past the swimming pool that he and Corey had swum and showered for the past two days. The dogs trotted along with him on their leashes enjoying the walk. The park ended and there was an area with shops and restaurants for several blocks. Then they came to a large marina with hundreds of boats moored to the docks that ran out into the lake. In one area there must have been at least a hundred sail boats, their tall masts swaying and their rigging ropes and buckles clanging against the steel masts making sounds like hundreds of small church bells.

He and the dogs continued walking on past charter boats, fishing boats and some big cruisers, all tied to their spots on the docks. There was a wide sidewalk along the marina. The sidewalk was atop a steel retaining wall along the water's edge and the dogs were fascinated by the smells coming from the water. There were many seagulls crying their hawkish calls. Ducks quacked from the water between the boats, looking for handouts and food.

Up ahead there was a large charter boat tied up with the bow pointing toward the shore. There was flat deck on the front and on the deck was a girl that Tag guessed was about fifteen or sixteen. She was lying on a lounge chair wearing a red bikini. Tag tried not to gawk but was very interested in her as he approached. She was wearing sunglasses and seemed to be sleeping.

As he got in front of the boat he turned and looked at her and she said, "If you had a camera, you could take a picture."

Tag turned about as red as the girl's bikini. "I'm...I wasn't trying to look, I'm real sorry," he stammered and began to walk quickly on down the sidewalk.

The girl laughed. "Don't run off, I didn't mean anything. What are your dog's names?"

Tag stopped and turned back. "Oh, this is Bob and this little guy is Harley."

The girl sat forward and took off the glasses. She was a beauty. Tag almost gasped as she stepped up to the rail of the boat. "Harley... he's adorable," she said. "Can I pet him?"

Tag nodded, his mouth hanging open.

The girl climbed over the railing and jumped to the sidewalk. "Hi, I'm Shelly," she said.

She stooped down and stroked little Harley's fir. Bob felt left out and wiggled in and got her share of the petting. "They're both adorable," she said. 'I used to have a little dog that was like a twin of Harley," she said picking him up and hugging him.

"Used to?" Tag asked.

Shelly looked at Tag sadly. "Yeah, he died about a year ago, he was sixteen. My parents got him for me when I was about one, so we had our whole life together."

"I'm sorry," Tag said. "I just got Harley, and I'm not sure how old he is, but I think he's about ten."

"Where did you get him? Do they have any more like him?"

"I didn't see any more," Tag said. Bob was now whining and feeling left out so Tag knelt down and began petting her. "Bob was a stray and she and I just got to be friends, and then she got arrested for running without a collar on. I found out where they took her and then when I went there to get her, I saw Harley. He was on his last day, no body wanted him, so they were gonna kill him. I stole him so he wouldn't get killed."

"Oh my God! They were going to kill him?" Shelly hugged Harley and kissed him on the head. His little tail was wagging so fast it was a blur.

Tag didn't know exactly what else to say. He felt awkward standing there talking to this beautiful girl who was wearing almost nothing. Shelly must have noticed his uneasiness. "Why don't you come aboard? I'll go put on some more clothes." She turned and climbed a gang plank up onto the boat, carrying Harley with her.

Tag picked up Bob and carried her up onto the boat. He let her down onto the deck and then stood there waiting.

"I'm such a dope," Shelly said, 'I didn't ask your name, and went on and on about the dog."

Tag smiled and then his mind worked furiously to think of a name. He was still in Chicago police jurisdiction and wasn't sure if his picture was on posters as a wanted man. "I'm Mark, Mark Twain," he said and regretted it immediately. "What? That's the best I could come up with?" he thought to himself.

Shelly looked surprised. "Mark Twain. Like the Huckleberry Finn guy?"

"Same spelling but no relation," Tag lied.

"Well Mark, it's nice to meet you. You've sure got some cute dogs, and you're not so bad looking yourself."

Tag felt his face get red. "I um, yeah, they're good dogs," he said, not knowing why or what else to say.

"You live around here Mark?"

"No, well I lived in the city before, but now I'm on my way to Wisconsin to meet with my parents."

"I live in Wisconsin, in Milwaukee," Shelly said.

"Really? How come you're here?"

"My dad is a charter captain. He had some fishermen out for a couple of days, then he picked me up and we brought the boat down here for some repairs. He's getting some parts at the Marina office. We're going to stay here tonight and then tomorrow we're going to fish on our way back to Milwaukee. Do you fish Mark?"

"Yeah, I do, I've never been out on a boat like this but I fish off the shore. Do you fish? I never knew a girl who liked to fish before."

"Sure I fish and I'm pretty darn good at it too, so where are your parents? Are you with them?"

"No they had business in Milwaukee so the dogs and I stayed behind for a day. I'm suppose to take the bus tomorrow and meet them but I lost my bus ticket, so I'm trying to find a way to get there. My mom will think I'm unreliable if I let her know I lost the ticket, so I thought I'd try to hitchhike to Milwaukee." He spilled out that lie very easily, quite proud of himself and how quickly he made all it up.

"Hitchhike! Jeez Mark, that's dangerous. There are lots of pervs out there. A cute boy like you would be just what they wanted."

"Maybe you're right," Tag said. "I'm not sure what I'll do just yet."

"My dad will be back in an hour or so, maybe he can help out."

"Oh I don't want to be a bother," Tag said.

"You won't be. How about a soda? Come on let's set up on the deck and relax."

They walked to the front of the boat and Shelly got out another deck chair for Tag. She went below into the galley of the boat and came back with two cans of Pepsi and a pan of water for the dogs. She also had a zip lock bag full of sugar cookies. "Take that backpack off and have a seat," she said to Tag.

He laid his backpack on the deck and sat back in the chair. Shelly handed him a soda and sat the pan of water down for the dogs. She opened her pop, and then offered Tag a cookie. She gave each of the dogs a cookie and then slipped off her shorts and tee shirt and lay back in the chair in her bikini. "So Mark, get comfortable, don't be shy."

Tag was anything but comfortable. He'd never been so close to a pretty girl, especially one that was almost nude. "I'm good, thanks," he said, trying not to look over at her too obviously.

Shelly grinned. "Do you have a girlfriend Mark?"

Tag blushed. "No, not right now."

Have you had a girlfriend before?"

"Well, no not really I guess."

"I can't believe a cute guy like you without a girlfriend. Are you gay?"

Tag almost choked on his soda. "No, I don't think so. I'm only thirteen, I haven't had much experience with girls or anything yet," he stammered.

"You're a really cute boy," Shelly said. "Lots of girls would love to go out with you."

"Oh, I don't know what to say to that," Tag said, completely dumbfounded now.

Shelly smiled. "Have you ever kissed a girl Mark?"

"Yeah... well maybe not, does my mom count?"

Shelly laughed. "Other than your mom Mark."

"Well then no... I guess. I got kissed by a girl... and by a boy too, but only once each."

"Want to try?"

Tag felt like his heart was about to stop. "What do you mean?"

"Do you want to try to kiss a girl Mark?"

"You?"

Shelly laughed again. "Of course me you ninny. Don't you think I'm good looking?"

"I think you're very good looking Shelly, but I don't know much about this kissing stuff."

Shelly leaned forward toward Tag. "Just close your eyes and I'll do the rest."

Tag sat forward in the chair and closed his eyes. His heart was beating so fast he thought it was about to explode. His hands felt cold and sweaty and his ears began to get hot. He could feel the heat from Shelly as she got closer and suddenly he felt her lips against his. They were warm and soft and she smelled like something wonderful and sweet. Her hands went up to his face and held it as she kissed him. Tag didn't know for sure what to do but soon he felt her lips open slightly as her tongue flicked across his lips. Then she was gone.

He opened his eyes and Shelly was sitting there looking at him smiling. "Well?"

"Wow!"

Shelly burst out laughing. "Was that a good wow or a bad wow?

"Definitely good!" Tag said smiling.

"So Michelle, who's your new friend?"

Shelly looked surprised and then she grinned. "Hi Daddy, meet Mark Twain."

Chapter 16

Tag's mouth dropped open. He looked over the bow of the boat at the man standing on the dock. The man looked to be around forty, tall, very tan and smiling at Tag. "Um, er hello sir," Tag said, his face turning a dark red.

"Hello Mr. Twain," the man said. "So how is it you're on my boat kissing my daughter?"

"I um, well, I was just walking by and Shelly, I mean Michelle…"

"Daddy! Quit that! Don't worry Mark, he's just messing with you."

Shelly's dad grinned. "Michelle's right Mark, I usually don't drown a boy for just kissing my daughter, but don't let it go past that."

Shelly laughed and stood up. "Are you through at the Marina Daddy?"

"Yup, all done…it didn't take as long as I thought it would. We might as well start back up the lake and then sleep on the water instead of staying here tonight."

Shelly turned to Tag. "Wait here a second, I want to talk to him." She got up and walked back to the side of the boat where her father was boarding. Tag watched them talking and saw Shelly nod his way a couple of times. He asked her something and she answered and then her dad shrugged and nodded to her. She threw her arms around him and hugged him, and then came skipping back to Tag.

"Daddy said you can ride up to Milwaukee with us Mark."

"Really? Wow that would be really cool," Tag said. "Can the dogs come too?"

"Sure, they can come. We've got a little sandbox thing that

Ponchie used to go potty in when he came with us on the boat, I'm sure they can use it if we show them." She took Tag's hand and led him back to the fishing deck of the boat. Her father was on the upper bridge getting things ready to leave the dock.

Michelle's father climbed down and walked up to Tag. He obviously spent a lot of time in the sun because he was very darkly tanned. His light brown hair was bleached out on the ends to make it almost frosted looking. "So Mark, Michelle tells me you're trying to get to Milwaukee. Good luck for you that we're going there eh? You lost your bus tickets? That's tough luck."

"Yeah my mom would be really mad at me but now she won't know, so this is good luck that I met Shelly, I mean Michelle," Tag said.

"So are you a fisherman Mark?"

"I fish on the shore, yeah I like to fish sir."

"Why don't you call me Andy?"

"Oh, ok Andy, sir."

Andy laughed. "Take it easy Mark. Michelle is a big girl, I'm not a father that butts in, and I trust her. How about going up on the dock and untying the bow line while Michelle gets the stern line?"

Tag nodded yes and climbed onto the dock, untied the rope from the cleat and tossed it onto the boat. Shelly did the same for the back and they both climbed aboard as her father started the engines. The dogs were very excited as Andy steered the boat and they worked their way through the marina toward the lake. Bob could stand on her back legs and see over the side of the boat, but Harley was too short, so he began barking and jumping up and down trying to see. Shelly scooped him up and held him in her arms as they began moving out into the big lake.

"Shelly, get those deck chairs stowed away and then we'll run up the lake a while and get to some fishing grounds that I know. Then we'll put out some rods and fish for a while. We'll anchor for the night and then go the rest of the way in the morning. You aren't scared to sleep on a boat are you?"

Tag shook his head. "I guess not." But inside his stomach, he felt a little jittery thinking of being out in the middle of Lake Michigan in the dark.

They began cruising up the lake and Shelly took Tag's hand in hers as they stood looking out over the stern of the boat. He looked over at her and she grinned and wiggled her eyebrows. His jittery stomach got more jittery.

After an hour of motoring across the water they started to slow down. "Michelle, run the boat while Mark and I rig some rods," her dad said from the bridge.

Shelly climbed up to the bridge and took the wheel while Andy climbed down onto the deck with Tag. He began showing Tag how to set the rods and to clip on the downriggers and planer boards.

The downriggers were lines that had heavy lead cannon balls attached to a steel cable that they lowered over the side from a large reel on the side of the boat. Then they let out several feet of line with a lure on the end and then clipped the line to the cable with a quick-release device, and lowered the whole thing down within a few feet of the bottom. "Those will catch lake trout, hopefully," Andy said. Next they let out line on two more rods and once they were the right distance behind the boat, they clipped the line onto a board that looked like a ski that was tipped sideways. The ski was attached to a long cord that they began to let out and as the line fed out, the ski took the line out, away from the boat with the fishing line attached to it. "The ski boards let us fish a wider path and they are set for salmon and trout that are closer to the surface," Andy explained. In a short time they had four rods set, two on downriggers for lake trout and two on side planers for salmon and rainbow trout. "Want to take the first fish Mark?" Andy asked.

"I'd rather wait and see how it's done," Tag said. "I'm not sure about how it goes?"

"I'll have Michelle come down and coach you," he said. Andy

climbed back up to the bridge and Shelly came down by Tag. "Is Daddy picking on you again?"

"No, he explained all this stuff and then he just asked me if I wanted to pull the first one in. This is all a little more complicated that the fishing I do. I just put a worm on a hook and then a plastic bobber and throw it out."

Shelly grinned. "I think he likes you. I'll help you with the first fish. That way I can teach you two new things in the same day."

Tag felt his face getting hot again. He turned to look forward and saw that Andy was watching his sonar and felt Shelly's breath on the side of his face. He turned and she kissed him quickly on the lips. Tag staggered and nearly fell overboard. "Holy cow, your dads right up there," he whispered. Shelly just laughed.

They trolled for about fifteen minutes when one of the planer board rods sprang up. "Fish on!" Andy yelled.

Shelly grabbed Tag's arm and pushed him toward the rod. "Pull it out of the holder and grab the reel handle," she said.

Tag did as instructed and could feel the strength of the fish on the end of the line as it raced across the back of the boat. "Holy smokes, it's strong," he said hanging on for dear life.

"Keep the rod up, keep the tip up!" Shelly said. "Good, you're doing fine, just let him go, for a bit but keep the rod tight."

Tag braced his knees against the side of the boat and held on. The fish made a run across the back of the boat, turned and ran back the other way. On the second trip across the fish began to slow down. "Now begin to reel, just steady don't be too rough, these fish have soft mouths, don't pull the hook out." Tag reeled and could feel the fish shaking its head.

"Now reel down almost to the water and then raise the rod up slowly...then back down, reeling as you lower it." Tag did as told and soon he could see the silver fish flashing behind the boat.

"I see it!" he shouted.

Shelly took the long handled landing net from a bracket on the side of the boat and stepped up to the rear railing. "Just lead him into me," she said.

The dogs were barking and very excited as Tag lifted the rod once more and the fish slid through the water toward Shelly's net. She put the net next to the water and waited, then swiftly slid the net under the fish and lifted it into the boat with water splashing off the fish onto the dogs and Tag. "Holy smokes, that's a beauty," Tag said finding it hard to believe he had caught such a nice fish.

"Good job you two!" Andy said from the bridge.

Shelly took the hook out of the fish's mouth and held it up for Tag to admire. "It's a chinook salmon... nice one too," she said smiling. Then she leaned over and kissed Tag.

He was surprised and scared at the same time. He turned and looked at Andy who was laughing. Tag laughed too, and kissed Shelly back.

Chapter 17

Shelly put Tag's fish in a cooler that was half filled with ice and they reset the rod. There were padded benches along the sides of the back deck that doubled as lockers for gear, so Tag and Shelly sat down on one of them. Shelly picked up Harley and held him in the crook oh her arm like a baby. She began rubbing his belly and soon he was sleeping.

Shelly turned to Tag, "He's so sweet, just like my Ponchie."

"Ponchie is gone I take it?"

Shelly blinked her eyes several times and Tag was sorry he had asked. "Ponchie was on the boat with us last summer. He loved to go fishing. He would jump up on the railing," she motioned to the four inch wide strip of wood on top of the sides of the boat. "Whenever we caught a fish he'd run to the back and jump up so he could see. It was kind of rough that day and while we were putting the fish away, Ponchie slipped and fell overboard. At least that's what we figured out afterward. We noticed him missing a few minutes later and I thought he was down in the galley going potty, so I didn't worry. A while later he hadn't come back and then we knew he was missing. We pulled all the lines up and went back as fast as we could but he was gone." She began crying softly and put her face down into Harley's fir. Tag put his hand on her shoulder.

"I'm real sorry Shelly," he said quietly.

Shelly sniffed a couple of times and turned and smiled. "Thanks Mark, I'm pretty well over it but seeing Harley just got me thinking of Ponchie again."

Just then one of the downrigger poles snapped up. "Fish on!" Andy yelled from the bridge. Tag and Shelly jumped to their feet and Shelly put Harley down on the deck. He looked around not knowing what was going on, having been awakened from a nice nap. Bob began barking as Shelly pulled the rod from the holder and began fighting the fish. Shelly knew exactly what she was doing and handled the fish expertly. This fish, unlike the one Tag had caught just stayed down near the bottom like a bulldog. Soon they could see it in the water below the stern. "Grab that net," Shelly said to Tag.

He picked up the long handled net and held it out over the stern. "Just put it so the front edge of the metal ring is in the water. I'll pull the fish to it. As soon as the fish is close, slide the net quickly under it and lift it up."

Tag nodded that he understood and thirty seconds later he was hoisting the large Lake Trout over the stern onto the deck. "A beauty," he said grinning at Shelly. "Jeez you're a heck of a fisherman, er fisherwoman."

Shelly laughed. "I've been doing it since I was about six, so I guess I have a little practice."

They put the fish in the cooler and reset the rod. "I'm going below and make some sandwiches," Shelly said.

Tag sat down on the bench and watched the rods.

"Mark, can you come up here a second?" Andy asked from the bridge.

Tag climbed up the four steps to the raised bridge. "Hi, what's up?"

Andy motioned for Tag to sit in the second stool on the bridge across from he was sitting. "I know it's not any of my business Mark, but that story about loosing your bus ticket and your parents being in Milwaukee is a little hard to understand."

"Um, what don't you understand?"

"Well for one thing, why would your parents expect you to take a bus and bring two dogs along when they were driving to Milwaukee?"

"Well, I had soccer and I brought the dogs cause, I..."

Andy looked quizzically at Tag. "And?"

Tag knew he was going to have to tell the truth. "My parents aren't in Milwaukee. I don't know who my dad is and my mom died about a week ago. I was in a foster home and got into a kind of a fight with a bully and left. I have a friend who lives in Wisconsin, and I'm trying to get to his place, and maybe I can find a place to stay up in Wisconsin and be with my friend. Bob was a stray who found me, and then she got arrested for not being on a leash and I went to get her back and Harley was in a cage and was going to be put to sleep the next day, so I rescued Bob and stole Harley. I've been kind of running from the cops for a few days."

Andy stood there absorbing all of this. "Michelle doesn't know the truth?"

"No she thinks I'm Mark and all that I guess."

"So this Mark Twain thing is also a lie?"

Tag nodded. "My name is really Tag, short for Taggert."

Andy nodded slowly. "I see, so what makes you think the cops are looking for you?"

Tag related the knife to the throat story.

Andy tried to look concerned but there was a slight smile on his face. "It sounds to me that you stood up for yourself. I'd be willing to bet that Clifford was too chicken to say anything about it. As far as the dogs, I doubt they're too worried about that either. They have way too many dogs that they can't find homes for. If a couple get "adopted" by someone as clever as you, I don't think they'd worry too much."

Tag felt relieved. "So you're not going to take me back?"

"No I'm not going to take you back, but I think you should tell Michelle the truth."

Tag nodded and stood up to climb down the steps to the deck. Andy held out his hand. "You're still welcome aboard my boat Tag."

"Thanks." Tag shook hands and felt much better as he climbed down the steps. He went down the three steps to the galley under the bridge where Shelly was just finishing up making sandwiches. The two dogs were sitting behind her begging for food. "Jeez, these two act like they're starved," she said handing each dog a slice of ham. "So I saw you go up on the bridge did you and Daddy have a talk?"

Tag nodded and then began to tell her the real story. Shelly sat enraptured as he related his short, but harrowing story. When Tag finished she said, "I'm so sorry about your mom." She put her arms around Tag and hugged him. Then she stepped back and smiled. "I knew you were more than just a pretty face when I first saw you. Jeez, you've had a busy week."

"No kidding, busy as can be."

Just then Andy shouted from the bridge. "Fish on!"

Shelly and Tag ran up the stairs. "Grab it!" Shelly said as she sat the plate of sandwiches on the side bench. Tag grabbed the rod from the downrigger holder and began fighting the fish. Shelly gave him encouraging suggestions and soon he could see a flash of the fish behind the boat. Shelly picked up the net and turned toward Tag and then yelled, "Hey you two! Get out of those sandwiches!"

Tag turned to look and Bob was on her hind feet, half a ham sandwich in her mouth, while Harley was up on the bench chomping on another. When Shelly shouted, Bob jumped down onto the deck. Harley tried to run with his sandwich and stepped up onto the railing, took about three quick steps and disappeared over the side. "Harley!" Shelly screamed. "Daddy stop, Harley fell overboard!"

Andy was turning to see what all the hollering was about when he saw Tag shove the rod into the downrigger holder, jump up on the railing and dive over the side. "Tag! Wait!"

It was too late.

Chapter 18

It felt like a thousand needles had been driven into his skin all at once when Tag hit the water. He went down for several feet before he could twist and head for the surface. "What the heck am I doing?" he thought to himself as he broke the surface. He blew out his breath and gasped as fresh oxygen flooded into his lungs. The initial shock of the cold water was long past and now all he could feel was the cold soaking into him.

"Tag! Behind you!"

Shelly was at the side rail of the boat pointing to his rear. He spun in the water and just then a small wave picked him up enough that he could see Harley dog paddling toward him. But, the boat was steadily moving away from both of them. Tag turned and swam toward the little dog. By the time he reached Harley he was beginning to get a cramp in his left calf. "Harley, come on pal, come on!" Harley was swimming for all he was worth, and a few seconds later he tried to climb onto Tag's shoulders. Tag grabbed the dog and held onto him, pressing him to his chest. "You're ok now, just hold on buddy."

Tag spun himself around in the water and saw that the boat was now over fifty yards away, but was beginning to turn back toward them. Shelly was in the stern reeling furiously to get the lines up so they didn't get all tangled up with the turn. Her dad was shouting and looking back at Tag and Harley.

Tag was beginning to tire out and the cramp in his calf was not helping him tread water. He tried to lay over on his back and let Harley ride on his chest. It worked pretty well, with him just moving his hands a little to keep himself up and kicking occasionally with his good leg. He looked toward the boat again and saw that it had made the turn and was heading their way.

"They're coming Harley," he said to the dog who licked his face.

The cold of the water was sinking into his body and his teeth began to chatter. He thought of how deep the water was and how far it was to the bottom and his pulse quickened with the thought of falling slowly through all that water to the cold bottom of the lake. There was a little chop on the water and every so often a wave splashed into his face making it difficult to keep afloat.

The boat seemed to be moving in slow motion but it was coming his way. He lifted one arm from the water and waved it just to make sure they saw him. Andy returned the wave and signaled that he was coming along the right side of the boat. Shelly was at the railing with a life ring in one hand and the long handled net in the other. "I'll throw you the ring. Then I'll stick the net out. Put Harley in the net and hang on, we'll pull you in!"

Tag nodded. Shelly threw the ring and it landed right on target. Tag slipped one arm and shoulder through it and by the time he had it situated the net was coming his way. "Here you go Harley," he said. Shelly extended the net right next to Tag and he plopped the wet pooch into it. Even though Andy had cut the engine, the boat was still moving and Tag was quickly being dragged through the water as he held onto the net. Harley was thrashing around in the water inside the net. Shelly was slowly pulling the net closer to the boat and Tag was being pulled along with it. Andy was now in the rear of the boat and began pulling the rope that was tied to the life ring. "Let go of the net," he said to Tag. Shelly lifted the net, with Harley inside, over the side of the boat as Andy pulled Tag closer. Tag felt the pull of the rope and slid through the water easily. A few seconds later, strong hands gripped his arms and he was lifted into the boat. His teeth were chattering and he couldn't get to his feet because of the shakes. He tried to get up but the cramp in his calf wouldn't let him just yet.

"Just lay still Tag, you're safe now. Jeepers, you almost gave me a heart attack!" Andy said shaking his head. Then he smiled.

"You're a pretty brave kid."

Tag nodded through his chattering teeth and looked at Shelly who was crying. "Is he ok?"

"He's cold but I think he's fine." She bent down and put her arms around Tag. "You're the bravest person I've ever seen." She put her face against Tag's chest and began to cry.

"Come on, let's get these two dried off, they must be freezing," Andy said.

He helped Tag to his feet and they shuffled down the stairs into the galley. Shelly carried Harley down to the galley and opened a drawer and pulled out several bath towels. She put Harley in one and began to dry him off. "Get those clothes off, and we'll get you warmed up," Andy said.

Tag was still shaking but managed to slide his sneakers off. Andy helped him pull off his socks and Tag pulled his tee shirt off over his head. He began to unbutton his pants and then stopped and looked over at Shelly. "Turn around Shelly," Andy said.

Shelly turned her back and Tag dropped his pants and underwear. Andy gave him a large towel and picked up the wet clothes. Once Tag was dry Andy gave him another dry towel and told him to wrap it around himself. He did and sat down on one of the bunks.

"Are you decent?" Shelly asked.

"Yeah," Tag said, "you can turn around now."

Shelly held up Harley who was all nice and dry and seemed to be in good shape. "He's just fine, thanks to you." Harley was all wrapped up like a newborn baby inside a dry towel, looking very satisfied. Shelly sat down next to Tag and wrapped her arms around his bare shoulders. "Thanks for saving him, you're my hero."

Suddenly Tag wasn't as cold as he had been. In fact he was beginning to feel pretty warm. Andy came back down the steps. "Well, I think everything's ok. The lines are all in and I'm going to anchor for the night. I think we've all had enough entertainment for a while. Honey, why don't you start to get our dinner ready?"

Shelly nodded and turned to Tag. "I'm going up and start the gas grill. You do have some dry clothes in your backpack don't you?"

"Yeah, they're all nice and clean too. I don't have any shoes but I guess I can go barefoot for a while."

Shelly and Harley went up on the deck and Tag opened his backpack and found a pair of underwear and put them on. He heard a noise and looked up the stairs to see Bob standing there looking down at him. "Hey Bob, do you feel left out?" He got up and reached up and took Bob in his arms and hugged her. "Don't feel bad, you're still my number one girl." Bob's tail wagged happily.

Tag dressed in a clean tee shirt and some khaki shorts and picked up Bob and climbed up on the deck. Andy had put the anchor out and they were just sitting in the middle of the lake. There was water as far as he could see. 'How far is it to shore?" Tag asked.

"About four miles," Andy replied.

Tag looked over the side. 'That way," Andy said pointing to the other side. Tag grinned.

"I'm glad you know where we are, I'd never find my way back."

"Don't worry we're just fine out here. The weather will be great tonight, very little wind, nice moon.....a nice night to spend on the water."

Shelly had the small propane grill going and soon she went below and began cooking something on the stove. After a while she came up on deck with a package of steaks and put them on the grill. "I've got the salads and potatoes almost done, watch these and I'll finish them up." Tag nodded and stood guard over the steaks.

Andy pulled up what Tag thought was just a panel but it turned out to be a table once it was opened up. He got some folding deck chairs from a cabinet and soon Shelly brought up the rest of the food from the galley. The steaks were done, so they sat down and Tag realized how hungry he was. The dogs each got a dish with steak and potatoes and gobbled theirs up hungrily, then begged for more.

'Wow this is great," Tag as he bit down on slice of steak. "We've been kind of eating on the run for a while, it's nice to sit and have a meal like this."

They ate and talked about the rescue of Harley and many other things. After dinner, Tag and Shelly cleaned up the dishes while Andy cleaned the two fish they had caught, and put them in a small freezer in the galley.

They sat in the deck chairs while the boat bobbed on the waves of the lake. The sky darkened to a dead black and soon the moon began to peak up over the horizon casting a silver slash across the water. "Wow that's kind of cool," Tag said. "I've never seen the moon come up over the lake like that."

He was resting his hand on the arm of the chair when he felt Shelly's warm hand on his. He turned toward her and she winked. He smiled and squeezed her hand.

Chapter 19

"Is it safe to be out here in the dark?" Tag asked Shelly as they watched the stars begin to twinkle on in the night sky.

"I'll turn on the lights," Andy said. "There are a green and red light on the bow and a white one on the stern. Any boats that come near will see them and steer clear of us. Don't worry Tag, we're plenty safe. We've done this many times."

"Those benches in the galley can be turned into two beds," Shelly said. "We've got cushions that we put on them. They're a little smaller than a single bed."

Tag nodded that he understood. "I'll just sleep on the floor with the dogs," he said.

"No we can share a bunk," Shelly said.

Tag looked surprised. "I um, I'll be ok on the floor."

"It's deck, not floor, and I don't think Daddy will have a problem with us sharing a bed. He'll be about three feet from us," Shelly said grinning.

"And I'm a light sleeper," Andy said.

Tag looked worried and Shelly and her dad both broke out laughing. "Don't worry Tag, it'll be just fine."

They coaxed the dogs into using the sandbox and then took turns in the small bathroom below the deck which Tag found out was called a *head*. Then Andy slipped off his shorts and climbed into one of the bunks. Tag looked at Shelly who grinned and slid off her shorts but kept on her tee shirt. Tag took his shorts off too and then she motioned for him to climb up on the bunk. He did and slid over as far as he could to the far side. Shelly lay down next to him and pulled a blanket over them. Tag lay with his back to Shelly, almost afraid to breathe.

"Tag," she whispered.

"Yeah?"

Shelly's arm slipped around his chest. She put her face up next to the back of his neck and kissed him on the neck. "Thanks for saving Harley."

He turned and looked into her eyes which were just inches away. He nodded. Then he closed his eyes and leaned forward and kissed Shelly. When they finished the kiss, Shelly giggled. "Wow, you're a fast learner!"

Tag smiled. "That was ok?"

"More than ok."

Tag rolled over on his side and closed his eyes with a smile on his face. Less than a minute later he was sound asleep.

He woke several hours later when the boat began to rock slightly. Waves were hitting it from the side made by another boat that must have passed them. At first he couldn't figure out where he was but then he felt the warmth of Shelly against his back. She had her arm around him and was spooned up against his back. "I can't believe this," he said to himself. "I've never even talked to a pretty girl like this and here I am in bed with her." He shook his head not believing his luck.

Just then he felt a bump and Harley jumped up onto the bed and snuggled down between Tag and Shelly's feet. Tag grinned as the body heat of the little dog warmed his feet. A few minutes later he heard Bob whining. He lifted his head and saw Bob standing by the bunk with her front feet on the edge. "Come on up," he coaxed Bob with a whisper. He patted the bunk above his head and Bob jumped up. He lifted her and put her down between him and the side of the boat and she snuggled down next to his chest. A minute later, everyone was asleep again.

It was light and the boat was rocking slightly when Tag next woke. Bob's soft silky left ear was against his cheek and the dog was snoring lightly. He raised his head and looked around to see that Andy was gone. That was probably why the boat was moving a bit. He turned and saw that Shelly was looking at him, smiling. "Good morning handsome," she said.

Tag smiled. "Good morning beautiful." He blushed when he realized what he had said.

Shelly pulled him closer and nestled her face next to his neck. She kissed him on the neck. "Did you like sharing a bed with me?" she asked.

"I'm just hoping I won't wake up and find out this was all a dream." He smiled. He leaned over and kissed her forehead.

Just then Andy came down the steps. "So are you two going to lie in the sack all day or are we going to try for a couple more fish on the way in?"

"Uh, do I have a choice?" Tag asked grinning.

"No," Andy laughed. "How old did you say you were Tag?"

"Thirteen, why?"

"You're an *old* thirteen by the way you were kissing my daughter just now, I think it's time to go fishing."

Shelly laughed and sat up. "Daddy, quit picking on Tag. He was just expressing his gratitude for the ride to Milwaukee."

Andy laughed. "I'll take a hand shake then."

By now the dogs were up and in a big hurry to use the sandbox. Shelly got up and washed up and then began making breakfast. Tag got up, put on his tee shirt and shorts and walked up on deck. It was foggy. Andy had the anchor up and was starting the boat.

"We'll get things warmed up and then after we eat, we'll begin trolling toward shore."

Tag nodded. "That sounds good. Um, I want to apologize for kissing Shelly this morning."

Andy just laughed. "Forget it Tag, Shelly's a big girl, she knows what she's doing. If you tried something that bothered her she'd probably break one of your fingers, I'm not too worried about her."

"Really? Jeez, it's a good thing I'm a gentleman."

"What are you telling him Daddy?"

Tag and Andy laughed as they went below to eat breakfast.

After they finished, Andy put the boat in gear and let it idle slowly while he and Tag put out the rods and reels. By the time Shelly had the galley cleaned up, they were fishing toward Milwaukee.

Chapter 20

They were still out of sight of land and Tag and Shelly were sitting in the back of the boat watching the rods for a strike. Shelly was holding Tag's hand and he was feeling uncomfortable about it. He kept looking at Andy watching for him to get angry.

"Are you worrying about Daddy?" Shelly asked grinning.

"Well, kinda. He said he's cool with you and I being friendly, but I'm kinda nervous about it."

She laughed. Daddy likes you Tag. But I'm afraid he might do something when we get back that you won't like.

He looked at her. "Like what?"

"He doesn't feel right about just putting you on the shore and saying good bye. He wants to go and contact Social Services to get you some help."

"I don't need any help. I'm going west. Once I get there I'll be fine."

"I told him that but he doesn't want to see you on your own in Milwaukee. It's kind of a rough town if you don't know where to go, or more like it, where to not go."

"I can take care of myself. I came from Chicago, that's not a real safe town either and I got along just fine."

She nodded. "He's going to make some excuse to go into town while we wait on the boat. Then he's going to call them, so I'll help you to get away while he's on shore."

Tag smiled. "You're the best Shelly."

A little while later Tag could begin to see the shore far ahead. It started out looking like the lake surface was rough and slowly began to rise, looking more and more like solid land. As they continued west across the lake it got closer and closer. "Michelle, you and Tag pull up the lines, we're getting into shallow water," her dad said.

The two of them reeled up the poles and Shelly stowed them

in a long locker at the side of the boat. Once they were all up, Andy gave the boat more gas and they took off for the harbor at Milwaukee.

"That's where we moor the boat," Shelly said over the sound of the motor, pointing ahead to a harbor where hundreds of boats were lined up along docks. Andy slowed down and threaded the boat through narrow openings into a berth at one of the docks. When he got next to the wooden dock Shelly jumped out over the side and wrapped the stern rope around a cleat and stopped the forward motion of the boat. Andy shut down the engine and jumped out and tied off the bow as Shelly tied down the stern.

"You do that like you've done it a few times," Tag said to Shelly as she hopped aboard again.

"I've been Daddy's first mate since I was about ten. My mom hates the water and won't go out with us, so Daddy and I have been fishing together for many years.

"Uh, I'm going up to the Harbor Master's office and see about some dock charges. You guys wait here and I'll be back in a little bit. We can take Tag into town and let him off someplace so he can continue on his journey," Andy said.

"Ok Daddy, hurry back," Shelly said walking down into the galley as if she were going to make them some sandwiches.

When Andy was out of sight, she came back up. "You've got to hurry Tag. Go to the end of this dock and then take a right and follow that dock all the way to the end. Then turn toward the shore and stay low until you're on land. The Harbor Office is on the other side of the harbor, so they shouldn't see you if you move fast and low."

Tag picked up Harley. "Shelly, Harley really likes you..... I was wondering if you'd take care of him. I'm going to have enough trouble getting rides with one dog, let alone two. Maybe since Harley was saved from the Lake, it's like your other dog coming back to you."

Shelly took Harley in her arms and cuddled him. "Tag are

you sure?"

He nodded.

Her eyes filled with tears. She put Harley down on the deck and put her arms around Tag. "I'll take good care of him, I promise."

"I know you will," he said.

He put his arms around Shelly and felt her sobbing into his chest. She looked up at him and they kissed tenderly. "Don't you forget me Taggert," she said.

He smiled and kissed her on the cheek, "Not a chance."

"Wait a second," Shelly said, running down into the galley. In half a minute she returned with a slip of paper. "Here's my phone number, will you promise to call me if you get into trouble?"

"Sure I will, but I'll call you from where I'm going, I promise." Tag scooped up Bob and held her next to Harley. "Tell Harley bye Bob, he's going to stay here."

The two dogs sniffed each other and their tongues came out and they licked each other on the face. Tag climbed up onto the dock. "Gotta go. Thanks Shelly, I'll never forget my first real kiss and the most beautiful girl who gave it to me."

He turned and ran down the dock. When he got to the end he turned onto the right dock and began trotting down it. He looked back and waved to Shelly.

"Bye gorgeous," Shelly whispered. "I hope you find what you're looking for."

Tag walked low until he was on shore and then worked his way across the parking lot staying behind cars and trucks parked there. Once he got to the other side, he started down a street that was heading west away from the lake. He knew the lake was on the eastern shore of Wisconsin, so to get where he wanted to go, he had to head away from the water.

Tag and Bob walked a long time and soon they were getting hungry and tired of walking. "I'll get us some lunch soon," he said to the dog who wagged her tail happily. The part of the city they were in was mostly older houses with tree lined streets. After several more blocks he saw a small corner grocery ahead, so when they got to it he tied Bob to a bike rack with a couple of bikes in it and walked into the store.

It was a small place with isles of food and snacks. There was an old man behind the counter who looked him over as he entered the store. Tag nodded to the man and began looking for something for lunch. He found the bread section and bought a package of hamburger buns and then went to a cooler and bought a package of big bologna and some sliced cheese. As he rounded the corner the two kids who's bikes must have been outside nearly knocked him down as they came laughing around the corner. "Whoops, sorry," one of them said as they giggled and continued down the aisle.

Tag smiled and said, "No problem," and continued on toward the chip display, picking up a bag of Cheetos. He picked up two bottles of water and went to the front of the store to pay for his purchases. The two kids were just walking out of the store as he put his food on the counter. The man began totaling up his bill and put the items into a plastic bag. "Four sixty seven," the man said. Tag handed him a five dollar bill and received his change. "You're new around here aren't you son?" the man asked.

"I'm just passing through, on my way west," Tag said.

"Where west?"

"Um, a place near the Wisconsin river."

The man looked surprised. "That's a quite a way off, you planning on walking there?"

"No," Tag said laughingly, "I'm taking a bus. I came here on a bus to see my grandma, and I'll be going back on one too."

"Who's your grandma?"

"Oh crap," Tag thought. "Um, do you know Mrs....." He scanned the shelves for a name. "Mrs. Swanson?"

"Swanson? Nope, where does she live?"

"I don't know the address, but it's just a couple of blocks from here. Well gotta be going, thanks." And he hustled out the door.

Bob was sitting on the sidewalk waiting and was very interested in the bag of groceries. "Let's see if we can find a place to stay tonight," Tag said as he untied her leash and started down the street.

They walked and walked and the houses began to get smaller and more run down looking. It was getting late in the afternoon and they were hungry but Tag didn't want to just sit on the sidewalk and eat, so they kept going. A little way farther they came to a large six lane street that was very busy. It was lined with stores and businesses, so Tag figured he was getting into the downtown part of Milwaukee. They crossed the street when the light turned and headed on west. A few blocks later they saw a small neighborhood park ahead on the left, so Tag headed toward it. There wasn't a slide but there was a picnic shelter and a ball field.

Tag and Bob walked over to the ball field and went inside the fence toward one of the dugouts. It was a good place to stop for supper and maybe a place to stay for the night. They sat down and ate and then Tag poured out part of a bottle of water into Bob's dish so she could get a drink. He drank the rest of the water and then lay back on the bench and closed his eyes. As tired as he was, it only took a few minutes for him to drop off to sleep.

It was dark when he woke to Bob's growling. "Bob, shh, what's wrong?" Bob was staring toward the park and the hair on her back was standing up. Tag got up and looked out around the end of the dugout. There were three cars parked at the parking lot and a half a dozen guys were in the picnic shelter laughing and partying. They were all wearing red bandanas on their heads or tied around their arms. Some were drinking beer and others seemed to be passing around a bottle of wine or some other liquor. Tag got down and stayed behind the dugout wall. "We gotta be real quiet Bob, those guys look like gang members." Bob wagged her tail.

Tag peeked up around the wall now and then to see what

was going on but the guys were still just partying. He sat back down and a short while later he heard a loud car drive up. Four guys got out swaggering toward the group in the picnic shelter and things quieted down. The new guys weren't wearing red bandanas but were dressed much like the others. Two of them walked up to each other, one from each group and began to talk. The talk got louder and soon they were shouting. "This looks bad Bob," Tag whispered

It wasn't long and the two were joined by the rest who began shouting and then began pushing back and forth. The argument was escalating to a fight. Tag saw a flash as a knife was pulled by one of the guys. It had no more than appeared when one of the new ones pulled a gun from behind his back and began pointing it at the others. Things happened fast then and soon all of them were fighting when a shot rang out. Bob jumped and began whimpering and Tag picked her up and tried to keep her quiet. Soon two more shots rang out and the fight was getting louder and more violent. Another shot came and it was much closer. Tag was trying to decide what to do when a kid wearing one of the red bandanas ran around the wall of the dugout and dropped down, holding a gun. The kid peeked out and then hid again as the fight continued. He hadn't seen Tag when he hurriedly dove into the dugout.

Bob began to growl and Tag began to shake as the kid turned quickly pointing the gun at him. "What you doin here?"

"I was just sleeping here."

The kid kept the gun on Tag. "You carryin?"

"Carrying what?"

"A piece fool."

"You mean a gun? Cripes no, I don't have a gun, I'm only 13."

"Lots of brothers got guns when they 13."

"Not me."

The kid looked him over. "You keep quiet."

Tag nodded yes.

Off in the distance a siren was whining and getting closer.

"Cops comin, I gotta blow, you stay here and stay cool. You be ok."

"I will, thanks for...well, for..."

The kid grinned, "Not shootin you?"

Tag smiled. "Yeah."

The kid winked and snuck down the length of the dugout and then slipped off into the darkness.

The rest of the gang members broke up quickly as the police got closer. The police car pulled into the park and shined the spotlight around, and then sat for a short time and pulled out.

Tag sat down and held Bob. "Wow Bob, I think the sooner we get out of Milwaukee, the better."

Chapter 21

The rest of the night was quiet and after the excitement of the gang fight, Tag had trouble getting back to sleep. He finally managed and when he next opened his eyes it was morning. Tag put his backpack on his back and clipped Bob's leash on her slip collar. They walked along keeping on a side street, rather than the main street that led from the harbor that he had been on the day before. He figured if Andy got to the Social Services people they might be out looking for him and he'd be safer if he stayed off the main street.

They came to a gas station and Tag tied Bob to a pop cooler and went inside. He bought two hot dogs off a roller grill and got a soda and a glass of water for Bob. "Do you have any maps of the city?" he asked the clerk.

"Sure, right there," he said pointing to a rack.

Tag took down one of the maps and opened it trying to figure out where he should go to get to the west side of Milwaukee where he could find a highway heading toward his goal. He had no idea where he was to start off, so he took the map up to the counter. "Could you show me where we are on this?"

The clerk, a college age kid spread the map out and looked for a minute and then saw the street they were on. He tapped the map with his index finger. "Right here is where we are."

Tag looked at the spot. "So where do I want to go to get to the west side of the city? I want to get to Madison or someplace in that direction."

The clerk moved the map around and then pointed to a freeway. "This is the fastest way to Madison, but I don't think you'll be able to hitch a ride. They don't allow hitchhiking on the freeway. You'd be better off to go a little north on one of the smaller highways and then you could get to Madison from there."

Tag looked where the kid was pointing. "Ok, that sounds good," he said.

"Hey kid, you in trouble or something?"

"No, I'm just trying to get to someplace to meet an old friend, and I kinda got lost."

"I see. Well you be careful around the middle of the city. Milwaukee has a couple of gangs that are kind of fussy about their turf. You don't want to be messing with any of them. You got any money? You'd be a lot safer to take a cab."

"I got a little money," Tag said, not wanting to tell the guy how much he had. "But I want to make it last all the way and a cab ride would take most of it. I'll be careful." He already had first hand knowledge of the gangs and their turf battles.

He paid for the hot dogs and soda. The cashier took a white paper bag and slid half a dozen cookies from a glass case into it. "Here, the pooch looks hungry and I don't think a hot dog will fill him," he said looking toward Bob.

"Thanks, Bob will be real happy for that," he said.

"Take care kid, good luck."

Tag went out to the parking lot and untied Bob. They walked to the edge of the lot and sat down next to a big tree and ate their hot dogs. Bob was wagging her tail like mad as Tag opened the cookie sack and broke off a piece and handed it to her. He drank his soda and poured the water in Bob's dish. She had a good drink and then he dumped the rest out and put the dish back into his back pack. "Well it looks like a long way across this town Bob. We better get going so we can get someplace good to sleep before it gets dark. I don't want to get in a fix like we almost did last night." He looked up at the sky. "Looks like it's gonna rain too."

They started off down the sidewalk putting the lake and that part of their journey behind them. They walked for several hours, taking rest breaks when they found a small park or a gas station that had a place to get some food and water. By late afternoon the clouds were getting dark and it was thundering in the west. They were walking down a residential area that was pretty run down. The houses were in poor shape and there were junk cars and other junk scattered in many of the yards. Just ahead was one small house that was all freshly painted with flowers in the small yard. He was almost to the house which was on the corner. Tag saw two kids coming his way from the sidewalk to the right. They were wearing real baggy jeans that were half way down over their butts with their boxers showing above them. One was wearing a white undershirt with just straps, no sleeves. The other was shirtless. They both had blue bandanas tied around their heads, and several gold chains looped around their necks. They got to the corner just before him and stopped.

Tag looked away and kept walking as he got closer. "Yo, you gotta pay a toll to walk on our street homie," the kid in the undershirt said, smirking at his buddy. The shirtless kid put his hands on his hips and blocked the sidewalk.

"What?" Tag asked.

"This be our street man. There's a toll charge to walk here."

"Are you kidding? How can you own a street?" Tag asked.

"One of the kids grabbed Tags shirt. "You mouthin us. You little honkie punk!"

The shirtless kid pulled Tag's back pack off and started down the driveway of the small house with it. Tag tied Bob to a small tree next to the sidewalk and ran after the two kids. "Hey, give me that back!" Tag yelled.

The kid with the shirt stopped and grabbed Tag by the front of his shirt. "And what is your skinny ass going to do to us if we don't?"

"Get your hands off him!"

The voice came from behind Tag. The two gang bangers looked up, trying to look tough but obviously when they saw who had yelled their attitude changed completely. The kid let go of Tag's shirt. He turned to see a tall man standing there on the back porch of the well kept house. "What are you punks doing, messing with this kid?"

"Hey Ryan, no we was just foolin him," the kid in the undershirt said, grinning and moving back a step. "We wasn't gonna do anything to him, just messin with him a little...just havin a little joke with him."

Tag looked over his savior. He was quite tall, maybe six foot three or four, thin but well built. He was wearing regular jeans, a Marquette University tee shirt and loafers. He was very nice looking, with light brown skin, brown eyes with long lashes and longish curly hair that was full of loose curls. He had very white teeth and smiled at Tag. "You lost kid?"

"No sir, I was just walking along trying to get toward the west side of town. I didn't know that anyone owned this street."

Ryan laughed. "First, don't call me sir, I'm only 20. Call me Ryan. Second, these two turkeys don't own the street, they're lucky if they own the shoes they're wearing. I don't think either of you bone heads is named Lexington is it?"

"You know it isn't Ryan," the shirtless kid said.

"And what you doing going through his back pack...give that back to him!"

Just then the back door opened at the house. A tiny woman with white hair, light brown skin and wearing a flowered house dress stepped out onto the porch. "You little shits let this baby alone! I'll turn my grandson loose on you and he'll give you a whoopin!"

The shirtless kid tossed Tag's back pack to him and he slid his arms through the straps.

"They're messing with his belongings and trying to charge him for walking down a street that isn't their street, Gram. Am I getting it right?" Ryan said stepping up to the two punks.

"Yeah you right, our mistake, our street be over one," the other kid said. "We be seeing you Ry. See you too Ryan's Gram."

The two of them turned and hustled down the street. Ryan grinned. Just then it began to sprinkle rain.

"Ryan, bring that baby inside before he get all wet," the

Grandmother said as she stepped inside the house.

"Come on kid, let's get out of the rain," Ryan said.

"I've got a dog with me," Tag said.

"Where is he?"

"He's out by the street tied to a tree, I tied him there when those guys took my backpack."

"Run and get him, Gram likes dogs."

Tag ran to the front, untied Bob and they both ran back and up onto the porch where Ryan was waiting. He held the door open and they stepped inside.

"Bring that baby in and I'll make him some hot chocolate," Ryan's grandmother said from the kitchen. Tag followed Ryan into the small, spotless kitchen where the Grandmother was stirring a pan with chocolate milk in it. A plate of cookies was already sitting on the kitchen table. "Sit down, have a cookie while I heat this up. Does your dog like cookies?"

Tag grinned. "Bob likes everything."

"Well give him a cookie and I'll get him some regular milk."

Ryan grinned and shrugged his shoulders. "Grandma's always think a boy is hungry," he said in a whisper. Tag nodded and grinned.

Soon Grandma sat three cups of steaming hot chocolate on the table and sat down with the boys. "What is a baby like you doing walking around this neighborhood?" she asked Tag.

"Well, ma-am, I'm not a baby, I'm thirteen. I'm on my way west of here to meet a friend of mine and I kind of got lost."

"West Milwaukee?"

"No, I'm heading for the western part of Wisconsin."

Grandma nodded her head and scowled. "Where are your parents child?"

"I'm on my own ma-am. But I've been on my own for a while and I started in Chicago, so I think I know what I'm doing."

Grandma's eyes raised with a surprised look. "You have no parents?"

"No ma-am, but I'm on my way to meet a friend, who will

take me in.....I hope." Tag said under his breath.

They drank their hot chocolate in silence for a few minutes and then Grandma got up and motioned for Ryan to follow her. "I think that child is in trouble, he needs someone to look after him," she said quietly.

Ryan nodded and grinned. "I suppose you think I'm that someone?"

"Yes I do, you take him home with you and see what's going on. He shouldn't be on his own in downtown Milwaukee. Besides it's raining, he needs shelter."

"I'll take him home with me if he'll go."

"He'll go."

They walked back into the kitchen as Tag was feeding a cookie to Bob. "Ryan thinks you should go with him to his apartment and wait out the rain," Grandma said.

Ryan nodded and pointed out the window to a car parked across the street and said to Tag, "We'll run over to my place and see how long this rain lasts." Then to his Grandma, "See you later Gram, thanks for the backup." The old lady grinned and went to a drawer and took out a zip lock bag and filled it with cookies which she handed to Tag. "You take these in case you get hungry later." She stooped and patted Bob on the head. "You take care of these guys, Bob."

Tag thanked Grandma and she patted his back. "You be careful child."

Tag and Ryan stepped out into the light rain and Ryan motioned to an older Toyota parked at the curb. They ran down the driveway and when they got to the car Ryan unlocked the door, jumped in and unlocked the passenger door just as the sky opened and the rain began to pour down. Tag jumped in with Bob in his arms. "Lean forward, I'll take your back pack off," Ryan said. Tag did and Ryan tossed it into the back seat. "Whew, it's a good thing I was parked close or you'd have gotten real wet."

"I'd have probably gotten more than wet," Tag said. "I think those guys didn't like me."

Ryan laughed. "They think they're tough guys, but all it takes is someone to stand up to them and they're not so tough. This used to be a nice neighborhood. Grandma has live here for 40 years. I was just there delivering her groceries. She calls me every week with her list and I shop for her. She's getting pretty old and can't get around real well any more. Gram saw those kids screwing with you and told me to kick their butts,' he laughed.

"Well I'm glad you were there and that you helped me," Tag said. "My name is Tag, short for Taggert."

Ryan offered his hand to Tag. "Ryan, short for Ryan. Pleased to meet you Taggert."

Ryan had a firm grip but his hands were smooth and gentle at the same time. "So tell me young Tag, what's this story of a friend waiting for you out west?"

Tag started at the beginning and told Ryan about his entire adventure. Ryan was transfixed as Tag talked about Corey and Shelly and his kidnapping the dogs. He had a grin on his face when Tag finished. "Wow, you've been a busy kid."

Tag nodded, "That's for sure. I never expected to meet so many people and to have such an adventure. All I wanted to do is get to where my friend lives."

"Where were you planning to stay tonight?" Ryan asked.

"Don't know. I was hoping to find a park with a tube slide or someplace where I could sleep, but with this rain, I'm not sure. Those tube slides make good places to sleep. I've got a little money but I don't want to spend any for a motel room. "

"My apartment is over near the university. I'm a student there. I'd be happy to have you as a guest for the night."

"Really? Wow that'd be great."

Ryan started the car and turned on the defroster to clear the windows. He rolled his down a little way and waved. "Granny is watching. She wanted me to let her know if you'd agree to stay with me tonight."

"It must be nice having a granny."

"She raised me. My dad was a gang banger and my mom was all screwed up on drugs. The old man was shot when I was about two. I don't remember him at all. Then my mom got all messed up and I ended up with Gram. My mom died of an overdose when I was about four. So Gram is all the family I have. Dad was black and my mom was from Brazil, but was blond. That's why I'm lighter skinned and haven't got such kinky hair."

They were driving through the rain as Ryan told his story. "So are you a basketball player?" Tag asked.

Ryan broke out laughing. "I'm the worst basketball player in all of Milwaukee. Just because I'm black and tall doesn't mean I'm a hoops player Tag. Actually I'm a musician. I play six instruments. I'm majoring in music and American literature."

Tag blushed. "I'm sorry Ryan, I didn't mean anything by the basketball question. You just looked pretty athletic, so I assumed."

"I've got a black belt in Judo," Ryan said. "Those two punks know it too, and thankfully they were smart enough to back down."

"Wow Judo," Tag said. "Maybe you can teach me some moves."

Ryan laughed. "You already know the best move Tag. You talk your way out of a fight, rather than fight. That's the best move of all."

They pulled into a driveway of a well kept two story house. "I've got a little place on the second floor in back. Come on, *me casa e su casa.*"

Chapter 22

Ryan parked in the driveway at the side of the house. The rain was pouring down but they only had a few feet to run to get to the stairs leading to the apartment. "Ready?"

Tag nodded. Ryan grabbed Tag's back pack and Tag carried Bob and they jumped out of the car and ran for the stairs that went up the side of the building. "Whooie!" Ryan yelled as the cold rain drenched them. It only took half a minute for them to reach the top step and ten seconds for Ryan to get the door unlocked, but in that short time they both were dripping wet. They crashed through the door laughing.

"Holy smokes!" Tag laughed. "That's not a rain storm, it's a monsoon!"

He put Bob down on the floor and she shook off, splashing water over the rug. "Don't worry about the water," Ryan said. "You've got more clothes in the back pack I expect?"

"Yeah, I've got more shirts and socks and underwear but no more jeans. But I've got a pair of shorts."

"Why don't you go in the bathroom and take a shower to warm up. Toss your wet clothes out here and I'll put them in with mine and some I've got in my laundry basket. I'll run them down to the basement. There's a coin washer and dryer down there."

"Gee thanks Ryan, that's real nice of you."

Tag went to the bathroom and stripped off his soaked clothes. He opened the door and laid them on the floor outside the bathroom and then added the dirty clothes from his backpack. Then turned on the shower and got in and enjoyed a nice warm shower. When he finished, he dried off and then put on a new pair of boxers, a tee shirt and his shorts. When he walked out into the apartment, he smiled when he saw Ryan lying on the couch with Bob on his chest sleeping. Ryan held his finger up next to his lips. "Shhh, Bob's real tired," he grinned.

Ryan had changed into a dry tee shirt and also had on shorts and was barefoot. Tag tiptoed across the room, looking it over as he walked. The whole apartment was just one medium sized room. On the outside wall there was a sink and some cupboards and a stove and small refrigerator. There was a little table with two chairs next to the cupboards. Along the inside wall was a book case filled with hundreds of books. There was a small television on a little table, an overstuffed easy chair and the couch that Ryan was lying on. Bob raised her head as Tag walked past. "Oops, sorry Bob, I didn't mean to wake you," he said as he bent to rub her head.

"She's a sweetie," Ryan said. "But I was surprised to see that she's a girl. How did you arrive at the name Bob?"

Tag laughed. "When we met, I never thought to look under there to see what she was. She reminded me of a kid named Bob who went to my school, so that's what I called her. Then when I noticed that she was a girl, I hated to change her name. She was already used to being called Bob, so I just left it rather than confuse her."

Ryan broke out laughing. Bob jumped down from his chest and walked over and jumped up in the chair and curled up to sleep. 'Well it looks like Bob feels right at home," he said. "Would you like something to eat?"

"I'm about starved," Tag said. "Can you cook?"

"I'm a pretty good cook as long as you don't want something fancy. You like spaghetti?"

"Yeah!"

"Make yourself to home, I'll get it started."

Ryan went to the kitchen and began making the food and Tag walked over to the bookcase and started looking at all the books. There were many that he had once owned or read. "You like a lot of the same books that I do," he said.

"You a reader Tag?"

"Yeah, I've been reading since I was just a little kid."

"Me too...that's why I'm getting a double major, one in music and one in literature. I love books and hope I can teach kids the

123

joys of reading."

Suddenly Tag noticed a book that was by the same writer that his favorite book was written by. He took it off the shelf. 'Ryan, how was this book?"

Ryan looked. "Great, it's about some kids on the Wisconsin river back in the early 1900's. I really liked it. Have you read it?"

Tag went to his back pack and took out his book. He showed it to Ryan. "This is my favorite book, and it's by the same writer!" He held the book out to Ryan. He paged through it and grinned as he read.

"So this is the character that you are going to meet?"

"Well, not the character, but the kid that the character is modeled after... the writer says in the *Forward* that he's a real person. He's my age and seems like he'd be a great friend to have. So that's where I'm headed, to see if I can find him."

Ryan looked like he was thinking. "Tag, the book that I have by this writer is his 5th book. That means that your book is at least five or six years old. Don't you think this kid might be older now?"

"I never thought of that." Tag said quietly.

Ryan stood next to him and squeezed his shoulder. "Hey, don't worry about it. He might be a little older but if he's a good guy like you say, that wouldn't make any difference would it?

Tag smiled up at Ryan. "No it'd be cool to have an older friend...like you."

Ryan tousled Tag's hair. "Thanks Tag. I'd love to be your older friend. Why don't you take a look at that book while I finish the spaghetti. I think you'll like it."

"Yeah cool. Here try this one while you watch stuff cook. It's about wrecked after that fat ass Clifford ripped it, so you can't hurt it much." He handed Ryan his prized book and gently moved Bob over to the side of the big chair, sat down, curled his feet up under him and opened it. Soon he was back in the early

1900's meeting new characters and reading about their grand adventure.

Ryan had things on the stove and was sitting in one of the kitchen chairs reading and keeping an eye on the food as it cooked. Every so often he'd begin laughing. "You're right, this is a great book," he said.

Tag nodded. "This one is too."

Half an hour later Ryan told Tag to come and eat. He put the book down and went to the table. There was a huge bowl of spaghetti and a bowl of meat sauce and a platter of garlic bread. "The sauce is from a jar, but I think it's pretty good," he said.

"Wow it smells great Ryan. You'd make somebody a good wife." They both laughed over Tag's joke. Then they dug into the food. Bob was whining for a share, so Ryan got a small pan out of the cupboard and fixed her a bowl of spaghetti and sauce. It didn't take long for the food to disappear. Tag leaned back in his chair. "Wow Ryan, that was great!"

"I'm glad you liked it," Ryan said. "I like to cook. My girlfriend is a horrid cook, so I do most of the cooking when we're together."

"You've got a girlfriend?"

"Yeah, why did you think I'm gay or something?"

"No, cripes no. I guess since you didn't say anything about it before I thought that maybe you didn't have one. Most guys just brag about their girlfriends all the time."

"Melinda is working today. I think she'll stop over later. You'll like her, she's really nice."

"How long have you been going with her?"

"We've been friends since third grade but we've been officially a couple for about three years...but we're going to wait to get married until we're both graduated from college. You got a girlfriend Tag?"

"Me? Cripes no!"

"I'm surprised...you're a good looking kid."

Tag blushed. "I'm only thirteen Ryan."

"And you're smart too. You've got lots of time for girls."

Tag got up and began to pick up the dishes. "I'll wash dishes since you cooked."

"You don't have to, I can do it."

"Just show me the soap and go sit down."

Ryan grinned. "Yes sir!"

He reached under the sink and got a bottle of dish soap and a dish rag and handed it to Tag. "Holler if you need me."

Tag began washing dishes and Ryan went and lay down on the couch, and began reading Tag's book. Tag was just finishing the dishes when there was a knock on the door and a girl walked in. "Hey Ry, oh who's your friend?"

Ryan got up and sprinted across the room, put his arms around the girl and kissed her on the lips. "Mel, this is Tag, we met over by Gram's house today and he's spending the night here." He leaned forward and said something into her ear. She smiled and walked across the room.

"Hello Tag, I'm Melinda."

Tag shook hands with her and felt like his face was on fire. Melinda was at least as pretty as Shelly and even better built. She looked like she had some Spanish blood in her background, making her skin a light brown that looked like she spent a lot of time on the beach. Her hair was medium brown with blond highlights in it that looked terrific. She was wearing a snug pale blue tee shirt with a bare belly, tight jeans shorts and white sandals. Her legs were long and shapely and looked great. She was stunning.

"Hi. I'm Tag... oh, you know that... Well ok, hi then."

Her hand was warm in his. She held onto his hand and smiled at him. "You're a very cute boy Tag. Too bad I'm not about five years younger or I'd dump that tall musician and take you for a long ride in the country."

Tag's mouth dropped open and he turned three shades of red.

Ryan burst out laughing. "Mel, stop that! Tag she's just

screwing with you."

He came over by them and took her in his arms and kissed her. "We're going for a little walk. Will you be ok here for a few minutes?"

Tag nodded. His knees were shaking from holding onto Melinda's hand. She winked at him and turned to go. Tag saw that from behind she was also very well built.

Ryan and Melinda left and Tag sat down next to Bob. "Holy smokes Bob. Did you see that girl? Holy smokes." He picked up Ryan's book and tried to concentrate on reading.

Half an hour later Ryan and Melinda came back into the apartment. Tag jumped up from the chair and Melinda came up to him. "I have to go home now Tag, I enjoyed meeting you. I hope you have good luck on your quest." She put her arms around him and kissed him on the cheek. *"Via con Dios Tag."*

She kissed Ryan again and left. Tag stood there kind of in a daze. "Wow Ryan, wow."

Ryan laughed. "You ok kiddo?"

Tag nodded again. "Wow, you're one lucky son of a gun," he grinned.

Ryan hugged his shoulder. "You'll find one just as great someday Tag, I just know it. Well, it's getting kind of late, you about ready for bed?"

"Yeah, I'm getting real sleepy. Should I sleep on the floor?"

"The couch is a hide-a-bed, it opens up so it's like a double bed. If you don't have a problem sleeping in the same bed as another guy, you can share it with me."

"I've slept with guys and girls so it doesn't bother me," Tag said.

Ryan looked surprised. "You've slept with guys and girls?"

"Yeah, but it was only twice with another guy and once with a girl."

"Wow, I'm surprised that at your age you're so far advanced."

"What do you mean? Advanced?"

"Most people aren't sure of their sexuality at such a young

age. And you're cool about both."

"Wait a minute! What do you mean sexuality? I've never done any sex with anyone."

Ryan shook his head. "Oh, jeez I'm sorry Tag. I was talking about sharing a bed. When you said you slept with guys and girls, well that usually means having sex with someone. It's a polite way to say you had sex. It's kind of how people say it."

Tag's eyes went wide. "Holy smokes! I didn't mean that! I meant Corey and I slept next to each other in a playground tube and Shelly and I slept in the same bunk, but I didn't have sex with either of them, unless you can count a kiss."

Ryan laughed. "Kissing is ok but it doesn't count. Sorry, my mistake. So just to be sure, do you want to share my bed?"

"I'd be glad to Ryan."

Ryan opened up the hide-a-bed and then put sheets and a blanket on it that he took from a little cupboard. He got two pillows and put them on the bed. Then they both stripped down to their boxers and Ryan got in the bed and moved over to the back side. Tag got in and Bob jumped up and lay next to him.

Ryan reached up and turned off the light.

"Ryan, have you ever slept with anyone?" Tag asked. "I mean the way you told me, like a polite way to talk about having sex." He turned toward Ryan and could see his smile in the half light.

"Kind of nosey aren't you?"

"I was just wondering. Maybe I'm doing something wrong. I just was wondering if you have done that."

"Tag, you're not doing anything wrong. You're only thirteen. Sure there are kids your age who do it but that doesn't mean you should. The right thing to do is to wait. You've got to find the right person first. When the time is right, you'll know....and for your question if I have," his smile widened. "It's none of your business."

Tag grinned, "Goodnight Ryan."

"Goodnight Taggert."

Chapter 23

Tag woke the next morning as thunder boomed outside the apartment. Another wave of storms were moving through the area and it looked like it would be raining all day. He looked to the other side of the bed and saw that Ryan was gone. Then he noticed the sound of the shower running. Bob crawled up next to his chest and laid her head on his neck. He smiled and stroked her head and ears. A few minutes later Ryan came out of the bathroom with a towel wrapped around his waist. "Morning there kiddo."

"Good morning Ryan, wow I slept like a log."

"You snore too," Ryan said laughing.

"Really? Jeez I didn't know that."

"Don't worry about it, so does Bob. Are you hungry?"

When Ryan asked, Tag realized how hungry he was. "Yeah, now that you mention it, I'm starved."

"Why don't you jump in the shower and I'll fix breakfast. Would you rather have eggs or pancakes?"

Tag thought for a second. "Pancakes sound great."

"Pancakes it is," Ryan said as he opened the closet and got his clothes. As Ryan was dressing Tag noticed a guitar sitting in the closet along with several other suitcases that looked like instrument cases.

"Can you play that guitar Ryan?"

Ryan turned back to him. "Yeah, I play guitar and the rest of these insturments too. I play the guitar, banjo, violin, trumpet, trombone and French horn. So far, I can play three string instruments and three brass instruments. I'm learning clarinet, sax and bassoon right now, so I'll be able to play three woodwinds too."

"Holy smokes... all I can play is the CD player."

Ryan laughed. "Maybe I can teach you. That's how I make part of my living. I teach kids how to play these instruments and also tutor them in their school subjects."

"I'd like to learn guitar."

"Get your shower. We'll give it a try after breakfast. The way it's raining I don't think you want to get back on the road today... do you?"

Tag looked out the window and shook his head. "I doubt that anyone would stop and pick up a wet kid and a wet dog on a day like this. I think I'll stay here where it's warm and dry if that's ok with you."

"You're welcome for as long as you like," Ryan said smiling.

Tag went to the shower and when he was finished he dressed in clean underwear, a clean tee shirt and his shorts. The apartment smelled great when he opened the door from the bathroom. Ryan had the table set with two plates and a platter of pancakes in the middle. "Come and get it," he said.

They ate and talked and fed Bob bites for the next fifteen minutes. After breakfast Tag did the dishes and Ryan straightened up the bed into a couch again. "Ryan, would you play something on the guitar for me?" Tag asked when he was finished.

"Sure, any requests?"

"Nope, whatever you like is fine with me," he said.

Ryan took the guitar and sat on the couch while Tag sat in the easy chair. "This is a song about a man who is saying goodbye to his son who is going off to war. It's kind of sad but very beautiful."

Bob jumped up and curled herself into Tag's lap and Ryan began playing some chords on the guitar and then began singing.

Oh Danny boy...The pipes the pipes are calling.
From glen to glen... and down the mountain side.
The summers gone... and all the roses falling,
It's you, it's you... must go and I must bide.
But come ye back... when summers in the meadow,
Or when the valleys hushed... and white with snow.

It's I'll be here... in sunlight and in shadow...
Oh Danny boy, oh Danny boy, I love you so.

And if ye come... and all the flowers are dying.
And I am dead... and dead I well may be.
Ye'll come and find... the place where I am lying.
And kneel and say... an Ave there for me.
And I shall hear... though soft you tread above me.
And on my grave... will warmer, sweeter be.
And ye shall bend... and tell me that you love me.
And I shall sleep in peace... until you come... to...me.

The song ended with a high clear tenor note that made Tag's eyes fill with tears. He blinked and a large tear ran down his cheek. "Ryan, wow that was beautiful. You have a wonderful voice."

Ryan smiled. "Thanks Tag. I've been blessed with a little talent for singing and music. I guess that's why I want to pass what I can onto others."

Tag wiped his face. "Sorry to be such a wuss. I've heard that song before but never listened to the words...it's really sad but beautiful too."

Ryan patted the couch. "Come here, I'll show you the chords, you can try it.'

Tag sat next to Ryan and he handed him the guitar and showed him how to hold it correctly. Then he put Tag's fingers on the correct frets and strings. "Now slide your thumb across the strings," he said. Tag did and the sound of a chord came from the guitar.

"That's a C chord."

Tag smiled. "Wow, show me more."

For the next two hours, Ryan showed Tag chords and they sang lyrics together. Ryan had a lovely tenor voice and Tag's while not as mature was quite good too. "You have a good ear Tag. You could become a very good singer if you did more of it."

"I sang in the school plays," Tag said grinning.

Ryan had his arm around Tag's back showing him where his fingers when for another chord when they felt some cool air blowing on them. They looked up to see Melinda standing in the doorway, shaking out her umbrella. "What are you two up to today?" she asked smiling.

"I'm teaching Tag to be a musician," Ryan said, getting to his feet and crossing the room. He put his arms around Melinda and kissed her. "And he's learning real fast. Come and listen."

Melinda sat in the chair and Ryan sat next to Tag again. "Go ahead, C, D-major, G."

Tag placed his fingers on the strings, played the three chords and then looked up. Melinda clapped. "Bravo!"

Tag blushed.

"How about I make you musicians some lunch and you can serenade me?" she said.

Tag handed Ryan the guitar and he began playing. He and Tag sang together while Melinda made soup and sandwiches. When she was ready they went to the kitchen and ate. Melinda and Ryan kissed often and were touching and holding hands constantly. Tag felt like he was intruding. "Why don't I go take Bob for a walk. It's stopped raining now. I'll be gone for an hour at least," he said trying to look serious.

Ryan raised his eyebrows. "See you later."

Tag and Bob walked down the stairs and down the street to a small playground where Bob had a grand time sniffing and running. Tag wiped off one of the swings and swung while keeping an eye on Bob. As much as he liked being with Ryan and Melinda, he felt he should get back on his quest. He knew that they'd never say anything to him about it, but he felt that they wanted to be alone and he was in the way. By the time the hour was up, he had decided that he was going to keep moving on. He waited an extra fifteen minutes and then walked back to Ryan's apartment. When he got to the stairs, he made lots of noise to make sure they knew he was coming back.

Ryan and Melinda were sitting at the kitchen table when he opened the door. Tag looked surprised. "What? Thought you'd catch us all naked and nasty?" Melinda said laughing.

Tag turned red. "No...jeez, you say stuff that I don't expect."

Ryan and Melinda laughed. "I've got to go to work. Ryan has lessons soon too, so come on in, the show's over."

Tag and Bob came into the room. Bob climbed up on the big chair and curled up. "Looks like Bob is comfortable," Ryan said.

"Um, I was thinking when I was at the park. I think I should be getting back on the road. You guys have your own lives and you don't need a kid hanging around here. Besides, I've got to find my friend...it's something I've promised myself I'd do."

Ryan looked sad. "Tag of course it's up to you. But, don't think that you're any bother. Mel and I really like you. If you need some time, you can stay as long as you like. No problems."

"Thanks...I appreciate that. And, you've been really great to me. I've just got to do this. If I don't I'll always wonder about him. Do you understand?"

Ryan nodded and Melinda put her arms around Tag. "You go find this guy. If he's what you thought he was, great. If not, you come back here and we'll take care of you." She hugged him and kissed him on the cheek. "Stay tonight and then tomorrow Ryan and I will take you to the bus station and you can ride the bus to where you're going."

Tag nodded. "Ok, thanks Melinda."

There was a knock on the door and Ryan opened it to two kids standing on the landing holding instrument cases, the boy about Tag's age and the girl a little younger. "Come on in," Ryan said. "Get your horns out. We'll start in a minute."

The kids came in like they'd been there before. Ryan put his hands on Tag's shoulders. "Is it ok to stay one more night?"

Tag nodded. "Sure, I really don't want to leave Ryan. I just got to, you know?"

"I understand. Come on, how about some trumpet lessons."

Chapter 24

That evening Melinda came over and made tacos and enchiladas for them. They feasted on the spicy food and had a great time talking. Tag found himself becoming closer and closer to these two young people who were complete strangers just days ago. He liked to sit and watch the two of them when they talked together, their love showing in their eyes and expressions. Often one of them would touch the other on the arm or hand, eliciting a smile from the person touched.

After dinner Melinda began cleaning up and Ryan got the guitar and began singing and playing. "Maybe I should go for another walk," Tag said.

Ryan laughed. "You don't have to do that Tag. Melinda and I aren't like dogs in heat, we're fine."

Melinda motioned for Tag to come closer. "Maybe I'll send Ryan out for some ice cream," and then she wiggled her eyebrows.

Tags mouth dropped open. Melinda began laughing and put her soapy hands on either side of his face and kissed him on the cheek. "You're such a cutie Tag, one of these days some girl is gonna grab you and just eat you up."

Tag's face was as red as could be, but he managed to grin.

Later Melinda left for her apartment and Tag and Ryan got ready for bed. They crawled under the covers and Bob climbed up and nestled down. Tag put his face against Bob's silky ear and smelled her scent as she sighed contentedly. "So you're sure you want to leave tomorrow?" Ryan asked as he turned toward Tag in the darkness.

Tag nodded. "It's not that I want to leave so badly, but I just gotta go and see. Maybe I won't find him, but I've thought about this for so long. If I don't find out for sure, I'll always wonder. Do you understand?"

Ryan brushed Tag's hair away from his forehead. "Sure I understand. It's just that Mel and I have become very attached to you. We hate to see you out in the cold world all alone."

"I made it this far on my own."

"Yeah you're right. But I'm going to give you my and Mel's cell phone numbers and if something bad happens, or your friend isn't there, we want you to call us and we'll come and get you. Will you promise me that you'll call?"

Tag smiled. "Sure I'll call either way, good or bad. You've been the closest thing I've ever had to a dad or even a big brother. I could sure think of a lot worse things than being with you and Mel."

"Ok, kiddo. That's the plan then. Good night Tag." Ryan gave Tag a hug and turned to the other side of the bed.

"Good night Ryan."

Ryan woke to find Tag missing but he could hear the water running in the shower, so he knew where he was. He got up, began making breakfast in his boxers and Tag soon emerged from the bathroom all bright and clean. "Morning Ryan, what's for breakfast?" he smiled.

"I've made scrambled eggs, bacon and toast. We need to get a good breakfast into you for your trip today."

After they ate, Ryan showered and dressed. While Ryan was getting ready, Tag gathered his clothes and put them in his back pack and left it sitting next to the door. "Mel should be here any minute," Ryan said.

Melinda came through the door a short time later wearing white shorts, a tight red blouse with white tennis shoes. She had large gold hoops in her ears. "Wow, Melinda, you look mega good today," Tag said.

"Thanks gorgeous, you don't look too shabby yourself."

They picked up Tag's bag, hooked Bob's leash to her collar and loaded up in Ryan's car. They drove to the west side of Milwaukee and Ryan stopped in the parking lot of the Greyhound Bus station.

The three of them got out and went inside, and walked up to the ticket counter. Ryan opened his wallet to purchase the ticket.

"Wait! I've got money," Tag said.

"My treat," Ryan said.

Ryan bought a ticket to the closest town to where Tag was going and handed it to him. He negotiated with the ticket man about Bob riding along. The policy was that an animal had to be in a pet carrier, but Ryan talked the man into letting Bob get on without one. "As long as Bob sits on your lap, she can go along. But be sure to keep her in your arms or on your lap."

Tag nodded ok.

Then Ryan handed him a small business card with his and Melinda's phone numbers on it. "You keep this and call us from anywhere you like, collect. No matter which way this turns out, you'll call ok?"

Tag nodded and took the card and put it in his pocket. He turned to Melinda and she put her arms around him. He buried his face at the side of her neck as she kissed his cheek. "You be careful little man," she whispered. "I hope you find what you're looking for."

Tag hugged her hard and then kissed her neck. "Thanks, Melinda."

He turned to Ryan and they hugged. "Remember, any time anywhere. You need us you call," Ryan said.

Tag's eyes were full of tears. "I don't know how to thank you Ryan. You're the best."

Tag stepped back, put his backpack on and picked up Bob.

"The bus leaves at 4:30.....that gives you a couple of hours to wait. I've got three kids coming in for trombone lessons in half an hour, so we gotta take off, you going to be ok?" Ryan said.

"Sure, Bob and I will just sit in there and watch the TV. We're good. I'll call you when I get there," Tag said smiling bravely, even though his heart was breaking inside.

Ryan and Melinda got into the car and pulled out of the parking lot onto the street. Ryan honked and his hand came out of the window as they drove away. Tag stood watching until they were out of sight. "Bob, this meeting people and then leaving them is not much fun is it?" He stroked Bob's soft head sadly as he felt the loneliness creep into his heart. "Well, let's go sit and wait for our bus."

Chapter 25

The bus depot was large, dirty and kind of drab. The bottom half of the walls was a kind of a mud brown with a tan color from the middle of the wall up to the ceiling. There were rows of orange plastic chairs all hooked together on rails running up and down the space. On one wall there were metal lockers with coin operated locks. In the back corner there was a doorway that led to rest rooms. The ticket desk was near the door where Tag walked into the room. People were scattered all over the room in singles and groups, waiting for busses. There were several televisions attached to metal brackets on the walls, so Tag walked to an area where there wasn't anyone sitting and sat down in front of one of the television sets. He slipped off his backpack and laid it on the chair next to him. He clipped Bob's leash onto her collar and put her on the chair next to him on the other side. "You sit here and stay, ok Bob?" Bob curled up, tucked her nose under her back leg and went to sleep.

The television was tuned to CNN. Tag tried to get interested in the news but most of it was not very interesting to him. He looked around and some of the other sets were tuned to other stations. "Stay Bob!" he said and he walked to the ticket window. "Excuse me ma-am, but how do you change the channels on the TVs?" Tag asked when he got to the window.

There was a large black woman behind the counter. "We've got remotes, you need one?"

"Yes, if you don't mind. I'm not too interested in CNN."

The lady smiled and handed Tag a remote. "You be sure to bring it back here when you get on your bus. Normally we don't let passengers have these but you look pretty honest."

"Oh I'm real honest," Tag said taking the remote. "Thank you very much."

On his way back to his chair he noticed a bank of machines

with snacks and sodas. He stopped and bought a package of chocolate chip cookies and a carton of milk. When he sat down Bob noticed the cookies and sat up waiting for her share. Tag and Bob ate the cookies. Tag drank part of the milk and then rummaged in his backpack and found Bob's dish, and poured the rest of the milk into the dish so she could get a drink. After she drank, Bob curled up and went back to sleep. Tag surfed through the channels and ended up on a re-run of *Everybody Loves Raymond.*

About half way through the show, a man sat down a few seats away and began watching with him. He was an older man who looked like a traveling salesman or some kind of accountant. He was wearing a wrinkled suit like he'd been on a bus all day. The top of his head was bald but he had let the side hair on one side grow long and had combed it over and pasted it down with some gel, Tag thought. When the commercials came on, he said to Tag, "You like that show huh?"

Tag turned and nodded. "Yeah, it's pretty funny."

"I like Frank...jeez he's a funny old guy."

Tad nodded. "Me too."

The show began again and they continued watching. As the episode of *Raymond* was over the man moved over to the seat next to Tag and sat down. "So where are you going on the bus?"

"I'm going west, to a town called Richland Center," he said. "How about you?"

"Minneapolis."

"You meeting your parents there?" the man asked a few minutes later.

"Um, no I'm meeting a friend close to there."

"So you're traveling alone?"

"I've got Bob with me."

"I see," the man said.

Just then, another episode of *Raymond* started and they began watching. The man laughed and they talked now and then during the commercial breaks. After the second *Raymond* was over Tag got up to go to the rest room. "Will you keep an eye on Bob?" he asked.

"Actually I've got to go too, can't you tie her to the chair?"

Tag decided that would work so he tied Bob and walked to the rest room, the man walking behind him. He stopped in front of a urinal and the man took the one next to him. "So I bet you got lots of girls who like to fool around with you huh?" the man said.

"What? No, not really, I mean not so far."

"You do like girls don't you?"

"Sure, I guess so."

Tag looked up from his business and saw that the man was looking over the partition toward him. He stood closer, finished up and zipped up. He walked to the sink, washed his hands, pulled a bunch of paper towels from a dispenser and walked out, drying his hands on the way. He dumped the towels in a waste basket and sat down next to Bob again.

Soon the man came out and sat down next to him. "So, you're not sure you like girls?"

Tag looked at the man, "What?"

"You said you weren't sure you liked girls. Maybe you like boys?"

"I gotta take Bob out for a walk Mister." Tag got up, put his backpack on and woke Bob up. "Let's go Bob, make a potty?" Bob got to her feet and jumped down from the seat. Tag started for the door.

"You coming back kid?" the man asked.

Tag didn't answer but opened the front door and looked for a place to take Bob for a walk. He turned and saw that the man was following him out of the bus station. "Come on Bob, let's get out of here!"

He walked quickly to the corner and saw that there was a little playground just down the street. "Hey kid!" He turned and saw the man walking toward him. Bob started across the intersection and gave a tug on her leash. Tag wasn't paying attention to her and the leash slipped from his hand and the dog ran out into the street. "Bob!" he shouted. He stepped into the street and ran toward Bob and suddenly he heard the sound of tires screeching. He looked to the left and saw the tractor from a semi truck bearing down on him and Bob. He scooped Bob up in his arms and turned to run. His right foot was still in the air when he felt a jolt in his left side as the truck slammed into him. Bob flew from his arms and he went tumbling end over end across the pavement.

Chapter 26

The sound of a siren wailing seemed very far off, but as he lay there, Tag could hear it getting closer and closer. Soon he could hear it very loudly and could feel his body being pitched back and forth as if he was in some vehicle that was moving very fast.

"He's coming around," a voice said.

Tag's eyes fluttered open and he was looking up at the ceiling of a vehicle with cabinets and gauges along the sides and a high ceiling above him. He tried to turn his head to see to the side but it wouldn't move. Then a face came into view above him. "Just lay still son," the face said.

Tag was confused. He couldn't figure out where he was or who the face belonged to. Then the young man leaned over him again. 'Can you tell me where it hurts kid?"

"Where am I?" Tag asked.

"You're in an ambulance on the way to the hospital. You got hit by a truck, do you remember that?"

Tag thought hard and then he did remember the truck bearing down on him but he couldn't remember it hitting him. Then he remembered he was holding Bob when he saw the truck. "Where's my dog!"

"He's ok, the guy who hit you picked him up. I think he put him in his truck, he's behind us."

"He's got Bob?"

"It that the dog's name, Bob?"

"Yeah, it's her name, the guy's got her?"

The face appeared again. He held a small flashlight up and shined it into Tag's eyes one at a time. "You're eyes are clear, but I think you might have a concussion."

"My head's fine, it's my left side that hurts, but you're sure Bob's ok?"

"Bob is your dog right?"

"Yeah, she's my dog."

The young man's face appeared again. "Your dog is a girl dog named Bob?"

Tag grinned. "Yeah...but it's a long story and I'm too tired to tell it right now."

The young man smiled. "I think you're ok kid. And I'm sure your dog is ok. The guy who hit you was real worried... he'll take care of the dog."

It wasn't long and the ambulance slowed to a stop, went in reverse for a little way and stopped again. The young man got up and opened the back doors and Tag felt the gurney being lifted from the vehicle. He could see the young man upside down at the end of the gurney as he was wheeled through a doorway and down a hall to a room full of lights and machines. There was a lady that looked like she was a nurse guiding the gurney from the other end. The young man came to the side of the gurney. "You're in good hands now kid, nice meeting you."

"Thanks," Tag said. "Nice meeting you too."

Soon a doctor and several nurses began working on him, taking off his shoes and socks, cutting his tee shirt off and sliding his pants and underwear off. The room was very cold and as soon as his clothes were off, a nurse covered him in a soft blanket. "How are you doing sweetie?" she asked.

"I'm ok ma-am. Has anybody come in with my dog?"

143

"Not yet, but don't worry about the dog right now, we've got to check you over to see if you're hurt."

"Ok, but keep an eye out for a man with a dog will you?"

"Sure sweetie, just lie still and let us check you over."

A few minutes later the doctor, a young man who looked to be from Pakistan or India came up to the bed and began checking Tag's arms and legs and asking him if anything hurt. When he moved Tag's left leg Tag winced. "That hurts a little, but not too bad," he said.

The doctor checked his foot and ankle and then his arms and shoulders. There was a scrape on his right elbow probably where he had hit the pavement after he had been bumped by the semi, but little other damage. The doctor removed the collar from his neck and felt carefully. "Take him and get an X-ray of that left hip and his neck," he said.

Soon Tag was wheeled down a hallway to a room where a man moved an X-ray machine over his hip and then over his neck and took several pictures of each. A nurse wheeled him back to the emergency room, bandaged his elbow and put a hospital gown over him and then covered him back up with the blanket. "We'll wait for the X-rays now. You have a visitor too."

She pulled a curtain around his bed and left. A minute later a man who Tag didn't know walked in looking very nervous. He looked to be about forty with a slight paunch. He was wearing a baseball type cap that said *Mort's Trucking* on it and he shuffled up to the bed. "How you doin kid?"

"I'm ok I think," Tag said. "Are you the guy who ran over me?"

The guy coughed and looked uncomfortable. "Well, I didn't actually run over you, but yeah I'm the guy who hit you. I'm real sorry kid. You just came out of nowhere. You're real lucky I DIDN'T run over you."

"It was my fault mister. I was trying to catch Bob so she didn't get hit and I got it instead. The ambulance guy said you picked her up, is she ok?

"Yeah, she's happy as a lark. She's snoring up in the sleeper of my truck. She didn't get touched by the truck. When you went flying she landed right on her feet, but she's just fine, don't worry I'll take care of her until you're out of here."

Tag was relieved to hear that. "Thanks mister, I'm real sorry to have caused you all this trouble."

"Don't worry about it kid, I'm just real glad I didn't kill you. My name is Don," he said offering his hand.

"I'm T....I'm Thomas Harris, please call me Tom." Tag decided to use a different name just in case the Chicago police had contacted the Wisconsin police to be on the lookout for him.

"Nice to meet you Tom," the man said shaking his hand. "I've got good insurance... it will pay for all your hospital bills. But I should call your parents and let them know you're here, do you have a number for them?"

"Oh no, you can't call them. They're out of town....well they're actually out of the country. They're on a trip to Denmark. I was waiting for a bus to take me to my grandma's house in Richland Center. There was some creepy guy at the bus station asking me about girls and stuff so I walked out to get away from him. I guess I wasn't paying attention and walked in front of you."

"Maybe I should call your granny. Is she expecting you today? She'll get worried if you're not on the bus."

"Oh no, she didn't know I was coming today. Well, she knows I'm coming but not which day. She plays bingo almost every day so she just sent me a key to her house so I could come when I wanted to." He was making it all up as he went and getting pretty good at these stories.

The man looked at Tag curiously. "Hmm...Well, let's see what the doctor says and then we can go from there."

The nurse came back and checked his blood pressure, and took his temperature. "How are you feeling?"

"I'm ok. My hip hardly hurts anymore. Can I go soon?"

"The doctor needs to look at the X-rays and then we'll see. I think you're a pretty lucky boy."

Just then the doctor came in. "Well there's nothing broken. It looks like all you've done is get a good bruising. He turned to Don. "Are you the parent?"

"No I'm the guy who hit him. My insurance will take care of the bill."

"I'd like to keep him overnight just to be sure," the doctor said. "Is there any problem with that?"

Don shook his head. "I'm laying over tonight anyway. I've got a load going back tomorrow."

"What about Bob?"

"I've got a sleeper cab in the truck. Bob can stay with me tonight. Tomorrow I'll come back and if you're ready to travel, you can ride with me back to Sauk City. That's half way to where you're going. You can take the bus from there if you feel like leaving. Or if you want to rest a little longer you can stay with my family and me. I've got three boys and two girls myself."

"That's real nice of you Don."

"It's the least I can do after almost making road kill out of you," Don laughed.

"Doctor, could I see my dog for just a minute?"

The doctor smiled. "Just a few minutes, and don't let the nurses catch you."

Don went out and smuggled Bob into Tag's room. She was very glad to see him, whining and licking his face. "You go and stay with Don tonight and tomorrow I'll see you ok?" He hugged the dog and held her back up for Don to take.

"I'll take good care of her. Is there anything I can get for you tonight?" Don asked.

"Do you have my backpack?"

"Yup, it's in my truck."

"There's a book in it, if it isn't too much trouble, I'd like to have it to read as long as I have to lie here."

"No problem, I'll get it and be right back."

Don left and an orderly came into the room and told Tag he was going to take him to his room. "Will you leave word for my friend so he can bring up my book?" Tag asked.

The orderly told the nurse which room Tag was moving to and then wheeled him down the hallway, into an elevator and then down another hallway into a room. He raised up the head end of the bed a little and showed Tag how to use the call button, gave him some water and left. Tag laid back and closed his eyes.

When he woke an hour later his book and a bag full of candy bars and snacks was lying on the bed. There was a note on the bag. *"See you in the morning Thomas. Sleep well."* Don Mortimer.

Tag smiled. He'd wondered why the man's hat said *"Mort's Trucking"*.

Chapter 27

During the night, a nurse came into Tag's room several times. Each time she woke him, took his temperature, blood pressure and checked his pulse. By morning he was so tired from being awakened all night that he was sleeping like a log when a nurse's aide brought in his breakfast. He didn't hear her but woke when he smelled the food.

The aide was quite young, maybe nineteen or twenty and very cute. "Oops, sorry did I wake you?" she asked when she noticed Tag looking at her.

"No, that's fine, I smelled the food. I'm starved."

She put the tray on a table that extended across the bed and pushed a button on the control that raised the head end of the bed. As the bed came up she took the cover off the tray revealing a bowl of cereal, toast, scrambled eggs and juice. Tag grabbed a fork and began eating. "My, you are hungry," she said. "Is this going to fill you?"

Tag was about to reply when he heard a voice say, "I've got some egg McMuffins if that doesn't fill him up."

Tag looked up to see Mort standing in the doorway with a McDonalds bag in his hand. "You look like you're feeling better Tom...at least your appetite didn't get bruised."

"I'm feeling ok, thanks Mr. Mortimer."

"Call me Mort. Everyone else does. So is your hip still hurting?"

"It's a little tender but I'm fine," Tag replied.

Mort opened the bag and laid a McMuffin on Tag's tray with a little bag of hash browns. He took a second sandwich from the bag and a cup of coffee and sat down on a chair next to the bed.

"I stopped and talked to the doc on the way up here Tom. They're releasing you this morning."

"That's good, I'm just fine, no reason to stay here any longer."

"I was wondering, are you planning on going on to Richland Center to your grandma's then?"

"Yeah, I guess so. I hope my bus ticket is still good."

"Oh I think they'll still honor it. I wouldn't worry about that."

"Good, then yeah, I guess I'll be going today then."

Mort nodded. "I was talking to my wife this morning before I came to the hospital. She wants me to bring you to our house for a couple of days to be sure you're not hurt more than you think."

"Oh, you don't have to do that. I'm fine."

"My wife will have a fit if I come home without you. Why not ride with me to Sauk City? Stop in and say hi and then you can catch the bus from there."

"Well, I guess that's ok too," Tag said.

"Good, I'll go down and get all the paperwork taken care of. You get dressed. There's a little furry girl downstairs that is very worried about you. Here," Mort said holding out one of Tag's tee shirts from his backpack, "I think they ruined the one you were wearing...I'll have to buy you a new shirt to make up for that one."

Tag got his clothes from the closet in his room and dressed. His left hip was hurting a little but he tried to walk normally so they wouldn't make him stay any longer. He walked down to the nurse's station, said good bye to the ladies and he and Mort took the elevator down to the garage floor. They walked out of the garage and onto the side street where Mort's truck was parked. When they got close Tag could see Bob standing up on the passenger seat with her paws on the dash. When she saw Tag she began barking and jumping up and down. He opened the door and she flew out and landed in his arms, licking him and whining.

"Bob, oh my poor girl," he said hugging her.

"I think she missed her buddy," Mort said laughing at the dog. "Well, climb up in there and we'll head west."

His hip hurt a little as he climbed the steps up to the cab of the semi. Tag had never been in a semi before and was amazed at how different everything looked from up so high in the air. They drove a while and turned onto a side street and Mort backed up to a trailer that was parked along with many others. He got out and hooked up the trailer, went into the office and got his paperwork and soon they were heading out of Milwaukee.

They talked about dogs and fishing and Mort told Tag about his kids. Tag was surprised to find out that he had twin boys who were just a little older than he was. "So do they look really alike?"

"They drive me nuts. I have a heck of a hard time to tell them apart. My wife can but she's their mother. They love to prank me. I think they are trying to drive me crazy."

After a while Mort handed Tag his cell phone. "Why don't you call your grandma and let her know what's going on? She must be getting worried that you're not there yet."

Tag took the phone and then hesitated. "Mort, can I trust you?"

"What do you mean Tom? Sure you can trust me. What's wrong?"

"Well, my name's not Tom and...I'm not going to my granny's."

Mort looked over at him. "Go on..."

Tag told Mort the whole story starting with Clifford and ending with Ryan and Melissa. Mort just shook his head in wonder. "That's quite a story. I was wondering about this bingo playing grandma."

"Yeah, I guess it's quite a story but that's the truth, I promise," Tag said. "I'm sorry about lying to you, but I thought maybe I was on some Most Wanted list and the hospital might turn me in."

Mort laughed. "Tag, I doubt that you're on any list of desperate hombres. I think the police have better things to do than look for a kid and a dog. If anything they're looking for you to return you to safety."

"I don't need any safety. I've done just fine on my own. Once I find my friend, I'll be ok."

Mort nodded as if he was thinking. "You know Tag...my twins are going on a church canoe trip. They're going to canoe for a week and go all the way from Sauk City to the Mississippi river. They'll go right past that town where you want to go. I've gone on the trip a few times over the years as a counselor. I could talk to the pastor, I think he'd let you go along with them. That way you could have a little canoe and camping adventure and you'd get to where you want to go at the same time. The trip isn't until next weekend, but you can stay with us until then."

"Wow, do you think the pastor would let me go along?"

"There's only one way to find out," Mort said. "When we get to Sauk, we'll go and ask."

Chapter 28

Mort drove into the parking lot of the trucking firm he worked for and unhooked the trailer from his semi. After he delivered the paperwork, he parked the semi in the back of the lot. "We'll take the pickup home," he said pointing to a red pickup parked in the corner of the lot. He and Tag got out, locked the semi and walked to the pickup, with Bob running ahead to the grass and squatting to go potty. Mort unlocked the pickup and they climbed in.

"We'll go to my place first and then I'll talk to the boys about the trip. Then we can go over to the Pastor's house and see what he thinks."

They drove through town and stopped at a large house with several bikes, a trampoline and a huge tree house in a large oak at the side of the house. There were two little kids playing in a sandbox next to the driveway. They both jumped up and ran to their daddy. One was a blond little girl about five or six and the other was a little boy, also blond who was only three or so. They all had a big hug and then turned their attention to Bob who was overjoyed to see the kids. Mort introduced Tag to Sophie and Timmy who shyly shook hands with him. Timmy sat down and coaxed Bob into his lap and began petting her and hugging her. Tag left Bob with the kids and followed Mort inside.

They walked into the house through the garage and found another girl who was about 12 helping her mother in the kitchen with some baking. "This is Sonja and that is my wife Susan," Mort said. His wife came over and shook his hand.

"Welcome to our home Tag. Mort called and told me about almost running you over. I'm certainly glad he stopped in time."

"Me too, or I'd a been road kill," Tag said grinning.

152

"Sonja, come and say hello," Mort said.

The girl was very pretty but very shy. Her face turned bright red as she came forward and quietly said hello. She turned quickly away and began busying herself with some flour.

"She's kind of shy," Mort said quietly.

"She's just beginning to notice boys," Susan said. "I suppose a cute boy like you is used to girls blushing at you all the time."

It was Tag's turn to blush. "I'm um, I'm not too familiar with girl stuff, I guess."

Mort laughed. "Come on let's find the boys," and they started through the house.

They checked the family room and then Mort said, "They're probably in the tree house."

They walked to the yard and could hear two voices talking from the house in the branches of the tree. "Hey you two come down here," Mort said.

Two faces appeared in the window hole of the house. They looked to be about fifteen, with blond hair, blue eyes and impish grins on their faces. "Hey pop, who's that, the kid you almost squashed?"

"Come on down here, we need to talk," Mort said.

Soon two sneaker clad feet appeared on the ladder and then the first twin came through and climbed down wearing shorts and a white tee shirt. The second was also wearing sneakers and shorts but had on a blue shirt. When he got to the ground they walked over to Tag, both smiling and held out their hands. "I'm Curt," the one in the white tee said.

"And I'm Craig," the other said.

Tag looked them over. It was like seeing double. They were identical in every way, same eyes, same hair, same nose, same crooked grin. "I can see why your dad gets you confused," he said grinning.

The twins laughed. "Poor pop, he doesn't know his own sons."

Mort shook his head. "If there's any doubt, I just beat them

153

both to make sure I got the right one." They all laughed.

Mort told the twins about Tag and his quest. They were fascinated at his adventure. "So tell us more about this Shelly," Craig said.

"Craig, jeez, that's not polite," Mort said. "I told Tag about your canoe trip on Saturday. Do you think Father Frank would let him go along?"

"I'm not sure... if he knows he's a runaway," Curt said.

"Maybe we could tell Father that Tag's our cousin or something like that," Craig suggested.

"Lie to a priest?" Mort said.

"Well, just a little lie. He actually looks like a cousin or something. He's got the same hair and eyes. We'll go to confession when we get back from the trip." The twins were both grinning now.

Mort smiled. "I guess it's for a good cause. Are there any open spots in the canoes for extras?"

"We usually ride three to a canoe anyway. Two people paddle and the other person just rides and then we switch and take turns after a while. We don't have anyone for our middle seat right now, so Tag could ride with us."

"How about Bob?" Tag asked. He called the dog over from the two little kids she was playing with.

Craig knelt down and scooped up Bob in his arms. "We've taken dogs along other years. I think Joey is taking that mutt of his."

"Yeah he is, I heard him talking about it. I know Odel is taking Emmet, he never goes anywhere without his twin brother Emmet. I don't think it's a problem as long as the people sharing your tent don't care, and that's us, so I don't think it's a problem."

"Well, that sounds good to me," Tag said.

Just then little Timmy came around the house and Bob ran to greet him. The little boy was delighted when Bob ran up to him. "Can Bobby come back and play with me?" he asked with his tiny voice. Tag nodded yes and Timmy and Bobby took off for the sandbox, Bob jumping and nipping at the hem of the little boy's shorts, almost pulling them down off his little butt. He squealed with glee as they disappeared around the side of the house.

"Looks like Timmy and Bob are getting along ok, let's go see Father and tell him cousin Tag just arrived from Chicago."

"I'm going to tell your mom where we're going, I'll meet you guys in the pickup," Mort said walking toward the house.

"Bob you want to come?" Tag asked the dog as they walked past the sandbox. Bob looked up and then climbed up onto Timmy's lap and began licking him. "Timmy you keep Bob here and make sure she doesn't get out in the road ok?" he said.

"Ok, I will," the little boy said hugging Bob.

Tag and the twins walked to the pickup which had an extended cab. Craig opened the small back door and then he turned and giggled. "Let's switch," he said to Curt.

The two boys each took off his shirt and traded. "This drives pop crazy," Curt said.

Tag laughed and climbed into the front seat. Soon Mort arrived and got in. They backed around and headed downtown to the parsonage. They stopped in the church parking lot and went to the house. The priest's housekeeper answered the door and told that Father Frank was in the garden. They walked around the side of the house to see an old man in bib overalls spraying some bug spray on the tomato plants. "Morning Father," Mort said.

The old priest looked around. "Well, good morning to you all, what can I do for you on this fine day?

Mort told the little lie about Tag and introduced him. "Tag, that's a name I've never heard before," the priest said.

"Short for Taggert," Tag said. The old man nodded thoughtfully. "Don't think I've ever heard that one either. To my knowledge there isn't a Saint Taggert either. Would you folks like some lemonade?"

The boys nodded yes and Mort said he'd like some too. "Mrs. Simms, would you please bring us five glasses and a pitcher of lemonade?"

The housekeeper said she'd be right out. They sat down in some lawn chairs under a willow tree. "Ah, so you want to go on our little canoe adventure. Have you ever canoed before Tag?"

"No Father, but I'm a quick learner."

"Curt and Craig have gone... what now...four years"

"This is the fourth Father," Craig said.

"I'm sure they can give you all the instruction you need," the priest said.

"Craig, would you help Mrs. Simms?" the priest said to the boy wearing the white shirt.

"That's Curt," Mort said grinning at the priest's mistake.

"No, I'm Craig," the boy in white said.Mort looked mystified.

"You said you were Curt when you came down from the tree."

The boys burst out laughing. "Pop, you'll never figure it out.'

"Well, whoever you are, go help with the lemonade."

Chapter 29

They finished their lemonade and thanked Father Frank and left for home. When they got there Susan had lunch ready so they all sat down to eat. After lunch Craig asked Tag if he'd like to see their tree house, so the three boys climbed up the ladder and into the house through a trap door in the floor. Tag was impressed. "Wow, this is just like a real cabin except it's in a tree!" he said looking around.

The tree house had some old chairs and a small table and several sleeping bags on the floor in one corner. There was a wire running up the side of the tree that lead to an outlet where a lamp was plugged into one space and a radio to the other. "We come up here to listen to baseball games lots of times," Craig said. "We sleep up here a lot of nights in the summer too."

"It's really cool," Tag said. "I've always lived in an apartment, we never had any trees."

"So Tag, tell us about that girl Shelly on the boat," Curt said grinning.

"What do you want to know?"

"What did she look like? Dad only told us you spent a night on the water with her and her dad, what happened?"

Tag blushed. "Her dad was like three feet away."

"Ok, so where did you sleep?"

"Well, Shelly and I slept in the same bunk, but we just kind of hugged and kissed a little. I was afraid her dad would throw me in the lake if he thought I was doing anything else."

"Wow, so she was pretty?"

"Yeah, really pretty, and a good kisser too," Tag said proudly.

"And then the gang banger guy, what did his girlfriend look like?" Craig asked expectantly.

"Her name was Melinda. Ryan isn't a gang banger, he's one of the coolest guys I've ever met. He saved me from getting a beating or worse."

"Oh, sorry, but how about Melinda?"

"Jeez, you guys have dirty minds," Tag said laughing.

"Right you are, so how about her?"

Tag described Melinda, much to the twins' delight. Then he told them about the creepy guy in the bus station and getting hit by their dad's truck. "Boy it's a good thing dad didn't have a trailer on behind him. He probably wouldn't have got stopped and you'd be a pail of mush at the morgue."

"That's a cheery thought," Tag said. "I was pretty lucky I guess. I've been pretty lucky since I started this trip."

The twins agreed. "So you think this kid is still there where you want to go?" Craig asked.

"I hope so. He may be a little older than he was in the book but I'm hoping he's still living there. If not, I'm not sure what I'll do."

"You could come back here, Mom would be happy to have an extra kid," Craig said.

"Yeah, six or five, not much difference," Curt said.

They talked the afternoon away until they were called to dinner by little Sophie. Mort had the grill smoking like mad as they trooped past him into the kitchen. The table was set with dishes of potatoes, a platter of ears of corn and salads. Soon Mort came in carrying a tray filled with hamburgers, hot dogs and brats. They all dug in and the room was filled with the smells of good food and lots of chatter and laughter. Tag stopped eating and looked around the table at the obviously happy family as they ate and talked. How he wished he had something like this, he thought to himself.

After dinner, the twins washed the dishes and Tag helped by clearing the table. Once everything was put away they whole family climbed into Susan's van and they went to the local park to watch the twins play baseball for their team. Afterward they stopped at the A&W for root beers and then went back to the house. "Can we sleep in the tree house?" Craig asked.

"Maybe Tag would rather sleep in a bed than in a tree," Mort said.

"No that'd be fun, I'd like to sleep in the tree," Tag said.

"Cool, is it ok if we take up a few snacks?" Craig asked Susan.

"Can Bobby sleep with me?" Timmy asked as the older boys got their snacks together.

"Well, I don't know," Tag said. "What will your mommy say if Bobby is in your bed?"

"Mommy, can Bobby sleep in my bed?"

Susan smiled. "I guess that's ok if it's ok with Tag," she said.

"I think she'd like that better than in a tree," he said. He stooped and picked up Bob. "You stay with Timmy tonight ok?" Bob licked his face and he put her down on the floor. She scampered over to Timmy's outstretched arms and he scooped her up and headed up to his room.

"She'll be so spoiled you won't be able to stand her," Craig said.

A short while later the three boys were climbing up the ladder with a small cooler filled with sodas and a bag containing chips, and cookies. They turned on the light and the radio to a local station and sat and talked and ate until it was nearly midnight. "Hey Tag, want to go skinny dipping?"

"What? Like swimming?"

"Yeah, there's a public pool about five blocks from here. The bath house is just cement block walls with no roof. We boost one guy over and then he goes in and unlocks the door from the inside. Then we go and swim. We do it all the time."

"Aren't you scared you'll get caught?"

"No, as long as we're quiet. There's no houses close, it's in a little park."

Tag was excited about the thought of doing something daring like this but a little scared too. "Well, sure, let's do it."

They climbed down the ladder and with Curt leading, headed

down through an alley toward the pool. They stayed in the alley until they came to the park, crossed by staying in the bushes and trees and snuck up to the pool. Tag could hear the sound of the water as it cycled through the filtering system. Curt stopped next to the block wall and laced his fingers together. Craig used Curt's hand as a step and hoisted himself up and got his shoulders over the top of the wall. Then Curt pushed up on his butt and he went up and over the wall. When Craig disappeared, Curt whispered to Tag. "Come on, quick!"

They snuck around the corner of the building and into a doorway on the front. Soon they heard a click and the door opened. There stood Craig, naked as the day he was born, grinning from ear to ear. "Last one in is a fart smeller," he whispered and took off for the other door that led to the pool. Curt and Tag undressed as fast as they could and raced to the pool. Tag was just a step ahead of Curt and he jumped over the side into the water, with Curt right behind him.

They had a great time, splashing and laughing and soon Craig was doing a cannon ball from the high diving board. They had been in the water for about half an hour when Craig suddenly whispered. "Holy crap! Look, the cop!"

Tag looked where Craig was pointing and sure enough. A police car was coming down the street toward the parking lot of the pool. "Come on!" Curt said swimming toward the side of the pool next to the parking lot. Tag followed the twins and soon they were tucked in tight against the pool wall, with just their faces out of the water. The policeman drove up to the wire fence and shone his lights across the water. With the boys next to the pool wall, he couldn't see them. He sat with the car idling for several minutes. Tag was so frightened that he began shaking violently. Then he felt one of the twins hand on his back. "Just stay cool, he can't see us," the voice whispered.

A few minutes later they heard the car back up and drive off. One of the twins, Tag couldn't tell which was which now that they didn't have on a colored shirt, peaked up over the side.

"He's gone but he'll probably be back in a while, we better get out of here."

They swam to the other side of the pool, got out and sprinted across the grass to the changing room. They pulled handfuls of paper towels from the dispenser and wiped themselves off and dressed as quickly as they could. Then they snuck over to the door, and Craig opened it a crack. "It's clear!" he whispered and they slipped through the door. Curt closed it behind them and they ran as fast as they could across the grass to the bushes and trees at the edge of the park. They checked for the cop again and then ran for the alley. Once they were in the alley they felt pretty safe, so they slowed down to a fast walk. "Jeez, I thought we were going to jail," Tag whispered.

"Nah, I don't think he'd do that. But it might be better in jail than if he took us home and woke up Ma. She's have a bird. We'd never be able to sleep in the tree again," Craig said.

A few minutes later they were climbing up the tree and a couple seconds after that they were safe and had the trap door closed. "Whew, that was pretty exciting," Tag said grinning.

"I thought you were gonna have a heart attack or something in the pool," Craig said.

"Sorry, I was trying to hold my breath and I just panicked."

"No problem, it worked out fine. Well, who's hungry?"

They chowed down on the remaining food and then stripped down to their underwear and each climbed into a sleeping bag. Craig reached over and turned out the light. "Night guys," he said.

"Night," Curt said.

"Good night...and thanks for the fun time," Tag said. Soon Tag could hear the twins breathing slow down and become steady. He smiled to himself. "I've sure met some cool people on this trip. Now if *he's* only this cool..."

Then he remembered he needed to talk to God before he went to sleep. "Hi God, Tag here again. Sorry I haven't talked to you for a while but I've been pretty busy. I suppose you know all this cause you can see everything and all that, but I'm still ok and doing good. I met a nice family today and am sleeping in a tree. My two new friends Craig and Curt and I went swimming naked but don't tell Mom about that. Maybe better not tell her about sleeping in a tree too. I don't want her to worry. Well, I'm getting tired. Tell Mom I love her. I'll talk to you again tomorrow night. Bye, Tag."

The dream of the long road to infinity came again that night. Now Tag expected it and wasn't surprised to see even more people standing along the road than before. As usual he couldn't see their faces but he felt that he knew them, just as he knew the person waiting for him at the top of the knoll. He was getting closer to the mystery person each time he had the dream. He knew that one of these days, he'd get close enough to see his face and he wasn't sure what to expect.

Chapter 30

The sun was shining in through the window hole in the side of the tree house. Tag woke to feel sweat on his forehead as the sun beam heated up his sleeping bag. He looked to either side to see Curt and Craig both still sleeping soundly. He unzipped the bag and threw it open to cool off.

His movement disturbed the twin on his left and soon a pair of blue eyes blinked and looked at him. "What time is it?" the twin asked.

"Don't know," Tag answered. "The sun's up high enough to shine in here though."

The twin sat up and looked around. "Curt, you got your watch?" he said to the sleeping twin. Curt stirred and held up his left wrist. Tag looked at the watch.

"Almost 8:30," he said.

Just then the trap door opened and Sonja's head appeared. "Time for breakfast," she announced. She looked over at Tag sitting in his underwear and her face turned bright red. "Oh sorry," she said and disappeared down the ladder.

"Sonja is sweet on you Tag," Craig said grinning.

Tag blushed. "I think she's real cute, but she's too young for me."

"What? She's 12, you're 13. Or does the famous Tag like older women like Shelly and Melinda?"

By now Curt was up and laughing along with his brother. "Tag the ladies man!" He began poking Tag and soon the three of them were in a pile wrestling. They were all laughing and trying to get the other down when Susan yelled up from the yard.

"You boys come to breakfast, hurry up, it's getting cold."

They untangled themselves and began dressing. One of the twins put on the blue tee shirt.

"Ok, Curt?" Tag asked. The twin grinned.

"Can't tell?"

"Cripes no!"

The other twin got up and sat down next to the one in the blue shirt. "Look close, there's a difference."

Tag looked from one to the other. Exact same face, same hair, same eyes, same nose, same grinning mouth, same teeth. He looked at their arms, hands, feet. They were exactly the same. "I can't see any difference," he said shaking his head.

"Look at the eyes."

Tag looked into their eyes. They were identical. "No, look lower, on the cheek," the one twin said.

Then he saw it. One of them had a tiny mole on his cheek below his left eye. "Ah, a mole," Tag said.

"I'm Craig," the twin said. "The name Craig has an I in it, so when you see the mole, think of a dot below the eye, and an I in the name."

Tag broke out into a big grin. "Dot the eye, Craig has an I, that's easy."

"Mom knows it but Dad doesn't. Mom doesn't tell him because she thinks it so funny that he can't tell us apart," Curt said laughing.

"She's evil!" Tag said

"Nah, she just likes to pull a fast one on the old man," Craig said. "We'll wear the same thing today, and now that you know who's who it'll drive Pop crazy."

They climbed down the ladder and headed to the house. When Tag was half way across the yard Bob came running to him and he scooped her up. "Well Bob...how was your sleep over with Timmy?" Bob was glad to see him and gave him a big wet lick.

The three boys walked into the kitchen to find everyone but Mort sitting at the table waiting. They filled their plates with scrambled eggs, bacon and toast and everyone had a grand time eating and talking. Tag felt right at home here and loved having so many people around him. He was used to being alone a lot and this was way better.

After breakfast the three boys went up to the twins room and took turns showering and cleaning up. Curt and Craig put on cut off blue jeans on and each put on a red Wisconsin Badgers tee shirt. Tag put on his last clean shirt and some tan cargo shorts. "Tag, you like to fish?" Curt asked.

"Yeah, I used to fish on the bank a lot in Chicago. There are bluegill ponds in some of the parks. I fished in Lake Michigan too and I caught a mega big salmon with Shelly's dad."

"We thought about going down to the river for a while and fishing, want to try it?"

"Sure, I've never fished in a river but I'm game. You got an extra pole?"

"We've got lots of stuff, don't worry."

The twins dug in the closet and found three pairs of flip flops, took a pair each and gave one to Tag. "These are best on the river bank. Sometimes we like to wade and it's muddy, so these work better than shoes," Craig said.

Tag slipped on the sandals and they went down to the garage and got their fishing gear. The twins had metal baskets on their bikes that held the poles and tackle box. They opened an old refrigerator in the garage and got out a small cooler that had fish worms in it. Craig asked Sonja if Tag could borrow her bike and she said yes, so the three of them biked down the street, through town and to the river bank below the dam. They laid the bikes in the grass and walked down to the edge of the river.

"This is the last dam on the river before it meets the Mississippi," Curt said. "It's a good place to catch walleyes and saugers and bass. Sometimes we catch catfish too."

"Cool," Tag said. "Mostly what I caught in Chicago were sheep head and carp and bluegills."

They spread out along the bank and Craig took an old

165

butcher knife out of the tackle box and cut three forked sticks to hold up their poles from getting in the sand. They baited up and threw their lines out into the current and then sat back to wait. It wasn't long and Craig had a bite and caught a small walleye. He let it go because it was too small. A few minutes later Curt caught one just like it. He was removing the hook when Tag's pole began jumping. Tag grabbed it and set the hook and fought a nice bass to the shore. "That's a keeper if you want it," Curt said.

"Do you guys usually keep them?"

"We usually just put everything back. Kind of fish for fun," Craig said.

Tag removed the fish and let it go back into the river. "I've never done that. In Chicago there was always someone who wanted every fish that got caught."

"We like to eat fish, but usually let them go. That way we don't have to clean them either," Curt said.

They were settled back enjoying the sunshine when suddenly a huge fish jumped out of the water, did a summersault and disappeared. "Holy smokes what the heck was that thing?" Tag shouted.

The twins laughed. "It's a Paddle Fish," Curt said. "They're like a pre-historic fish that feeds on plankton. They come up here from the other parts of the river and spawn. Dad says they get little parasites on their gills and they jump like that to get rid of them. I think it just looks like they're having fun."

"It was huge!" Tag exclaimed.

"Yeah, they're big. Some are over six feet long. Did you see that long snout? They look like a sword fish. But they're not aggressive. They just swim around with that big mouth open filtering out plankton. Pretty neat huh?"

"Yeah, so you never catch them?" Tag asked.

"Sometimes they swim into someone's line and get hooked. Then you have to try to get them in so you can get your line back. If you don't they take all the line off your pole."

Just then another Paddle Fish or the same fish from earlier, jumped and did another flip. "Wow, they're pretty cool," Tag said shaking his head. "It's hard to believe they get so big just eating plankton."

"The biggest fish in the world is a Whale Shark, and it's a plankton eater too," Craig said.

"You guys know a lot about this stuff don't you," Tag said.

"We've lived on this river all our lives," Craig said, 'I guess we learned it by accident."

They fished for another hour or so and then waded in the shallow water and found some clams. Tag was amazed to find out that there were several species of clams in the river. Curt and Craig showed him several different kinds and told him their names. "I always just thought a clam was a clam," Tag said.

"See, you learned some stuff today and didn't even have to try hard," Craig said.

Tag nodded in agreement. He liked these two new friends. They were clever, smart and fun to be with. He was looking forward to the canoe trip that was starting the next day.

Chapter 31

Tag and the twins spent the afternoon being lazy and listening to music in the tree house. Craig and Curt had a baseball game that evening and they didn't want to use up all their energy beforehand. Bob was playing with Timmy in his room and the rest of the family was scattered out around the house. Mort arrived late in the afternoon and soon everyone was getting cleaned up to go to the game. "We'll eat at the park," Mort told Tag.

Timmy wanted to be sure Bob could go along, so Tag got her slip collar and leash from his backpack. Susan had washed his clothes, so he had clean stuff to change into after his bath. The twins were in their Sauk City Warriors uniforms and were having a hilarious time confusing Mort as to which was which.

They arrived at the ballpark and gathered around the refreshment stand. Mort began taking orders and relaying them to the attendant in the stand. When he came to Tag he asked what he wanted. "I can buy my own, you don't have to pay for me," Tag said.

"Don't be silly," Mort said. "Tell the man what you want, and get an extra hot dog for Bob.'

After everyone got their food the whole family sat around a picnic table eating and having a grand time. As soon as they finished, Craig and Curt ran over to the ball diamond to begin warming up with their teammates.

The rest of the group followed and took their places in the bleachers, with Bob sitting on the bench next to Timmy. "You like Bobby pretty good huh?" Tag asked.

"Bobby is a nice guy," Timmy said petting the dog. Tag grinned.

The game started and soon they were cheering as the twin's team took a three run lead on a long double by Curt or Craig,

Tag couldn't see the mole from where he was sitting. A while later Timmy pulled on Tag's shirt sleeve. "Tag, can you take me to the bathroom?"

"You gotta go?"

"Yup, gotta go and Bobby does too I think."

Tag told Susan that he was taking Timmy to the bathroom and helped the little kid down from the bleachers. Bob hopped from seat to seat until she was on the ground and then followed Tag and Timmy across the park to the bathrooms. Tag took Bob's leash while Timmy went inside and went to the bathroom. He came out grinning. "I did it all myself and didn't even pee on my shoes." Tag laughed.

"That's good, and Bobby didn't pee on her feet either." Timmy took Tag's hand and together they walked back towards the ball field. When they got near the refreshment stand Timmy said, "Do you like ice cream Tag?"

"Yeah, I do, how about you?"

"Yeah I do too, want to get one?"

Tag smiled at him. "Sure, you got any money?"

"Nope, do you?"

Tag reached into his pocket and pulled out a wad of bills. "I got plenty," he said.

They walked up to the counter and Timmy told the attendant that he wanted a chocolate soft serve cone. The man got it and handed it over the counter to him and went to get a vanilla cone for Tag. Timmy thanked Tag and turned to give Bobby a lick when a boy stepped up next to them and stepped on Bob's foot. The dog yelped and tried to get out of the way. Timmy looked up at the kid and yelled at him to watch out. Tag was just turning to see what was going on when the kid slapped Timmy in the side of the head. He was a short squat looking kid with a shaved head and three spikes in his left ear. He wore braces and had bad acne.

"What the heck are you doing?" Tag said loudly.

"That little punk and his dog are in my way," the kid said

stepping up nose to nose with Tag. "What you gonna do about it?"

Tag didn't have time to reply. Timmy reached up and stuck his cone on the front of the kid's shirt.

"Why you little shit!" The kid grabbed for Timmy but he was too quick. He was already running and Bob was right beside him. Tag was so surprised he just stood there. Then the kid turned and grabbed him by the front of the shirt. He pulled Tag's shirt up and used it to wipe the ice cream off his shirt.

"That brat your little brother?" he asked.

"No, he's my friend's little brother."

"Well you ought to tell him not to act like such a little shit," the kid said letting loose of Tag's shirt.

Tag looked down at his ice cream covered shirt. Then he looked up at the much heavier boy. He motioned for the kid to come closer. "I've got something to tell you," he said quietly.

The kid looked confused but stepped up closer. Tag leaned forward and as the kid leaned in to listen to what he was going to say...Tag bought his knee up and kneed him in the crotch as hard as he could. "Ooooooooooooaaaaaw!" The kid said as he doubled over in pain. Tag took his ice cream cone and smashed it down on the kid's head. When he felt the ice cream on his head he looked up and Tag hit him in the face with his fist as hard as he could. The kid sprawled over on his back on the concrete.

"Way to go Tag!" Timmy said smiling as he walked back from a safe distance.

"Way to go kid," the attendant said. "Wait let me replace your cones," he said as he turned and made two more ice cream cones and held them over to Tag and Timmy. "Here these are on the house." The bald biker kid was lying on the ground clutching his crotch and moaning.

Tag and Timmy thanked him and walked across the grassy park to the bleachers. Timmy held Tag's hand and kept looking up at him and grinning. "What?" Tag asked.

"That was pretty cool what you did?" the little boy said.

Tag grinned too. 'It's better not to get into a fight, but sometimes you have to do what's right. I don't like people stepping on Bob's toes and I don't like people hitting my little friend."

Timmy nodded. "That guy is a big bully. Curt and Craig hate him. He's in their grade in school. His name is Odel. They call him Odie the Ugly."

Tag laughed. "Maybe we shouldn't tell your Mom we got in a fight. She might not like that."

"Ok, I won't tell Mom, but we have to tell Curt and Craig. They'll be really happy that you kneed his nuts."

Tag burst out laughing. "Jeez Timmy, how old are you?"

Timmy held up four fingers. "I'm not old but I know more than you think," he said grinning widely.

They had arrived at the bleachers again and sat down to watch the end of the game and finish their cones. "So what took you guys so long?" Susan asked.

"It took Tag a while to decide if he wanted crushed nuts on his cone or not," Timmy said nonchalantly not taking his eyes off the ball game.

Tag almost choked on his ice cream.

Chapter 32

When the game was finished, the whole family gathered and began loading up in Susan's van for the ride home. Timmy quickly pulled the twins apart and whispered to them about his and Tag's encounter with Odie the Ugly. Curt and Craig both looked surprised and then burst out laughing.

"What's so funny?" Mort asked.

"Just a little joke Timmy told us." Craig replied. "It's not that funny really," he whispered. Then he winked at Timmy.

When they got home, Tag ran upstairs to the twins' room and put on a clean tee shirt and then joined them and Timmy in the tree house. As he was climbing up the ladder he heard Timmy's tiny voice, "And then he said, something like I gotta tell you something and then wham! He kneed him right in the Family Jewels. Old Odie went...OOOOOOOAAAAAAA! Then Tag popped him right in the face. It was the coolest thing...and then...hey Tag!" Timmy stopped his narration as Tag's head came up through the trap door hole.

"Jeez, is it safe for us killer?" Curt laughed.

Tag grinned. "That Odel guy is kind of a smart ass. He slapped Timmy in the head, and it made me mad. I shouldn't have hit him but you know how it is."

"You should have hit him. He's the school bully. Usually he picks on kids like Timmy who are smaller and younger. He didn't know you and you look kind of innocent. Big surprise for Odie the Ugly."

"Guess what Tag?"

"What?"

"Odie is going on the canoe trip. He's got one of those English Bulldogs that look like a giant head and a little wrestler's body. He's taking old Everett along too. You'll have to watch out for him, he'll try to get even."

172

TAG

"I'm not scared of him or Everett. But as far as I'm concerned, it's over," Tag said.

Just then Mort hollered up that they should come in and get packed for the canoe trip. They were leaving the next morning, and had to pack their clothes so they could be at the boat landing at 9:00 am. They all trouped up to the twins' room and in a short while they had everything packed. The twins decided they'd sleep in their beds for the last night home so Tag spread out a sleeping bag on the floor.

"Tag, come and sleep in my room," Timmy said when he came in to see Tag arranging the bag.

"I can sleep here," Tag said.

"Come on, you and Bobby can sleep in my bed with me. I don't pee the bed any more, come on... please?"

Curt said, "Go ahead...we'll wake you in plenty of time."

Tag followed Timmy down the hall to his room. He slept in a single bed but since Tag was so slim and Timmy so small there was plenty of room. Bob snuggled up between them and soon she and Timmy were sleeping. Tag watched the two of them, so innocent and small.

He turned over on his back and folded his hands. "Hi God, Tag here again. Well, tonight is my last night here. These are really nice people. Tell Mom I'm doing good. I did get in a little fight today, but it was necessary. This guy was picking on Timmy. I suppose you know all about it, since you see all, but that's why I hit him. I don't think it's right to slap a little kid. Anyway, I don't think you need to tell Mom about that. Tomorrow I'm leaving on a canoe trip and in about three days and 50 miles of river, I'll be *there*. Then I'll really need your help to find him. Well, talk to you later, give my love to Mom." And then he closed his eyes and slept.

It didn't seem like enough time had passed when Tag woke to see Craig grinning down at him. "Time to wake up sleepy head."

Tag nodded and looked to the left to see Bob wrapped up in Timmy's arms sleeping. He grinned. "I'm gonna have to fight to get Bob away from your little brother." Craig nodded.

Tag got up, showered and dressed and soon joined the rest of the family in the kitchen. Timmy had gotten up and was still in his pajamas with Bob at his side, sitting at the table. He smiled at Tag when he walked in. "Did you sleep good?"

"Yeah, I did, you and Bobby didn't hardly move around at all."

They had breakfast and Mort began hurrying the three boys to get loaded up in the van for the trip to the boat landing. They had to take their clothes, sleeping bags and fishing gear. Everything else was provided by the Church and the counselors. When it came time to leave Tag went up to Susan and hugged her. "Thanks for a swell time," he said.

"You're welcome Tag. You're always welcome in our home, just remember that."

He hugged Sonja and then walked up to Timmy who was holding Bob's leash. "I want to thank you for taking such good care of Bobby while I was here," he said. Timmy's eyes were wet with tears as he held out the leash with Bob on it.

"I like you Tag, I hope you come see us again, and bring Bobby too," he said softly. Tag hugged him and rubbed his back.

"I like you a lot too Timmy. If I ever had a little brother I'd hope he'd be just like you."

Timmy picked up Bob and kissed her on the nose. "Bye Bobby," he said and then he put the dog down and ran from the room.

Susan's eyes filled with tears. "He'll be ok," she said. "Have a safe journey and I hope you find what you're looking for Tag."

Tag smiled and turned toward the driveway where the twins and Mort were waiting. He almost felt like he was leaving home. He had only been there a few days but already it felt like a home to him. It was hard to leave, but he was getting so close, he felt he had no other choice.

Chapter 33

The boat landing looked like some kind of a mock disaster drill. There were three pickup trucks with large trailers holding dozens of canoes parked next to the water and people everywhere were unloading cars and vans. There were several older kids wearing tan shorts and light blue shirts who were trying to get everyone organized. Some were unloading canoes and carrying them to the water's edge and others were hauling large plastic totes and coolers down to the river's edge. Moms were hugging kids and Dads were giving last minute instructions and warnings.

"So I guess I don't have to remind you guys that you really need to wear your life jackets when you're paddling. On the sandbars and islands you can take them off, but just be careful. The river current is really fast, and you can get swept downstream really quickly," Mort said as he handed the twins and Tag their gear.

"We know Pop, we've been on the river a million times," Craig said.

"Yeah, but it only takes once. I know you guys are river smart but Tag hasn't been on a river so you guys keep an eye on him." He winked at Tag. "I'm not trying to scare you Tag, but this is different than a lake or pool. Be cautious until you know what you're doing."

"I will Mort. I've made it this far, I'm not going to take a chance on drowning when I'm this close."

They carried their gear down by the river and a counselor came up and told them to take any canoe they liked and to get their gear stowed into it. The counselor handed them three large heavy duty trash bags so they could put their clothes and sleeping bags into them. "That way if you would happen to tip over, you'll have dry clothes and beds," he said.

They did as instructed and soon most of the canoes were loaded. Mort hugged the twins each goodbye and then hugged Tag too. "I hope you find him Tag," he said. "Let us know when you get there. You have our phone number?"

"Yeah, I do, it's in my book with the rest of them. Thanks Mort, I was pretty lucky to almost get run over by you," he grinned. "I've had a blast at your house."

Tag joined the twins and Mort walked up to the van, waved and then drove off. Tag watched him go and turned to Curt and Craig. "Your dad and mom are pretty cool," he said.

"Yeah, we know."

Just then Tag noticed Curt look to the right and he heard a familiar voice. "Well, if it isn't the pretty boy who likes to kick guys in the balls!"

Tag turned and there stood Odie the Ugly and right beside him was a kid that looked like a twin but a little younger. The younger one was holding the leash on the ugliest dog Tag had ever seen. The dog's head looked like it had slammed into a wall making his face flat and it had a big flat nose that rode up in front of his eyes. He had a huge mouth and his tongue was sticking out between large slobbering lips. The thing was mostly head, but his tiny body did look like a very small muscle bound wrestler. Odie walked up to Tag, nose to nose. "I didn't know you were going on this trip. Since when did you start going to our school?"

"He doesn't go to our school lardass, he's just visiting from Chicago. Not that it's any of your business!" Craig said stepping up to them.

"Nobody asked you Mortimer. I was asking the pretty boy."

"Odie, why don't you and Parnell there take that thing you call a dog and get into your canoe before we toss you in the river?" Curt said joining the group.

"There'll be no tossing into any river," one of the counselors said walking up. "Odel, are you having a problem?"

Odie looked at the kid who was most likely in college and much bigger and stronger than he was. "No problem. I just was asking about this new girl in town."

Odie's little brother snorted and began laughing. He was a head shorter than Odel and had short hair but not cut as tight to his head as his big brother's. He was built the same, short, stout and thick. The counselor turned and looked at him. "Did you have anything to add Parnell?"

"No sir...just had a sneeze."

"Well I suggest you two get your dog and get loaded up. We're about to have our group meeting and then we'll get going."

Tag turned toward Curt and Craig and they all grinned. "Jeez, you said their dog was ugly, you sure weren't kidding."

"Poor old Everett, he's not a bad dog, he just got adopted by a family of morons," Craig said. "I kind of feel sorry for him having to hang around with Odel and Parnell."

Just then one of the counselors blew a whistle and waved for all the kids to join him and the other counselors. "Come on everyone in here, we have some announcements."

The three of them walked up on the landing with the rest of the kids and the lead counselor stepped up onto a cooler. "Ok, many of you have done this trip before but some haven't so this is for those who haven't. Those who have, listen up too, just in case you forgot. When you are in your canoe you will have on a life vest. No exceptions. When we land on a sandbar for a break or lunch you can take them off. When wading or swimming, remember, the current is strong. If you get carried away from where you were wading, just go with the current. In a few minutes you'll be right back in shallow water. Do NOT, I repeat, do NOT, try to swim against the current.

Some canoes will have three kids, others just two. Those two person canoes will take a cooler or food tote with them. Dogs should be unleashed when in the canoe. If it would sink or get caught in brush, we want the dogs to be able to swim free. Safety first at all times...any questions?"

Everyone seemed to understand, so the counselor told them to load up and push off. Craig got into the front of the canoe and then Tag and Bob climbed in and sat on the bottom in the middle. There was an aluminum strut across the middle to make the canoe more rigid and Tag piled up a couple of sleeping bags against the bar and made himself and Bob a nice soft seat. Then Curt pushed them off and climbed into the back. They began paddling and the canoe wobbled back and forth a bit. "We'll quit that wobbling once we get our sea legs," Craig said over his shoulder.

All of the canoes were soon on the water. There were twenty eight of them in all, so it was quite a large commotion until everyone figured out how to steer and paddle. Odel and Parnell were heading upriver instead of down until one of the counselors yelled at them. When they tried to turn around, Everett climbed up on the side of the canoe and almost tipped them over. "Everett, sit down you idiot!" Odel yelled.

About a mile later they were passing under the highway bridge and heading down river. One of the counselors yelled to everyone to make for the right side of the river because there was a railroad bridge coming up with a very fast current and you needed to come at it from the right side. Shortly after that they approached the railroad bridge and Tag noticed how the current boiled at the side of the bridge abutment. Curt and Craig paddled like mad and soon they shot past the bridge. "Pretty exciting huh?" Curt asked.

"Yeah, like in the movies," Tag answered.

The group waited until all of the canoes were safely past the fast water, just back paddling below the railroad bridge. A couple of canoes came close to hitting the bridge but none did. Even Odel and Parnell made it.

The river straightened out before them and soon the group was scattered out over about half a mile of river. Tag lay back against his backpack and sleeping bag and took in the surroundings. "This is a really pretty river," he said.

"Yeah... you'll see eagles and lots of critters as well as scenery."

"Tag this is the longest stretch of water in all the mid-west that doesn't have a dam on it," Craig said.

"The Sauk City dam is the last one all the way to the Mississippi River," Curt added.

"It's really cool," Tag said. Bob lay down in his lap, he began to stroke her silky fir and in no time she began to nap.

Chapter 34

They hadn't gone too far when the sun began warming them up. It was clear and the sun was high in the sky, so Curt and Craig took off their shirts and tied them to the struts in the canoe. Tag noticed the twins were shirtless and decided to take his off too. "You better put some of that sunscreen on Tag," Curt said.

Tag looked down at his very white stomach and then saw how much more tan the twins were. "Yeah, I look like a snowman," he said reaching for the bottle. He spread it liberally over his legs and stomach. Then Curt motioned for him to slide toward the back of the canoe and he put some of the lotion on Tag's back. Just as he finished Odel and Parnell came up next to their canoe. "You guys married or just going steady?' Odel asked smirking.

Curt slapped his paddle in the water and Odel and Parnell began shouting as the cool water drenched them. Everett began barking and lapping at the water as it hit him in the face. "Hey, watch it, you moron!" Odel yelled.

"This is a big river Odie, why don't you and that troll you call a brother find another part of it to pollute?" Craig said from the front of the canoe.

"We got as much right to this spot as you fairies do!" Odie

said defiantly.

"Ok fine, take it," Curt said and began paddling away. A minute later they were several yards away and Odel and Parnell lost interest in them. "Jeez, what a couple of losers," Tag said. "I feel sorry for their dog." The twins burst out laughing.

They came along side a canoe with two girls and a Golden Retriever in it. "Tag these girls are in our class in school. This is Lisa and Teri. That's Lisa's dog Abby. Girls this is... our cousin Tag, from Chicago and that's his dog Bob."

Everyone said hi and they canoed along together talking for the next several miles. Tag got the distinct impression that the twins and the two girls were very good friends... or maybe something a little more. A while later they noticed that the canoes ahead of them were pulling up on a large sandbar so they followed. The counselors were getting things ready for lunch and some of the kids were setting up a net for volleyball in the shallow water next to the sandbar. In no time everyone was out on the sandbar helping with the food and getting things ready for the lunch. The dogs that were on the trip were all galloping around together. In addition to Bob, Everett and Abby, there was a wiener dog named Otto.

After lunch some of the kids waded into the shallow water and began playing volleyball. Tag, Curt and Craig were together on one team with several other kids and Odel and Parnell were on the opposing team. Every time Tag or one of the twins was in the front row of players next to the net, Odel would splash water in their faces as they tried to play. This went on for half an hour until Craig got the chance to spike a ball that was set up by Tag and he smashed it into Odel's face. The bully fell over into the water and came up with blood gushing from his nose. One of the counselors took care of him and grinned at Craig as he led Odel away. "You guys be a little careful," he said half laughing.

A while later the counselors decided it was time to get moving, so everyone loaded up their canoes and they began paddling again down the river. The rest of the day slipped past them like the swift water of the river and in a few hours it was time to set up camp for the night. They pulled up on a large island with a nice sand beach. Several of the counselors helped the kids set up their tents and others began making the dinner. Different campers were given jobs including gathering fire wood, helping with the cooking and digging a latrine in the woods. The campers were instructed to make sure the latrine was used, and for those with dogs, it was noted that each dog owner was responsible for depositing any doggie pooh in the trench. Tag and the twins set up their tent next to Lisa and Teri's tent. The girls introduced Tag to one of their friends named Cindi who blushed when she said hi. After the evening meal the counselors put the food away and then built a bonfire. All of the campers and counselors sat in the sand around the fire and talked and laughed. One of the counselors produced a guitar and soon they were singing campfire songs. Darkness fell and the air cooled their backs while their fronts were toasty warm. Cindi snuggled next to Tag and put her hand in his. Curt and Craig each snuggled with Teri and Lisa and were winking at Tag when he looked their way.

Abby and Bob were lying together on the sand between the boys and girls and soon Everett came over and snuggled down between them. Tag smiled at Everett. "He thinks he's a real stud next to those two girls," he said quietly to Cindi.

"I feel sorry for him having to live with that Odel," she said.

"Sorry for who? Who you sorry for?"

Tag looked and Odel was standing behind them glaring at them. "Nobody, we're just talking," he said.

"Well don't be talking about me," Odel said. "Everett, come on, we're going to bed."

Everett sighed and got up and followed his master off into the darkness to their tent. Tag watched him go and just as he was turning back toward the fire, Curt winked at him. "Later," he said.

A while later the counselors decided it was time for bed.

"Everyone to their own tents," one of them said, looking right at the twins.

Curt and Craig looked hurt. "What are you implying?" Craig said.

"Nothing...I just wanted to be sure you heard me," the counselor said.

They said goodnight to the girls and walked over to their tent. "Take your time," Craig whispered to Tag. They fussed with some garbage bags and straightened their gear in their canoe until everyone was settled into their tents. Craig reached under the canoe and pulled a package out that was wrapped in aluminum foil. He and Curt were giggling as they opened the package.

"What's that?" Tag whispered.

Craig held it over for him to see.

"Holy shit!" Tag exclaimed.

Craig laughed. "Exactly right. Everett did this right after we got here and of course Odel didn't take it to the latrine like he was suppose to, so I saved it." He was holding about a six inch dog turd.

"What are you going to do with it?"

"Watch!"

Craig snuck over across the sandbar to Odel and Parnell's tent. He went to their canoe and found Odel's tennis shoes still tied to the strut of the canoe. Carefully, he slid the dog turd into Odel's shoe and then pushed it down toward the toe end with a stick. He came sneaking back laughing and the three of them climbed into their tent. They each wiped the sand off their feet, took off their shirts and pants and climbed into their sleeping bags in their underwear. Bob climbed up between Tag and Curt and snuggled down.

Odie's gonna crap when he finds that turd," Tag laughed.

"How will we know where Odie ends and the turd begins?" Craig laughed.

They snickered and laughed for a while and then the twins

both drifted off. Tag was really tired but lay over on his back, folded his hands and closed his eyes. "Hi God, Tag here again. Well, I'm on the river, on my way. I'm getting close. I think it's about another 35 miles or so. I'm getting kind of nervous. Suppose *he's* not a real person, or not here anymore? Well, in a couple more days I'll find out I guess. I'm pretty tired tonight, so I think that's all I'll say. Please tell Mom hi. Bye for now."

Tag's dream came again that night. But this time the lonely road had more people standing along it. He couldn't see anyone's face but it seemed like he knew all of them. The figure at the crest of the hill was there again as usual, and the more Tag dreamed about him, the more he felt that he was someone he needed to know.

Chapter 35

Tag could hear pots and pans clanking as the counselors began making breakfast. He pulled his sleeping bag up around his neck and tried to ignore the urgent call to nature that he needed to attend to but Bob began rooting at him trying to get him up. "Stop it Bob!" he whispered. Bob kept pestering him so finally he sat up. The dog was sitting between him and Craig wagging her tail expectantly. "You gotta go out?" Bob began jumping up and down.

"Whoa, watch where you're putting your feet!" Craig said turning to his side. "You're stomping on my jewels!"

Curt began laughing and soon the three of them were sitting up and trying to get their cold damp clothes on. Tag finished first and untied the flaps on the tent letting Bob out. She ran for the edge of the water and peed, and then began looking for the perfect spot for the rest of her duties. Tag watched as she searched, found the spot, circled three times and then squatted and pooped. Bob came galloping back, all ready for the day. "I've got to pick up Bob's poop, and then I'm going to the latrine," he said to the twins. "See you at breakfast."

He went to the cooking area and got a piece of paper towel, walked over and picked up Bob's deposit and carried it to the latrine. One of the other kids was just leaving. "Morning," Tag said.

"Morning."

Tag threw Bob's deposit in the trench and then did his business. There was a plastic jug with water sitting next to the trench with a roll of paper towels for drying hands after washing up, so Tag used them. When he got back everyone was up and moving around in the cool morning air. There was a thick layer of fog hanging over the water and the sand was cool on their feet. Some put on their shoes for warmth. The breakfast was almost ready so Tag and the twins got in line to get their food. They were waiting when Curt poked Tag in the shoulder. He nodded toward the water. There was Odel waddling across the sand, scratching his behind...heading toward the canoe. They watched as Odel sat on the edge of the canoe and wiped off his left foot. He untied his shoe laces from the canoe strut and slid his foot into the shoe. Tag and the twins watched expectantly. Then Odel wiped off his right foot and slid it into the other shoe. He got a confused look on his face and pulled harder on the shoe. Soon the confused look turned to a scowl and he tugged harder on the shoe. Tag and the twins were about to burst, trying to hold back their laughter. Finally Odel pulled the shoe off and looked right at them with a look of hatred. His foot was coated in brown sticky dog poop. "You're gonna die!" he said getting up from the canoe and stomping across the sand. Curt and Craig stepped up shoulder to shoulder and waited for Odel to get to them.

"You got a problem Odie?" Craig asked.

"Yeah I got a problem and I'm gonna kick the snot out of you with my poop covered foot!"

Everyone looked down at Odie's foot covered with brown poop and sand, and began laughing. Odel grabbed Craig's shirt and was about to hit him when the lead counselor grabbed him. "Hold on Odel, what's going on here?"

"These pretty boys stuck shit in my shoe!"

The counselor looked at Curt and Craig. "How do you know

that one of these boys did it?"

"I just know. They think they're so smart, them and this pretty boy from Chicago, they all think they are so smart."

"Odel, that's the dumbest thing I've ever heard. Where did that come from in the first place?"

"I don't know, how should I know."

"It came from his dog, Everett," another kid volunteered.

"Oh really? And why didn't you take it to the latrine as you were told to do? The counselor asked Odie.

"I uh, I thought Parnell was going to do it. That doesn't give them the right to put it in my shoe."

"But you can't prove they did it can you?"

"No but, I know it was them."

The counselor shook his head. "Go wash your foot off and then come and get your breakfast Odel. No more arguing or we'll drop you off at the next town and have your parents come and pick you up."

Odel stood there about to explode and then stomped off to clean off his foot. The counselor turned to Tag and the twins. "Nice work," he said grinning.

The breakfast proceeded without any further disturbance, and when everyone was finished the campsite was cleaned up and everyone loaded up their canoes to set off for the day. By now the sun had burned through the fog and it was warming up. Craig sat in the middle of the canoe and Tag took the front paddle. They were paddling along enjoying the morning when Odel and Parnell came past them. Odel looked over and snarled, "Just wait you smart asses, I'll fix you." Parnell looked at Tag and the twins and shook his head slightly and rolled his eyes.

"Yeah we're shaking in our flip flops," Curt said smacking his paddle in the water and splashing Odel. 'Now get out of here before we capsize you. And get your lifejackets on. If the counselors see you without them you'll be in deep shit."

"Worry about yourself, Mom! I don't need no stinkin lifejacket." Odel steered away from them and soon was harassing someone else up the way. "He sure can be a pain in the butt," Tag said.

"I think his goal in life is just to piss people off."

"I think he was dropped on his head when he was a baby and it scrambled his brain," Craig said.

The river was beginning to widen out and there were more and more sandbars and islands as they headed west. The miles slipped by and soon they were beginning to feel hungry. It wasn't long and they saw the counselors waving to them to pull up on an island. All of the campers and counselors pulled up and several people pitched in and no time lunch was being readied, the volleyball net set up and everyone was relaxing in the sun. Tag and the twins had their shirts off as did most of the other campers. Tag had sunscreen oh his back again but had taken on a little color from the day before.

They played volleyball, ate lunch and had a rest and then everyone loaded up and they took off down the river again. Now there were many islands, and the campers were taking different routes down the river. Some stayed in the main channel and others went to the side of the islands and took the back channels. Tag and the twins were taking a side channel that was quite narrow with many trees hanging over the banks into the water. "Let's go inside the trees," Craig said.

They paddled over near the island and soon were shooting down a very rapid patch of water that ran inside of the tree tops that were hanging into the water. The bank had caved away and the tree which had stood on the edge of the river was now under water. The top of the tree was still green and sticking up out of the river, making a narrow slot between the branches and the shore. It was like shooting rapids. 'Whooie, that's cool," Curt said from the back of the canoe. He was guiding them by using his paddle as a rudder. They had just shot past a large treetop and were heading into a narrow cut. Just as they got near it, they were surprised to get a jolt from another canoe that had come up behind them. "What the...?" Curt said turning to look who was running into them.

"Odie you idiot! Be careful you'll tip us and you both over!"

Odel had a look of hatred on his face as he aimed the canoe at them. "I'll tip you fairies over, that's for sure!"

Just then his canoe slammed into the side of Tag and the twin's canoe. Tag turned to see a look of terror on Parnell's face. He had dropped his paddle and was hanging onto the side of the canoe with a death grip. Tag paddled hard on the right to keep the canoe going straight into the cut. Then in less than a second, they shot through the cut and heard a cry as Odel and Parnell's canoe turned sideways and slammed into the tree top. Odel and Parnell were leaning back from the tree and the current was very swift. When they leaned back, the upriver edge of the canoe was forced down and began taking on water. In just seconds the canoe flipped over and Odel, Parnell and Everett were dumped into the water and disappeared under the treetop.

Chapter 36

The current was very fast and so strong that Tag's canoe shot through the gap between the shore and the treetop like a rocket. "They tipped over!" he shouted to the twins. "Paddle to the island!"

Tag paddled hard on the left and Curt put his paddle into the water and turned them into the island. The front of the canoe slammed into the steep bank and Tag reached up and grabbed a small birch tree that was hanging out over the water. "Hold me against the bank!" he gasped.

Curt paddled as hard as he could and Tag managed to pull himself up onto the edge of the river bank. His legs were in the water but he pulled with all his might and heaved himself up and onto the bank. Craig crawled up to the front of the canoe and held onto the tree, keeping the canoe from drifting away. Tag ran up through the brush to the treetop upriver where Odel's canoe capsized. Just as he got to the tree, Everett popped up on the lower side of the tree and began swimming. "There's Everett!" Tag shouted. Curt and Craig yelled back that they saw him.

"Come on Everett!" Craig yelled. The dog paddled toward their canoe and Curt reached over the side and grabbed his collar and then hauled him into their canoe. "We got him!" he yelled to Tag, who was now climbing down the bank toward the treetop. Craig reached back and grabbed a rope that was lying in the bottom of the canoe and tied them off to the birch tree.

Odel was hanging onto a branch in the middle of the treetop and began yelling for help. His head and neck were out of the water and his body was being pulled down under the treetop. "Come over this way!" Tag yelled.

"I can't get there! The water's too fast!" Odel yelled back, terror on his face.

"You've got to come this way, I'll help you!"

Odel started working his way toward Tag pulling himself from branch to branch as his legs were being sucked under the treetop by the current. "Parnell's gone!" he yelled. "He's under the tree!"

By now Craig was up on the shore with Tag and he grabbed a long branch and held it out for Odel to grab onto. "Hang on and we'll pull you in!" he yelled. Odel took hold of the branch with one hand. Craig yelled again. "You've got to let go of the branches, we'll pull you, just hold on tight." Odel took a deep breath and let go of the treetop with his other and grabbed on for dear life to the stick Tag and Craig were holding to him. Tag and Craig pulled him through the open water between the treetop and the bank. When they got him close, Tag grabbed the collar of his shirt and helped him up onto dry ground.

"Parnell never came up!" Odel shouted, "oh no, Parnell's gone!"

Just then Curt yelled from the canoe below the snag. "I see Parnell...he's stuck in the branches under the water!"

Tag ran below the snag and looked and just then he saw one of Parnell's feet come up toward the surface and then dip down again as the current surged. He ripped off his life jacket and took a deep breath and dove into the river. As soon as he hit the water, Tag grabbed onto a branch from the treetop. He opened his eyes and could see pretty well in the clear water. He reached ahead and grabbed another branch and then pulled himself farther out into the river. The current was tearing at him and he had to hang on very tightly to keep from being swept away. Finally he had to come up for air, so he surfaced, hitting his head on branches, and took another deep breath and then began working his way toward where he had seen Parnell. Suddenly he saw Parnell's hand float past him and he grabbed it with his free hand. He pulled and felt something give and in another second he and Parnell were being swept downriver. Tag swam for the surface holding onto Parnell's hand. When he came up he was just a couple of feet from Curt in the canoe. "I've got him, grab him!" he shouted holding Parnell's hand up. Curt reached over the side and grabbed onto Parnell while Tag was swept down past the canoe. He began swimming as hard as he could toward the bank and soon felt his feet hit some roots and rocks. He grabbed onto a root and hauled himself up onto the bank. He was panting from the hard swim but got to his feet as quickly as he could and ran back toward the canoe.

Craig had run back and waded into the water up to his hips and helped Curt drag Parnell up onto the island. By the time Tag arrived Curt was doing compressions on Parnell's chest and Craig was breathing into his mouth. Odel was crying and blubbering about how his dad was going to kill him. "Shut up for a minute!" Craig said as he listened for Parnell's breath. He held his hand up for Curt to stop compressions and then smiled up at him. "I think we got him going again," he said.

Parnell was breathing and began coughing up water. Curt turned him on his side so he could get rid of the water and soon he opened his eyes. "Am I dead?" he asked.

"Nope not yet," Craig said.

"How did I get out of the river, I was caught in the tree?" he said weakly.

"Thank Tag, he went in the river after you," Curt said.

Parnell turned to Tag. "Did you really? You saved my life man!"

Tag smiled. "No problem Parnell."

Just then Everett came waddling over and licked Parnell on the face. "Hey Everett, you're ok too!" he said. He put his arms around Everett and began crying.

Odel got to his feet and consoled his brother and soon he turned to Tag and held out his hand. "Tag I'm sorry for being such a butt head. That was a brave thing you did, thanks a lot."

Tag shook hands with Odel. "No problem, maybe now we can

be friends instead of arguing."

"You bet!" Then Odel turned to Curt and Craig and offered his hand to them too. "Can you guys give me another chance?" he asked.

"You bet Odie," Craig said.

"Consider it done," Curt said.

Just then two canoes pulled into the bank with four of the counselors in them. They all wore concerned looks on their faces. "We saw what happened from upriver. Odel, Parnell, are you two ok?"

"We're fine thanks to Tag and the twins," Parnell said.

"Tag that was pretty brave to dive into that current," one of them said.

"That's the first time I ever swam in a river," he said grinning. "I was lucky to find him, but it wasn't a big deal."

The counselor smiled. "No, not a big deal, you must save a life every day or so huh?"

It didn't take long for word to spread among the campers that Tag had saved Parnell's life. It took six of the counselors to drag Odel's canoe from under the tree with ropes but when all was said and done, all they lost were his shoes and Everett's water dish. What could have been a disaster, turned out to be one of those adventures that they'd talk about for years to come around the campfires of future canoe trips.

That night as they sat around the campfire, Odel and Parnell joined in with the fun. They were astonished to find that Odel had a beautiful singing voice and after much urging, he sang the verses to *Michael Rowed the Boat Ashore,* while the rest joined in with the choruses. It turned out to be a pretty fine day. After many songs and much laughing they retired to their tents. Sleep came quickly to most of them except Tag who wanted to talk to God before he slept. "Hi God, Tag here again. Well, I had quite a day. The rest of the kids and the counselors are saying I was a hero but I think I just had a chance to do something good and took it. This kid Parnell got almost drowned in the river and I dove in and kind of saved him. It was pretty cool. I suppose you saw it all, but it's kind of fun talking about it. We've got about one more day before I get *there*. I'm getting nervous. I know you know if he's there and if he's gonna like me. I wish you'd let me know, but I suppose I got to find out for myself. I'll probably know by this time tomorrow. Well, if you want to tell Mom about me saving that kid, tell her it wasn't very dangerous. I don't want her to worry. I'll talk to you tomorrow."

He rolled over onto his side and Bob snuggled up against his chest. She put her face against his, let out a long sigh and soon they were both sound asleep.

Chapter 37

The tent was warming up nicely as the sun shined on the nylon. Inside the tent, the light had an orange tint as the sun burned against the bright orange nylon fabric . Bob began yawning and licking Tag's face and he opened his eyes. "Hey Bob, time to get up?" Bob's tail began wagging and she licked his face happily.

"So what's on the agenda today hero?" Craig said sleepily from his sleeping bag.

"Oh not much, maybe a couple of rescues and pulling a widow and her children from a burning building," Tag said laughing.

As they were getting dressed and Bob crawled out through the bottom of the door flap. They were just about dressed when there came a tapping on the tent flap. "You guys up?"

Curt untied the flap and there stood Odel and Parnell, with three glasses of orange juice. "Thought you guys might like some juice right away," Parnell said offering them the glasses.

"That's nice of you Parnell," Craig said taking a glass. Tag and Curt also accepted a glass of juice. "Thanks guys," they said.

They crawled out and the entire group was beginning to fix breakfast and break camp. "We'll get you some breakfast, just sit and relax," Odel said.

"Hey Odie, that's fine, you don't have to wait on us," Craig said.

"It's ok, I want to after yesterday," Odel said.

"Yesterday is over, let's just be friends and that will be

enough," Craig said.

Odel and Parnell both nodded. "Ok, but if you do need something let us know."

"Let's get our breakfast and sit and eat together," Tag said. They stood in line together, filled their plates and then sat down on the edge of the sand with their feet in the water and ate. "So you're from Chicago, Tag?" Parnell asked.

"Yeah, I grew up there."

"Are you going to school there this fall?"

Tag looked at the twins. They shrugged their shoulders. "I'm not going back to Chicago," he said. "My mom died a while ago and I was put into foster care. I had some trouble and took off. I'm heading to a town downriver from here to meet a guy who I want to meet."

Odel and Parnell looked surprised. "So you're not their cousin?"

"No their dad hit me with his semi in Milwaukee and I came home with him and one thing led to another."

"Show them the book," Craig said.

Tag jumped up and went into the tent and got his book and took it back and handed it to Odel. "This is the guy I'm going to try to find," he said pointing to the title character's name.

Odel and Parnell looked through the book reading the inscription inside the front. As they paged through it the picture of Tag and his mother fell out into the sand. Parnell picked it up. "This is your mom?"

Tag nodded.

Parnell's eyes welled up with tears. "She's real pretty," he said quietly. "I'm real sorry she died."

"Thanks, Parnell," Tag said.

"So you're not going all the way with us?" Odel asked.

"No, when we get to this town, I'm getting off and I'm going to try to find him."

"Wow," Odel said. "You're a brave kid. I don't think I'd be brave enough to go from Chicago clear to here."

After the group finished breakfast they loaded up the canoes. Everyone began casting off and soon the canoes were strung out along about a mile of river. Tag was riding in the middle with Bob and the twins were paddling. "We'll be there this afternoon," Curt said to Tag.

"Yeah, I figured that," he replied. "I'm going to get off there, I'm kind of nervous."

"Maybe we could ask the counselors and see if they'd let us stay behind with you, that way if he's not there you could come on with us down the river."

"I don't think they'd let you. Besides, if he is there, you guys would be way behind the rest if you took off after them. It would screw up the whole trip for you."

"Well, what are you going to do if he's not there?"

"I haven't thought of that I guess. I'll have to decide if and when that happens. I'll call you guys and let you know...we'll go from there."

"I'm sure Mom and Dad would let you stay with us...and we'd love to have you too," Craig said.

Tag felt a lump in his throat. "If it comes to that, I'd love to come back and stay with you guys too."

They paddled on and the river began to flatten out. The riverbanks became sandy and they were lined with trees and marshes. At noon they all gathered on an island and had lunch. As they were packing up the head counselor came over to Tag. "We're just about to your destination, Tag."

Tag nodded. "Yeah, I guessed that."

"Are you still sure about getting off there?"

He nodded, "Yeah, I have to see for myself. I've come a long way to find him, I'm not going to chicken out now."

"Ok, well, Curt and Craig know where to stop. The rest of us will go on. Good luck, I've enjoyed having you with us. I hope to see you again someday and I hope you find what you are looking for." The counselor shook hands with Tag and then gave him a firm hug.

Tag climbed into the canoe with the twins as the rest of the group loaded into their canoes and slid off into the swift water. Tag was feeling kind of empty inside, as he thought about leaving this group of friends, just as he had done many times in the past couple of weeks. It sure didn't get any easier the more he did it.

The sun was getting low in the west as they came around a bend in the river and could see a large bridge up ahead. "That's it," Craig said. "We'll pull in at that boat landing over there," he said pointing to the left.

They began to move to the left side of the river and the other canoes kept on course. The other paddlers waved to Tag and raised their paddles as they went on past. Tag waved back, feeling sad as all of these new friends left him. They were just about to the landing when Odel and Parnell pulled up next to them. "You weren't thinking of leaving without saying good bye, were you Tag?" Odel said grinning at him.

"No, I wouldn't do that," Tag said as they pulled along side.

Odel reached out and grabbed Tag's hand. "I won't forget you Tag. Thanks for being there for us." Tag nodded and felt his eyes welling up with tears.

Parnell slid along side and also reached over to Tag. His eyes were filled with tears too. "I'll always remember you as the guy who saved my life," he said. "Don't forget us will you?"

"No Parnell, I sure won't. Have a great life."

They let go and paddled off toward the middle of the river. They both waved again as they slid off into the swift current. Curt guided the canoe up onto the boat landing and they all got out. Tag retrieved his backpack and Bob hopped out onto the gravel. "Well, I guess everything I own is in this backpack, so I guess I'm off," he said.

"Why don't you keep that sleeping bag?" Craig said. "We don't need it and just in case, at least you'd have someplace to sleep."

"Yeah, ok," Tag said. "That way I have an excuse to come

visit. I'll have to bring your sleeping bag back.

They all stood awkwardly for a minute and then Craig put his arms around Tag and hugged him. "You're quite a guy, Taggert," he said with his crooked grin.

Curt stepped up and he and Tag hugged too. "You know where to come if this doesn't work out," he said. Tag nodded. Curt stepped back, "Well, brother, I guess we better be off."

The twins got into the canoe and pushed off. Bob ran to the edge of the water and watched them float out into the current. "Take care, Tag," Craig said as they turned toward the middle of the river.

Tag stood and watched as they paddled toward the bridge, then slid under it and on down the river until they were out of sight. He let out a long sigh and turned to pick up his backpack. "Well Bob...we're here," he said.

Chapter 38

Tag clipped Bob's leash onto her collar, picked up his backpack and slipped it on his back, then picked up the rolled up sleeping bag and walked up the boat landing to the street. He looked around and saw that there was a campground next to the landing, a park down a block and a baseball field. To his left on the riverbank about a hundred yards away was a look-out type of shelter. It was built right on the bank of the river with a wooden floor and roof and open sides with railings to keep people from falling over the bank into the river. The town seemed to be to the south of the river so he began walking down the street towards the buildings and houses.

After several blocks Tag came to a gas station that had a sign advertising pizza and sub sandwiches, so he tied Bob to a Handicapped sign and walked inside. There was a kid behind the counter so Tag walked up and asked if he could get a couple of sandwiches. The kid took his order and began making them as Tag shopped for some other food. He returned to the counter with a couple of bottles of soda, a package of Oreos and a bag of chips. The kid rang the food up on the register, Tag paid him and he went out to Bob. "Well, we've got food for supper," he said to the dog who wagged her tail excitedly. "It's getting pretty late in the day to go look for *him*, maybe we can just camp down by the river tonight." Again Bob wagged happily.

Tag and Bob walked back the way they had come and looked over the campground. He chose a campsite near the water and he and Bob sat down to eat their supper. As he was eating, he noticed a kid riding a bike down the street with a couple of fishing poles stuck in a wire basket on the back of the bike. The kid looked to be about his age or a little older. As he passed Tag he nodded and smiled, and then turned his bike, made a U turn and peddled into the campsite. "Hey, you camping here?" the kid asked.

"Yeah, I planned on it, is it ok to camp here?"

"Oh sure, but have you looked to the west? It's gonna rain, it doesn't look like you've got a tent, do you?"

"Nope, just a sleeping bag."

"Are you alone?"

"Yeah, I'm hoping to meet someone here but I didn't find him yet."

"You're gonna get wet if you sleep here without a tent."

"I don't really have anyplace else to sleep," Tag said.

"Come on with me down to the Gosey, I'll show you a place where you can sleep in the scenic overlook shelter."

"Is that the place down there by the river bank?"

"Yeah, nobody will bother you there, and you can stay dry if it rains."

Tag gathered up his stuff and walked toward the boy. 'My name is Tag," he said offering his hand.

"Phillip," the kid said shaking hands with him. "Come on, I'm gonna fish down there for a while. Unless you've got something more important to do, you can come and fish with me. I've got an extra pole."

"Ok" Tag said grinning.

Tag walked along as Phillip rode slowly. They walked past the river overlook building and on up the bank to a little area that had a nice grassy bank. Phillip sat down by a forked stick that was shoved into the river bank, baited up his hook with a worm and tossed his line out into the water. Tag sat down beside him, did the same with the extra pole, and Bob ambled off sniffing all the new smells of the river.

"So you're camping all by yourself." Phillip asked.

"Yeah, I've been kind of on my own for a few weeks," Tag

said.

Phillip looked at him. "Did you run away from home?"

"Well, not really but kinda. My mom died and I was put into a foster home and there was this kid who was a bully and I kinda got into it with him and left. I've been trying to get here for the last couple of weeks.'

"You wanted to come here?"

"Yeah, I'm looking for someone."

"Like who?"

Tag opened his backpack and took out his book. He held it toward Phillip. "I think this is where this guy who wrote this book lives," he said pointing to the author's name on the book.

Phillip looked at the book. "Yeah, he does, I know him."

"Really?" Tag was very excited. "Do you know where he lives?"

"Sure, it's on the other side of town. He is a cool guy. He comes to the schools around here and talks to the kids about his books and how to write."

"So he's written a lot of books?"

"Oh yeah, there are two more just about this guy," Phillip said pointing to the title character. "Then there are a couple about the Gosey, which is this place where we are, and a couple more novels. He writes another book almost every year."

"I didn't know that," Tag said. "I thought this was his only book when I started out to come here." He thought about two more books about his hero and was confused. "Is this kid in the story a real person?"

Phillip nodded his head. "I think he's older now, but his younger brother used to go to our school."

Tag broke out in a huge grin. "So he is real," he said.

"Yeah, he's real. Why?"

"You're gonna think I'm stupid, but I came all this way to meet him. I've read this book a dozen times, and I wanted to meet him."

"How far did you come?"

"I started in Chicago."

"Holy shit! You came all the way from Chicago to meet this guy?"

Tag nodded yes.

"Well, it's kind of late to go calling, but tomorrow I'll show you where the author lives. He'll know where the other guy is."

"That would be great," Tag said.

They sat in silence for a while and then it began to thunder in the distance. "We better get going, it's gonna rain," Phillip said.

They loaded up their stuff and walked down the river bank to the overlook. Tag checked it out and saw that it had a good roof that should keep him and Bob dry. "You gonna be ok here?" Phillip asked.

"Sure, Bob and I have spent nights in worse places than this."

"Well, ok then, I'll come down in the morning and take you to that guy's house."

Phillip got on his bike and rode off down the street. Tag crawled down over the river bank and filled Bob's water pan with river water and then they settled down on the floor of the overlook. Tag took off his shoes and spread out the sleeping bag and then Bob climbed up into his lap and they watched the darkness take over. Lightning was flashing on the western horizon and the fire flies were blinking on and off in the darkness when he heard the clinking of metal and looked to see Phillip riding up on his bike.

"I thought you might like some company," Phillip said getting off his bike.

"Sure, that'd be great," Tag said getting to his feet.

Phillip took a sleeping bag and a plastic bag of food from his bike and retrieved a large plastic tarp from the back basket. "I brought this, we can tie it and drape over one of these picnic tables to keep us dry if the wind begins to blow. He grinned at Tag.

There was enough light from a nearby streetlight for them to see and soon they had their plastic tarp situated so they had a snug little shelter built under one of the picnic tables. They both walked off by the river bank and watered the bushes and then took off their shoes and shorts and climbed into their nest with Bob right behind them. Phillip had brought a little battery operated camp lantern and he turned it on as they got ready for bed. They both got inside their sleeping bags and Bob nestled down between them. Phillip turned off the light and then nest went dark.

The lightning flashed blue as it shown through the blue plastic tarp and soon they could begin to hear the patter of rain on the roof of the overlook. "So, what are you going to do if this guy you're looking for isn't here anymore, or isn't who you hope he is?" Phillip asked.

Tag thought for a couple of minutes before he answered. "I've tried not to think about that. If it happens that way, I guess I'll have to figure out what to do. I've made some good friends on the way here...I might have to try to get back to one of them to see what other options I have. But, I'm hoping it won't be necessary."

"Well, tomorrow you'll know," Phillip said.

"Yeah, tomorrow," Tag said. He snuggled the sleeping bag up under his chin and shivered. "Tomorrow I'll know," he thought to himself.

He waited until he heard Phillip's breathing become slow and steady and then he turned onto his back and folded his hands across his chest. "Hello God, Tag here again. I guess you know...I'm finally *here.* I met a kid who knows where I can find the writer, and then we'll see. Now that I'm finally here I'm kinda scared. You know, what if he's not real, or gone someplace else...I've never thought about that too much, cause I was always just worrying about making it here. Well, tomorrow is the big day, so keep your fingers crossed. Tell Mom I'm ok. Amen."

Chapter 39

The dream that had become so familiar had come again as Tag dropped off to sleep. It was like it always had been except that now the side of the road was getting more and more crowded with people. As he walked down the road he could see them but couldn't see their faces. Up ahead the lone figure on the crest of the hill was still waiting. The dream began to fade as something disturbed his sleep.

Tag woke up when Bob began trying to crawl down inside his sleeping bag. "Hey Bob, what's up?" he said sleepily. As he came fully awake he was surprised to hear how hard the rain was falling and noticed that the shelter was shaking and rattling in the strong wind.

"It's really storming," Phillip said in the darkness.

"No foolin, are we safe here?" Tag asked.

"I don't know, we might be getting wet soon. If the rain keeps blowing like that, it's gonna run under our tarp." There was concern in Phillip's voice. "It's not like we'd die or anything but I don't like to sleep in a wet sleeping bag. I don't know about you though."

Lightning was crashing, lighting up the sky, followed by deafening claps of thunder. The wind blew in gusts shaking the plastic tarp to the point that the boys feared it would be blown away. Bob shivered inside of Tag's sleeping bag. "It's ok Bob," he whispered to the frightened dog as he stroked her head. Just then Phillip moved quickly toward Tag's side of the shelter.

"Whoa! I've got water running under my side!" he said frantically trying to move away from the flood. He turned on the lantern and they saw that there was a steady stream of water running in, and soon they'd both be soaked from it.

"We gotta get out of here!" Phillip said scooting to his hands and knees.

"Where we gonna go?"

"We can run to my house, it's only two blocks from here. You take Bob and I'll take your backpack. We can come and get the rest in the morning."

Tag nodded ok and they both slipped out of their sleeping bags. Phillip picked up Tag's backpack and Tag held Bob tightly in his arms. Phillip untied one of the ropes holding the tarp down and it blew up and began slapping against the next table in the shelter. He shinnied out under the seat of the picnic table. Tag followed him.

Outside it was like stepping into a nightmare. The trees were whipping back and forth, the thunder booming and the sky was flashing with lightning. The rain was coming down in buckets. "Follow me!" Phillip shouted and took off running across the wet grass. Tag ran along behind Phillip, slipping and sliding in the soaked grass, holding Bob tightly against his chest. They crossed the riverside park and were nearly to the asphalt street when Phillip's feet flew out from under him and he sprawled on his butt on the grass. Tag tried to put on the brakes but couldn't stop in time and slid right into Phillip. They both began laughing crazily despite the cold water and slick mud. Phillip got to his feet, his backside covered with mud. "Come on, let's go before we get struck by lightning and turned into crispy critters!"

About half way down the block Tag realized that he was getting hit with hail stones. The little balls of ice were about the size of a pea but there were many of them and they hurt like heck when they hit his face and body. He put his arm over Bob's head trying to protect her from the hail. "Holy smokes.....hail!" Phillip yelled as he held Tag's backpack over his head for protection. "Come on, it's just a little way farther!"

They took off running again and soon they were splashing down the street on the shiny wet asphalt. Hail stones were piling up in little piles as they ran along making their bare feet feel like they were running on stones. They ran the length of the block and then Phillip turned and ran across the yard of a small house and up to the back door. He opened the door and they both ran inside sliding on the vinyl floor of the kitchen. Tag's feet slid out from under him and he sprawled on his butt on the floor, laughing like mad. They were panting from their run and giggling from the excitement. Phillip turned on the kitchen light and turned to Tag. "Welcome to my home," he said, grinning through the mud and grass clippings that were plastered over his face.

Tag began laughing and looked down at their bodies and feet. "Jeez, we're covered with dirt, you're mom's gonna kill us," he said. Just then a lady stepped into the room wearing a bathrobe and slippers. She looked at the two nearly naked boys, covered with dirt and grass and shook her head. Then she smiled.

"Phillip, aren't you going to introduce me to your new friend?"

Phillip grinned. "Ma, this is Tag, and that's Bob," he said pointing to the wet beagle on the floor who was wagging her tail. "Tag this is my mom, Agnes."

"Pleased to meet you ma-am," Tag said, embarrassed at the idea of standing there in his underwear in front of a lady who was a complete stranger.

"The pleasure is mine, Tag," Agnes said smiling. "Why don't you two both get a shower and change into something dry? I'll make you some hot chocolate while you clean up."

Phillip motioned Tag to follow him down the hallway and Tag followed him into the bathroom. "Go ahead and get into the shower," Phillip said, "I'll get you some dry underwear and a tee shirt." Tag peeled off his wet tee shirt and underwear and turned on the shower. When it was hot he stepped in and rinsed off all the grass and mud. Once he was warmed up nicely he turned it off and stepped out and took a towel off a pile that was on a little table and dried off. He was just finishing when Phillip came back with two pair of underwear and two tee shirts in his hand. Phillip stripped and got into the shower. Tag dressed in the dry clothes and then took an old towel that Phillip had brought with him and dried Bob off. Soon Phillip was finished and got out to dry and dress. "There, that's better," he said when they both were dressed.

They walked down the hallway to the kitchen where Agnes had set two big mugs of steaming hot chocolate on the table next to a plate of cookies. "Sit and warm up your insides," she said. Apparently she had mopped up the wet floor while they were in the shower. She got a small bowl and filled it with milk for Bob and sat it down on the floor. "Did you say this little girl's name is Bob?" she asked.

Tag grinned. "When she and I met, I thought she looked like a buddy of mine from school, so I called her Bob. I didn't look to see what kind of plumbing he had and it turned out he was a she. But she seemed to like her name, so I left it at Bob."

Agnes laughed. "Bob is a fine name," she said. "Phillip, can I talk to you for a second?"

Phillip got up and followed Agnes down the hall. Tag could hear them talking and heard his name mentioned. Soon they came back. "Well, when you boys finish, just leave the stuff on the table. I'm going to clean up the bathroom and then go to bed. I'll see you two in the morning."

"Thanks Mrs....," Tag said.

"Just call me Agnes...and you're welcome Tag."

The boys finished their hot chocolate and Phillip turned out the light. Tag followed him down the hall to his room. Outside the storm was still raging but seemed to have calmed down a little bit. Phillip's room was small but had a set of bunk beds in it. "My older brother and I used to share this room, but he's gone now. I'll take the top bunk and you can have the bottom so Bob can sleep with you."

"Ok thanks," Tag said. "Phillip, is your mom ok with me being here?"

"Yeah, she didn't think you were a local kid and wanted to know who you were. I kinda explained about you and she was fine about it."

Phillip crawled up the ladder and got in bed and Tag turned back the covers and then turned off the light and got into his bed. Bob stood up with her front feet on the side of the bed and Tag lifted her up into the bed with him. She snuggled down under the covers against his chest and let out a long sigh. "I think Bob feels safer here," Tag said quietly.

"I do too," Phillip said laughing from above. "Good night Tag, again."

"Good night Phillip, thanks for taking me in."

Chapter 40

Tag woke when Bob began stirring under the covers. He laid there blinking, trying to figure out where he was when it all began coming back to him. He remembered the storm and running through the night to Phillip's house. The bedroom door was part way open and he could hear a TV going somewhere and Phillip voice talking to his mother. Just then he heard someone at the door.

"*Hello.*"

"Hello," Tag answered.

"*Hello.*"

Tag got a bewildered look on his face. "Hello," he said again. He got up on one elbow and looked toward the open door.

A bright red head about the size of a tennis ball appeared around the door and then a huge red parrot walked into the room. Tag's eyes got big as the huge bird walked up to the bed. It was red with blue and yellow wings and stood over a foot tall. It had a large hooked beak and a long tapered tail. He thought it was called a Macaw, but wasn't certain. The bird walked up and looked right at him. "*I want a peanut.*"

Tag was shocked. "Excuse me?"

"*I want a peanut.*"

Tag was staring at the bird trying to figure out what was going on when Bob stuck her head out from the covers.

"*Here doggy, here doggy,*" the bird said. And then it whistled.

Bob jumped up and tried to jump off the bed but Tag held onto her.

"Phillip!"

"*Phillip! Phillip!*"

Phillip came into the room on the run. "Oh there you are!" he said to the bird.

"*I want a peanut.*"

Phillip began laughing. "I bet you thought you'd gone nuts hey?"

Tag nodded yes. "Is that your bird?"

Phillip nodded. "Well, it's Mom's. His name is Taco."

"Does he know what he's saying.....He wants a peanut?"

"*I want a peanut.*"

"Look in that top drawer. I keep a bag of in-the-shell peanuts. I give him some each morning," Phillip said.

Tag swung his feet out of the bed and reached over to the top drawer and found the peanuts. He took one and handed it to the bird.

"*Thank you.*"

Tag looked up and burst out laughing. "I don't believe it. That bird is really smart."

Phillip shook his head. "You have no idea.

"Is it ok to let Bob down?"

"Yeah, Taco will keep her in line. If she gets too friendly that big beak of his can deliver a nasty pinch."

Tag let Bob down on the floor and she carefully approached the bird who by now had eaten his peanut and discarded the shells. "*Nice doggy.*"

Bob's tail began to wag and she sniffed the bird. "*Nice doggy.*" "*I want a peanut.*"

Just then Agnes called from the kitchen. "Come boys, breakfast is ready."

Phillip opened a drawer and handed Tag a pair of cutoffs and they walked out into the kitchen. Phillip had put his arm down for Taco and the bird had side stepped onto his hand, walked up his arm to his shoulder and was sitting on it, while he ate. "I can't believe that bird. I've never seen anything like that." Tag said.

"He was my mother's," Agnes said. "She died and left him to me. I've got him in my will and Phillip gets him when I die."

"How old is he?"

"He's 43 now."

"43! How old do they get?"

"They live into their 80's sometimes into their 90's. If you buy one, the first thing they tell you is to make a will because the bird will outlive you."

"Amazing!" Tag said. "Does he say a lot of stuff?"

"Does he say a lot of stuff? Awk!"

Tag laughed out loud. The bird was mocking him. Then it laughed exactly like he had. *"That's amazing,"* he said.

"He can mock any sound he hears. He about drives us crazy when he gets it in his head to make a sound like the phone ringing. He can be a little annoying sometimes."

"Nice doggy, Arf, Arf"

They continued to eat their breakfast and Taco sat on Phillip's shoulder getting bits of toast until he ran out. Then as if it was time for a concert, he began singing.

> *"Oh what a beautiful morning,*
> *Oh what a beautiful day,*
> *I've got a beautiful feeling,*
> *Everything's going my way...."*

"Oh boy, Oklahoma again," Phillip said. "Grandma loved that musical, and Taco knows it word for word. Sometimes he sings for hours."

> *"there's a bright golden haze on the meadow,*
> *there's a bright golden haze on the meadow,*
> *the corn is as high as an elephant's eye....*
> *And it looks like it's climbing right up to the sky....*
> *Oh what a beautiful morning..."*

"Come on Tag, let's go get the rest of our stuff while Taco serenades Mom."

Phillip put Taco on the back of his chair and the bird continued to sing as they thanked Agnes for the breakfast and walked out and down the street to the park. "That bird is about the coolest critter I've ever seen," Tag said.

"Yeah, he's fun but he can be annoying too. If he gets something in his head he can just say it over and over until you think you're gonna go nuts. We have a big cage with a cover that we put him in when he gets on our nerves. Then he shuts up. But he's cool. You ought to hear him cuss. Holy cow.....once the priest was here visiting Mom after she had surgery and Taco said *'Who the f—k farted?'* Mom about had a heart attack."

Tag was laughing so hard he could hardly walk.

They got to the park, gathered up their gear and walked back to Phillip's house. Taco was still singing and Agnes took their wet clothes and put them in the washer. Phillip found an extra pair of sneakers for Tag to borrow and they left. "So you want to see where the writer lives?"

Tag felt a knot in his gut but nodded. "Yeah, I'm kinda scared to finally get here but I came a long way and I can't go back now."

Phillip got his bike and they put Bob in one of the baskets and Tag rode double on the back carrier. Phillip drove down the main street of the small town and then turned down a street at the other end. They went three or four blocks and the he stopped on the corner. "That's his house right there," he said pointing to a place on the left. It looked like a normal house.

"That's it?"

"Yeah what did you expect?"

"I don't know. I guess I thought it would look more like a writer's house."

Phillip laughed. "What, a cottage with gingerbread on the outside? He's just a normal guy, he just happens to write books."

"Yeah, I guess I should have thought that too. Do you think he's home?"

"It looks like he's gone. He has a van and a car and the van is missing."

"Well, that gives me a little more time to get up my courage anyway," Tag said grinning.

"Come on...let's go back to my place. Mom should have your clothes done and I have summer baseball practice in half an hour."

They went back to Phillip's and got Tags clothes. He thanked Agnes for her hospitality and said bye to Taco. *"Bye bye."* *"Bye Bye doggy."*

As they walked across the yard Phillip said, "Listen, if this doesn't work out like you planned, come back here. Mom said you could stay for a while until you get things worked out. It's cool."

Tag put his arm around Phillip's shoulder. "Thanks for everything. I was lucky to run into you. I'll let you know one way or the other."

Phillip smiled and nodded. "Good luck."

Tag picked up his backpack, slipped it on his back, hooked Bob's leash to her collar and set out down the street to the other side of town.

Chapter 41

Tag and Bob walked along the street slowly. It was a nice little town, with clean streets and nicely kept homes. He passed the High School and across the street from it was an athletic field and public pool. When he got downtown, he came to a gas station, tied Bob to a post and went in and bought a couple of donuts, a pop and a bottle of water for Bob. Across the street from the gas station there was a little park with a small shelter, so he and Bob went over there and sat at a picnic table and had their snack. Tag watched people come and go and finally decided that he'd take a walk past the house and see if the writer was home yet.

He and Bob walked down the street and he saw that there was now a van in the driveway in addition to the car that was there earlier. He kept walking past and saw two dogs in an enclosure in the yard. One was a Golden Retriever and the other, a yellow dog that looked like it was part Golden. The two dogs began barking at him and Bob so he walked a little faster. He noticed a man looking out the window as the barking probably got his attention. Tag walked on past the house and down to the end of the block.

"Well, what are we gonna do now?" he said to Bob. "Should we just walk up and say hi?" Bob looked up at Tag and had no idea what he was talking about. Tag tugged her to her feet and decided to circle the block and go past again. Ten minutes later they were back in front of the house and the man was on the patio tending to a grill that was sending out some good smelling smoke. The dogs began barking again and the man turned and looked out to the street at Tag. He smiled and waved.

"Can I help you?" he asked.

215

Tag stopped. "Well, I was kinda looking for someone."

"Maybe I can help, come on over."

Tag walked up the driveway and the man opened the gate to the patio. "Hello," he said.

"I'm Tag, and this is Bob," Tag said nodding to Bob.

The man squatted down and petted Bob. "Hello, Bob," he said.

Just then his two dogs came running up. "This big girl here is Katy," he said pointing to the chunky Golden, "and this guy here is Kirby." Up close Kirby looked like a Golden and Collie mix. Tag petted both dogs who took a great interest in Bob. "Sit down, would you like a soda?" the man asked.

"Oh no thank you," Tag said, "I just had one a while ago." He sat down in a plastic lawn chair and the man sat in another.

"So, who are you looking for?"

Tag unzipped his backpack and took out his book. "If you're him," he said pointing to the author's name, "I'm looking for you."

The man looked surprised. He reached out and took the well worn book from Tag. "Well, you found the guy you're looking for." He looked over the well worn book. "You've read this more than once haven't you?" he said.

"Yes sir, I've read it lots of times."

"So, do you live around here?"

"Well no, I came here from Chicago."

The man looked confused. "You came from Chicago? Did you move here with your family?"

Tag shook his head. "I don't have any family. My mom died and I don't have a dad. I came here from Chicago to see if he's still around," he said pointing to the title character's name.

"Wait a minute. How did you get here?"

"I walked, rode on a boat, in a car, in a semi and in a canoe."

"You came all this way to meet this character?"

Tag nodded yes.

The man looked shocked. He opened the front cover of the

book and began reading the inscription. TO TAG WITH LOVE
FROM YOUR MOM, MERRY CHIRSTMAS. MAY YOUR LIFE BE
FILLED WITH GREAT ADVENTURES. He looked even more
shocked when he read the inscription. Looking up he said to
Tag, "Was your mom Sandy?"

Now Tag was the one to be surprised. "Yeah, how did you
know that?"

The man looked Tag up and down and a shocked look came
across his face. "I knew your mom when she was a high school
girl here. We were friends, well friends of a friend. She wrote to
me years ago when she heard about my first book and asked me
to send her a copy for you." Then his eyes got very wet looking
as if he would cry. "How did she die?"

"She was working in a quick gas place and a guy shot her
when he robbed her." Tag said.

The man shook his head. "She was a wonderful girl. I
thought the world of her," he said sadly. Then as he looked at
Tag he suddenly looked like he had discovered something. "Oh
my God!" he whispered.

Chapter 42

"Is something wrong?" Tag asked. The man sat looking off toward the yard with a strange look on his face.

"I just realized something," he said. "Will you stay for something to eat? I've got plenty."

"Well, sure I guess. We don't really have anyplace else to go anyway."

"Make yourself comfortable, I'll go in and get the rest of the stuff and be right back." The man went into the house and Tag sat down again and played fetch with the dogs. He heard him through the window talking to someone on the phone and soon he came out with a tray with buns and burger fixins' and sodas and chips. He removed the burgers and hot dogs from the grill and they put everything on the picnic table. They sat down and began to fix their food, the dogs gathering around for a handout.

Tag hated to ask but couldn't wait any longer. "So is he still around here?"

"Thunderfoot?"

"Yeah."

"He lives about 18 miles from here, so we don't spend as much time together as we used to, but we do see each other often. He's grown up some from when I wrote that book."

Tag was visibly sad. "So he's gone away and not a kid?"

"Well, he's still a young guy but not 13 any more. I don't know about him being a kid. He acts like one most of the time. He still likes to prank me when he gets the chance."

"Can you tell me where he lives? Maybe I can get there and meet him anyway."

"Oh you'll meet him. I called him when I went into the house...he's on his way here right now."

"Really? He's coming to see me?"

"Yeah, he is. I told him there was someone here who came a long way to meet him. He should be here any time."

Tag's stomach knotted up and he couldn't eat any more. He felt like he was going to be sick. "Can I use your restroom? I'm not feeling to well."

"Sure, just go in, through the kitchen and the second door on the right."

Tag walked into the house. It was kind of what he expected. Lots of prints of ducks and dogs, a large gun case filled with shotguns and rifles, several deer horns, a couple of turkey mounts and some fish mounted. He went into the bathroom, splashed cold water on his face and dried it off. When he felt better he began walking back out and he noticed a picture of himself standing on a book shelf. He walked up and looked at the picture. It was him alright, but he didn't remember ever having taken it and the shirt he was wearing in the picture was one he couldn't remember. Just then he heard a car drive into the driveway and looked out the window. It was a bright yellow Mustang convertible and there was a young man getting out. He hurried out to the patio.

The young man walked toward the patio. "Anything left to eat?" he said grinning.

"Sure," the man said. "You might want to meet this person I told you about first though.'

Tag came out the door as the young man came through the gate of the patio. They both stopped short and looked at each other curiously. The young man was in his late twenties and about Tag's height. He was handsome with short brown hair, a little darker than Tag's, bright blue eyes and a nice smile. He was well built and you could tell that he took care of himself. He looked curiously at Tag and then at the writer.

The writer spoke up. "Tag this is Jamie.......or as you've come to know him, Thunderfoot." Tag smiled and felt his stomach begin to knot up again. "Jamie this young man has come all the way from Chicago to meet you. I don't know how to tell you this so I'm going to just say it. Tag is a fan of the Thunderfoot book but he's more than that....he's your son."

Both Tag and Jamie turned toward the man with shocked looks on their faces. "What did you say?" Jamie asked.

"Tag is Sandy's son...and your son."

Tag and Jamie looked at each and other they knew. There was no doubt, it was true. The same eyes, same nose, same mouth...Tag was this man's son.

"I...I," Jamie stepped forward and put out his hand and then put his arms around Tag and squeezed him to his chest. "My son!" he whispered.

Tag was wrapped in the arms of this strange man and his head was spinning. How could this be? How did the writer know? Right then he didn't care, he knew it was real and he knew his journey had been right all along.

There were tears running down all three of their faces and after several minutes Jamie let loose of Tag and wiped his eyes. "I never knew," he said to Tag.

Tag looked at the writer and said, "How do you know this?"

The man sat down and motioned for them to do the same. Tag sat in a chair and Jamie sat right next to him with his arm around Tag's shoulder. "Yeah, you gotta tell us what's going on?" he said.

He looked at Tag. "Tag many years ago your mom lived here. She and Jamie were friends for years, starting way back in grade school. I first knew Jamie when he was 13 and shortly after we met...I met Sandy, the love of his life. Jamie and I had become friends and then one day he brought this cute little girl over so I could meet her. It was very sweet, this nice boy and girl so obviously in love and so young. Then as they grew a little older they became more and more in love. Sandy's parents were very strict and didn't allow any dating, but these two managed to keep it secret from her parents. Then about a month before high school graduation Sandy just vanished. Her parents thought Jamie had secreted her off someplace but that wasn't true. No one knew where she had gone. They searched and searched for her but didn't find a clue as to where she'd gone."

Jamie spoke up. "She never said a word to me. She just didn't show up at school one day and then the word was that she was gone. I tried everything I could to find her but she vanished. Her parents called the police. They questioned me for hours but I didn't know a thing."

The writer looked at Jamie. "A few years ago when *The Adventures of Thunderfoot* was published, I got a letter from Sandy. She had an old girlfriend here in town yet, who she kept in contact with and this girlfriend had told her about Thunderfoot and that it was about a character based on Jamie. Sandy told me that she had left because she was pregnant and couldn't face her parents. She didn't want to wreck Jamie's life with a baby, so she moved to Chicago, had the baby, got her GED and started a life for herself and her son. She asked me to send her a book inscribed to the baby, for a keepsake of the person who the book was named after, Thunderfoot.... his father. But she swore me to secrecy, and I promised never to tell. She knew you had moved on and didn't want to disrupt your life," he said turning to Jamie.

Tag looked at Jamie. "So you never knew about me?"

Jamie shook his head. "I never even knew Sandy was pregnant. You gotta understand Tag, we weren't like that. I mean we weren't having sex all the time. We loved each other very much but we were willing to wait until we got married. But one night we got a little carried away and things got out of hand. It was only that one time. I never had a clue that she was pregnant or that you were born. My God, how I've missed her and now she's gone forever." His eyes filled with tears again and he buried his face in his hands. Tag's eyes filled too and he put his arm around his dad's shoulder.

Jamie wiped his eyes and smiled at Tag. "I should have known the minute I laid eyes on you. You look exactly like I did at your age."

"Is that a picture of you in there with the blue shirt on?" Tag asked, pointing to the house.

Jamie nodded and smiled. "Looks just like you doesn't it?"

"I wondered how he got a picture of me, and couldn't figure out where that shirt had gone because I couldn't remember it."

"In all of my plots and stories I could have never dreamed up a plot like this," the writer said shaking his head.

"You've come up with some good ones but this would take the cake," Jamie said. He squeezed Tag's shoulder again. "I can't believe it," he said smiling.

Tag still felt a little knotted in his stomach. "So what now?" he asked tentatively.

"Now I think we need to get to know each other a little," Jamie said. "Do you like to fish?"

"Yeah I love it."

"Right answer," Jamie said grinning. "Can we borrow a couple of poles, some bait and some tackle?" he said to the writer.

The man grinned. "You've been using my gear and my bait for nearly twenty years, why change things now?"

They gathered up the gear and Tag asked, "Are you coming along?"

The writer shook his head. "This is time for you two to get to know each other. Come on back when you're finished and we'll have a talk."

The got into the bright yellow convertible and Jamie started it up and revved the motor. Tag looked over at his dad and grinned. "How fast does this thing go?"

They were both laughing as they laid rubber down the length of the driveway.

Chapter 43

Tag and his dad drove down the street toward the river. Jamie turned near the riverside park and headed down the street. "Are we going to the Gosey?" Tag asked.

Jamie turned with a surprised look on his face. "Yeah, we are, how do you know the Gosey?"

Tag laughed. "I fished there last night with Phillip," he said nodding to the house they were passing. "We camped out until the big storm and then ran back to his house."

Jamie shook his head. "I used to be good friends with Phillip's older brother. We used to fish down here a lot and I stayed over at his house many times. Did you sleep in his bunk beds?"

Tag nodded yes.

"Does he still have that big red bird?"

"Taco? Yeah, he came into the room and asked me for a peanut."

Jamie burst out laughing. "He still does that? What a cool bird."

They stopped at the riverbank and got out. Tag grabbed the two fishing poles and Jamie picked up the tackle box and bait, and they started down over the bank. There were a couple of forked sticks still sticking up out of the sand at the edge of the river so they sat down in the grass, baited up and cast out.

They both put their poles down with the rod sticking up in the forked stick and settled back. Neither knew for sure what to say, so they sat quietly for several minutes. Then Tag said, "So what's new?"

Jamie looked over at him and began laughing. "What's new? Boy that's the question of the year. What's new....a new son. I guess that's something pretty big."

"Tag, I feel terrible that I didn't know about you. All these years you had no dad. I want to make that up to you now."

"It's ok," Tag said, "Mom kept it a secret. It wasn't your fault."

"It wasn't anyone's fault, but I think of all we missed by me not being there for you and all I missed by not being with Sandy. How did she die?"

Tag told his dad the story of how his mother had been murdered, his placement in the foster home, his encounter with Clifford, and then the story of his journey. Just as he finished the part about the canoe trip he noticed his pole bouncing and grabbed it, set the hook and caught a nice catfish. Jamie grinned with pride.

"Should we keep it?" he asked.

"Nah, let it go, we'll just catch and release today."

Tag let the fish back and then he turned to Jamie. "So, now you know about me, tell me about you."

"Well, you know about a lot of things I did when I was a kid. My dad and mom divorced and we moved here. I met our writer friend and he kind of became like a big brother/father to me. After your mom left and I graduated from high school, I wanted to make some money rather than go to school, so I got a job and have been working ever since. I waited to hear from Sandy for years and finally I gave up and found a nice gal to marry. I have two kids, a boy who is 9 and a girl who is 6."

Tag nodded. "That's good. Well, you don't have to worry

about me, I've made a lot of friends on the way here, I'll get in touch with them and I'll have a place to stay."

"What do you mean? You're going to live with me and my family!"

Tag was shocked. "I don't expect you to change your whole life. What will your wife say about my mom?"

"She'll understand. I've told her about Sandy. The kids will love having a big brother. We have a real nice house with lots of room, there's no problem. There's no way I'm going to let you walk out of my life now that I've found you."

Tag's eyes filled with tears. "For true? I'm going to live with you?"

Jamie pulled Tag to his chest had hugged him hard. "For true, Tag, for true." Jamie rubbed Tag's back and they held tightly, father and son.

Suddenly Tag heard a rattling sound and looked as his pole was sliding across the forked stick toward the river. He jumped toward it, just missing and the pole slid off the stick and into the river. Tag didn't even stop to think, but dove in after the pole. The water was pretty clear and he saw the pole sliding along the bottom through the sand. He grabbed it and swam for the surface. "I got it!" he yelled holding the pole up in his hand.

Jamie was laughing so hard he could barely stand up. He worked his way down the bank and helped Tag to the shore. Tag fought the fish and in a short while pulled a big carp onto the sand. He turned and grinned at his father. "The big one didn't get away that time!"

They released the carp and gathered up the gear. "With all that commotion we probably won't get another bite here for a week," Jamie said laughing.

As they walked up the riverbank Jamie said. "I think we should take a trip back to Chicago and get you all squared away with the Child Welfare people. I'd like to meet all those people who helped you and thank them for what they did."

"That would be great," Tag said. "We better take a big

truck...I got lots of good junk in storage."

When they got to the car Tag looked at the nice clean seats. "I better walk...I'm all wet and muddy."

"Just a second," Jamie said as he popped the trunk.

He rummaged around and found an old raincoat. He put it on the seat. "Take off your shoes and socks and put them in the trunk," he said.

Tag tossed his wet shoes into the trunk and then carefully sat on the raincoat. They drove back to the writer's house, got the wet shoes and walked up to the patio where the writer sat. He shook his head and grinned. "The boy has many of your attributes. I can remember many times you and I came back just as wet and muddy. He's got to be your son for sure."

They all had a good laugh.

Chapter 44

"I'm going to drive home and have a little talk with the family," Jamie said. "I think rather than just show up with you, it'd be a good idea to prepare them. And this is something I should do in person and not over the phone."

"Tag can stay here and we'll get some stuff ready for a cookout. Bring them down with you and we can all have a little party to welcome Tag to his new life," the writer said.

Jamie ruffled Tag's wet hair and grinned at him. "See you in a little while." He got into his car and drove off.

"Well, it looks like you could use a shower and some clean clothes."

Tag nodded. "I've got clothes in my backpack, but my shoes are pretty wet."

"Don't worry...just go barefoot, nobody will mind. Come on, I'll show you where the towels are."

Tag showered, dried off and dressed and walked out to the patio where the writer and the dogs were waiting. Bob was having a great time with Katy and Kirby and came for a quick pet before running off with the other two dogs to play. "They seem to be getting along well," the man said.

Tag nodded. "So do you think Jamie's...Dad's wife will be ok with me?"

He nodded. "She'll love you Tag."

They sat and talked for a while and then Tag remembered his scrap of paper with the phone numbers of all the people he had made friends with along his journey. "Is there someplace where I can make some phone calls?"

"Who are you calling?"

"I met a lot of people along the way who helped me. I have

their numbers, and wanted to let them know I got here."

The writer reached into his pocket and handed Tag his phone. "Go ahead, make all the calls you want. I've got more minutes than I ever use." He got up and headed toward the house. "I'm going to get some food ready, have fun."

Tag dug in the bottom of his backpack and found his phone number list. He punched in the numbers for Mort and his family first. Susan answered the phone. "Hello Susan, this is Tag."

"Tag sweetie, where are you?"

"I made it. I found him."

"Oh my goodness how wonderful...the boys aren't home yet from the canoe trip and Mort's on the road with a load. So is he still your age?"

Tag smiled. "No he's in his twenties now."

"Oh Tag I'm sorry, but you did get to meet him?"

"Yeah Susan, I met him. It's not sad that he's older though. You're not going to believe this but he's my father."

There was silence. "Susan, are you still there?"

"What did you say Tag? He's your what?"

Tag began telling Susan the story and he could hear her sobbing. "Don't cry Susan, this is good, he wants me to live with him and his family."

"I'm not crying sad tears Tag, they're tears of joy. Mort and the twins will be so happy for you. You're not that far away, we can visit."

"I'd like that a lot, Susan. Thanks for everything." He gave her the number Jamie had given him on the drive back from the river. "That's his...er, Dad's number. I'll be there from now on."

Susan promised to call and would have the twins call as soon as they got home. They said their goodbyes and hung up.

Next he punched in Ryan's number and Melinda answered. "Hello, Melinda, this is Tag."

"Oh my Gosh! Tag honey where are you child?"

"I made it here, Melinda. I found him."

Tag could hear Melinda talking to Ryan. "Hey, Tag, it's Ryan, you made it?"

"Yeah, Ryan, I did. I had quite an adventure, but I made it."
"And...is he real?"

"Ryan, he's real all right...he's also my father."

"Tag, what did you say?"

"He's in his twenties, he was my Mom's boyfriend, he's my
father, and he never knew I was born."

He could hear Ryan relating the news to Melinda and then he
heard her crying. The phone changed hands and Melinda came
on. "Tag, are you serious? The kid you thought was a friend is
really your father?" she said sobbing.

"Yeah, Melinda, he really is." He related the whole story to
her and as he said it Melinda related it line by line to Ryan. It
was very confusing. Finally Ryan came back on the phone.

"Mel's kinda loosing it Tag," he laughed. "So are you going to
live with him?"

Tag told Ryan about his new family. "We're coming in a
couple of weeks to Chicago to get my stuff and get me all legal,
and Dad wants to meet you and Melinda and thank you for
helping me."

"Just let us know when Tag. We'll have a party." Tag gave
Ryan his number and they hung up.

Next he called Shelly. Her phone rang twice and she
answered. "Is Harley there?" he asked.

"Tag! Is that you?"

"Yeah, it's me, Shelly, how are you?"

"I'm great, Tag, but how are you, where are you?"

"I'm in Wisconsin, I found the guy I was looking for Shelly."

"Oh my gosh! You really found him? Is he still a kid like you
thought?"

"No, I was a little off there, but it's even better. Shelly, he's
my father."

Tag waited for a reply. "Shelly, did you hear me?"

"I'm sitting here with my mouth hanging open trying to
figure out what you just said."

Tag laughed and began telling her the story. When he finished she said, "Tag, that's one of the most fantastic stories I ever heard. I'm just about speechless."

"Well, it's true, we're going to Chicago in a couple of weeks to get things settled with the Welfare people and stuff, and he wants to meet you and your dad on the way back. Would that be ok?"

"Oh Tag yes, bring him and the whole dang family. We'll take the boat and go fishing or something."

Tag laughed. "Well, we'll see about that. How IS Harley? You didn't drop him overboard again did you?"

"No he's wonderful Tag. He's just so sweet. Right now he's sleeping on my bed like a little angel."

"Well don't wake him. I've got to go, Shelly, write down my number in case you want to call and I'll let you know when we're coming there to visit." He gave her the number and then they hung up.

Next he called Fred. After several rings an answering machine picked up the call, so Tag told an abbreviated version of the story to the machine...gave it his new number and hung up.

He had one more call to make. He didn't expect to get Corey when he punched in the number but planned on leaving a message. He was surprised when Corey answered on the second ring. "Hey Corey, it's Tag."

"Tag! My man Tag, where are you?"

"I made it, Corey, I found him."

"No fooling? I can't believe it, Tag. So is he as cool as you thought?"

"Corey, I didn't find a kid my age. I found a man who is in his twenties. But that's not the best part, I found my Dad. Thunderfoot is my Dad!"

Corey's voice quivered. "He's your father?"

"Yeah, Corey, he's my father."

As usual there was silence as Corey digested the information.

So Tag began with his story and told the whole thing to his friend.

"Tag, you can't imagine how happy I am for you. You're such a good kid, I'm so glad for you."

"Thanks Corey, I'm about as happy as I could be."

"Well, maybe I can make you just a little happier Tag."

"What?"

"Did you think it was funny that I answered my phone?"

"Yeah, I figured to leave you a message."

"Well, I don't have any trouble charging my phone battery any more Tag. When we got back from New York, Eric asked me to live with him. I moved in a week ago. I've enrolled in night class and am getting my GED. Eric is helping me to go to City College this fall. I've got a home, Tag, I'm off the street."

Tag's eyes filled with tears. "Corey, I'm so glad," he said, "I worried about you out there...that's the best news I've heard next to finding my Dad."

"Looks like we both found what we wanted Tag. I told you I thought Eric was the one. He's such a good guy and I'm real happy to be with him."

They talked a while longer and then Tag told Corey about their upcoming visit. "Will your Dad be ok with Eric and me?"

"Well, we didn't discuss that, but I'm sure he's ok with it. He's pretty cool."

They said their goodbyes and Tag closed the phone and sat back in his chair. This had turned out to be one heck of a good day.

Chapter 45

Bob came over and put her front feet up in Tag's lap, so he reached down and lifted her up so she could curl up for a nap. The other two dogs were tired out from playing and had lain down on the patio to sleep too. Tag ran his hand over Bob's silky fur, laid back in the lawn chair, and before he knew it he was sleeping too.

In his dreams, he saw himself and Bob walking down a long road. There were green hills and farm fields along the road. The sun was getting low in the west and he and Bob were walking along alone. Then up ahead he saw someone standing next to the road and Fred smiled at him as he walked past. He walked a little farther and Corey was standing along side the road grinning at him. He winked at Tag and then he saw Shelly holding Harley in her arms. As he got to her she blew him a kiss and waved one of Harley's little front paws at him. Just ahead Ryan and Melissa were smiling at him, Ryan standing with his arms around Melissa and smiling slyly. A little farther down the road the twins stood grinning with their lopsided grins at him. Mort and Susan and the other kids stood behind Curt and Craig smiling. They looked over their shoulder and Tag followed their gaze. Just past the twins and their family stood his Mom, smiling at him. He stopped beside her and she smiled and nodded her head to him, and then looked down the road to the hill. He knew that she was telling him things would be all right from now on. He smiled at her and began walking. In the distance at the top of a little rise, he could see the man standing, as if waiting for him.

He couldn't see the man's face. But now he knew who this man was. He broke out in a smile and he hurried down the road toward him. As he got closer the man opened his arms wide for Tag.

When he awoke he noticed that there were coolers and lots of food on the patio table. He turned as the door opened and the writer walked out. "Ah, having a beauty rest?" he asked.

"Jeez, I didn't think I was so tired, but I guess I dozed off for a couple of minutes," he said.

"Couple of minutes, more like an hour," he said laughing.

"Has Jamie...I mean has my Dad called yet?"

"He'll be here in a little while....he called a half hour ago."

"So, did he say how his wife and kids took the news?"

The man grinned. "They're so excited to meet you," he said.

Tag took a deep breath.

The writer sat down next to Tag and picked up a notebook and a pen. "Tag while we're waiting...why don't you tell me the whole story. It's a pretty good plot."

Tag looked at him. "You want to write about me?"

"Maybe... it depends on the story."

"Ok, well where should I start?"

"Well...it's always good to start at the beginning."

Tag thought back. "The rain came down steadily, not hard and driving, but a rain that seemed it would last forever, making a hissing sound as it hit the ground, trees and puddles..."

Postscript

If you've not read *Tag* yet.... Do Not Read This.

I'm often asked where I get my ideas for a book. It's a hard question because many times the idea just pops into my head and from there, I mull it around for a few days and sometimes that idea becomes a book, sometimes not. I've read other books that have inspired me, heard stories that inspired me and in this case, watched a video.

Anyone who ever watches YouTube knows that by clicking on a video, you have more choices of similar videos to choose from on the same page as the video you are watching. Often by clicking on a similar video you sometimes can get off to watching videos very different from where you started. This happened to me while I was watching a music video some time ago. I had searched for the title song from the musical *Oklahoma*. After watching it, I noticed another video titled *Oklahoma*, by Billy Gilman. Though I was not real familiar with his music, I decided to watch his version of *Oklahoma*.

When I watched this video, I knew right away that I had the idea for a new book. With a few days of thought the story of *Tag* was in my head, waiting for me to put it to paper. I urge you to watch this video and you'll know how I got the idea for this book. I also want to make it clear...this is fiction. The people, the events and the story all came from my head. And thanks to my friend *Thunderfoot* for letting me yet again make him part of one of my books.

By the way, when you watch *Oklahoma*, be sure to have a Kleenex with you.

About the Author

Dan Bomkamp has made his home in the Wisconsin River valley all his life with the exception of his college years in La Crosse. He has been an avid hunter and fisherman his whole life. For many years he was in the sporting goods industry and began writing in the 80's for outdoor magazines. He is active in the Foreign Exchange Student program having hosted 30 boys from 18 countries over the years. Golden Retrievers have also been a big part of his life. He has had at least one Golden sharing his home for 33 years.

His previous books are: *The Adventures of Thunderfoot; More Adventures of Thunderfoot; Thanks Thunderfoot; The Gosey; Big Edna—Back to the Gosey; Voyageur; and Lost Flight.*

Check out his website at: www.danbomkamp.com
Or you can email him: danbomkamp@live.com